THE
NOTHING
MAN

Also by Catherine Ryan Howard

Distress Signals

The Liar's Girl

Rewind

THE NOTHING MAN

CATHERINE RYAN HOWARD

CORVUS

First published in Great Britain in 2020 by Corvus, an imprint of Atlantic Books Ltd.

10 9 8 7 6 5 4 3 2 1

A CIP catalogue record for this book is available from the British Library.

Hardback ISBN: 978 1 8389 5106 1
Trade paperback ISBN: 978 1 78649 659 1
E-book ISBN: 978 1 78649 660 7

Corvus
An imprint of Atlantic Books Ltd
Ormond House
26–27 Boswell Street
London
WC1N 3JZ

www.corvus-books.co.uk

Printed and bound in Great Britain by Clays Ltd, Elcograf S.p.A.

To John and Claire, who have to share,
because to put one before the other just wouldn't be fair.

Jim was on patrol. Head up, eyes scanning, thumbs hooked into his belt. The heft of the items clipped to it – his phone, a walkie-talkie, a sizeable torch – pushed the leather down towards his hips, and the weight of them forced him to stride rather than walk. He liked that. When he got home at the end of the day and had to take off the belt, he missed the feel of it.

The store had only opened thirty minutes ago and the staff still outnumbered the customers. Jim circled the Home section, then cut through Womenswear to Grocery. There was at least some activity there. You could count on a handful of suited twenty-something males to come darting around the aisles round about now, eyes scanning for the carton of oat milk or pre-packed superfood salad they were after, as if they were on some sort of team-building task.

Jim stared into their faces as they rushed past, knowing they could feel the heat of his attention.

He made his way to the entrance, where the department store met the rest of the shopping centre beyond. He watched people coming and going for a few minutes. He checked the trolleys, all neatly lined up in their bay. He paused at the bins of plastic-wrapped bouquets to dip his head and breathe in deep, getting a whiff of something floral and something else faintly chemical.

One of the bins appeared to be leaking water on to the floor underneath. Jim pulled his radio off his belt and called it in. 'We need a clean-up by the flowers. Possible leaking bin. Over.'

He waited for the crackle of static and the drawl of the bored reply.

'Copy that, Jim.'

This time of the morning he liked to have a surreptitious read of the headlines. He moved to do that next. But before he reached the newspapers he saw, in his peripheral vision, someone duck behind the carousel of greeting cards about fifteen feet to his right.

Jim didn't react, at least not outwardly. He continued with his plan, walking to the far side of the newspaper display so that he could face the cards. He picked up a paper at random and held it out in front of him. He looked at its front page for a beat and then slowly raised his gaze.

A woman. For this time of the morning, she looked the part. Trench coat on but not buttoned up, large leather handbag resting in the crook of one arm, stylish but functional shoes. A harried look. A young professional on her way to work, trying to knock one thing off her endless list of 'Things To Do' before she had to go into the office and do more of them – or maybe that's just what she wanted you to think. There was something tucked under her left arm. Jim thought it might be a book.

A *ding-dong* sound interrupted the quiet muzak playing throughout the store before a disembodied voice boomed, calling someone named Marissa to Flowers. *That's Marissa to Flowers, please; Marissa to Flowers.*

The woman picked one of the cards and looked at it as if it was the most interesting thing she'd ever seen in her life.

Jim had the newspaper held up high. If she looked at him from this angle she would see the grey hair and the age-spotted hands, but not the ID hanging from his shirt pocket that said SECURITY in bright red lettering.

The book slipped out from under her arm and fell to the floor with a smack. She reached down—

The Nothing Man.

The words were printed in a harsh yellow across the book's black, glossy cover.

As she bent down and picked it up, Jim could see the same three words on its spine too.

Blood suddenly rushed into his ears in a great, furious wave, filling his head with white noise. It had an underlying rhythm to it, almost like a chant.

The Nothing Man The Nothing Man The Nothing Man.

He was dimly aware of the fact that the woman was now looking at him, and that it looked like he was probably staring at her. But he couldn't pull his eyes from the book. He was rooted to the spot, deafened by the chant that was growing louder all the time, only moments away from becoming a full-blown, wailing siren.

THE NOTHING MAN THE NOTHING MAN THE NOTHING MAN.

The woman frowned at him, then moved away in the direction of the tills.

Jim didn't follow to check that she was actually going to pay for the book, which he might have done under normal circumstances. Instead, he turned and walked in the opposite direction, towards the aisle where they stocked the stationery supplies, a small selection of children's toys and the books.

It's fiction, he told himself. *It has to be.*

But what if it wasn't?

He didn't have to search. Three entire shelves were taken up with its display. Every copy was facing out. A dark chorus, screaming at him.

Pointing at him.

Accusing him.

They hadn't been there yesterday, Jim was sure. The stock must have come in overnight. It must be a new book, probably just released this week. He stepped closer to look for the author name—

Eve Black.

To Jim, that was a twelve-year-old girl in a pink nightdress standing at the top of the stairs, peering down into the dim, saying 'Dad?' uncertainly.

No. It couldn't be.

But it was. It said so right there on the cover.

The Nothing Man: A Survivor's Search for the Truth.

Jim felt a heat spreading inside him. His cheeks flushed. His hands shook with the duelling forces of his desperately wanting to reach for the book and the part of his reptilian brain trying to stop him from doing it.

Don't do it, he told himself, just as he reached out and took one of the books from the shelf.

The hard cover felt smooth and waxy. He touched the title with his fingertips, feeling the letters rising to meet his skin.

The Nothing Man.

His other name.

The one the newspapers had given him.

The one no one knew belonged to *him*.

Jim turned the book over in his hands.

He came in the night, into her home. By the time he left, only she was left alive ... The sole survivor of the Nothing Man's worst and final attack, Eve Black delves deep into the story of the monster who terrorised Cork City, searching for answers – and searching for him.

After all this time ...

That little fucking bitch.

Jim opened the book. Its spine cracked loudly, like a bone.

THE NOTHING MAN

A Survivor's Search for the Truth

EVE BLACK

Iveagh Press

First published in the UK and Ireland by Iveagh Press Ltd, 2019

IVEAGH PRESS IRELAND LTD
42 Dawson Street
Dublin 2
Republic of Ireland

Material covered in The Nothing Man was featured in the article 'The Girl Who' first published by the Irish Times.

A CIP record for this book is available from the British Library

ISBN: 987-0-570-34514

For Anna
and all the victims whose names we
tend to forget, or never learn

THE VICTIMS

Alice O'Sullivan, 42

Physically assaulted in her home on Bally's Lane, Carrigaline,
Co. Cork, on the night of 14 January 2000.

Christine Kiernan, 23

Sexually assaulted in her home in Covent Court,
Blackrock Road, Cork, on the night of 14 July 2000.

Linda O'Neill, 34

Violently and sexually assaulted in her home outside Fermoy,
Co. Cork, on the night of 11 April 2001.

Marie Meara, 28, and Martin Connolly, 30

Murdered in their home in Westpark, Maryborough Road,
Cork, on the night of 3 June 2001.

Ross Black, 42, Deirdre Black, 39
and Anna Black, 7

Murdered in their home in Passage West, Co. Cork,
on the night of 4 October 2001.

The author was the lone survivor.
She was aged 12 at the time.

A Note on Sources

There are three sides to every story, they say: yours, mine and the truth. At the time of writing, the Nothing Man has not yet told his. Transcripts, reports, recordings and in-person interviews are as close as we can get to hard facts, and I have relied on them exclusively as sources for this book. I have made every effort to tell other people's stories – those of his victims, those of the man who tried to stop him – as accurately as possible. But this is also *my* story. I have done my best to tell it to you as I tell it to myself. That, I think, is as close as we can get to the truth.

INTRODUCTION

The Girl Who

When we meet, I probably introduce myself to you as Evelyn and say, 'Nice to meet you.' I transfer my glass to my other hand so I can shake the one you've offered, but the move is clumsy and I end up spraying us both with droplets of white wine. I apologise, perhaps blush with embarrassment. You wave a hand and protest that no, no, it's fine, really, but I see you snatch a glance at your shirt, the one you probably had dry-cleaned for the occasion, to surreptitiously assess the damage. You ask me what I do and I don't know if I'm disappointed or relieved that this conversation is going to be longer. I say, 'Oh, this and that,' and then ask what you do. You tell me and I make the *mmm* sounds of polite interest. There's a silence then: we've run out of steam. One of us rushes to use the last remaining card in play: 'So, how do you know …?' We take turns explaining our social ties to the host, casting for connections. We probably find some. Dublin is a small place. We grasp for other topics: the turnout tonight, that podcast everyone is obsessed with, Brexit. The room is uncomfortably warm and noisy and strange bodies brush against mine as they pass, but the real source of my anxiety, the thing that has an angry red flush flaring up my neck, is the possibility that, at any moment, the penny will drop, and you'll frown and cock your head and look at me, *really* look at me, and say, 'Wait, aren't you the girl who …?'

This is always my fear when I meet someone new, because I am.

I am the girl who.

I was twelve years old when a man broke into our home and murdered my mother, father and younger sister, Anna, seven years old then and for ever. I heard strange and confusing sounds that I would later discover were my mother's rape and murder and my sister's asphyxiation. I found my father's bloody and battered body in a crumpled heap at the bottom of the stairs. I believe that, having survived the attack, he was trying to get to the phone in our kitchen so he could raise the alarm. I survived because of my bladder, because of the can of Club Orange I'd smuggled into my bedroom and drank in the hour before I went to bed. Minutes before the intruder made his way up the stairs, I woke needing to go to the bathroom. I was then able to hide in there once it began. The lock was flimsy and there was no means of escape. If the killer had tried the door it would have yielded and I'd be dead as well. But for some reason, he didn't.

We were the last family this man attacked but not the first. We were his fifth in two years. The media dubbed him the Nothing Man because the Gardaí, they said, had nothing on him. With the sole exception of a momentary glimpse in the beam of headlights on the side of the road one night, no one saw him coming or going. He wore a mask and sometimes shone a torch directly into his victims' faces, so no survivor could provide a useful physical description. He used condoms and left no hair or fingerprints that anyone was ever able to collect. He took his weapons – a knife and then, later, a gun – with him when he went, only ever leaving behind the strands of braided blue rope that he used to restrain his victims. The rope never gave up any secrets. He spoke in a weird, raspy whisper that offered no clues as to his real voice. He confined his crimes to one county, Cork, Ireland's southernmost and largest, but he moved around within it, striking places like Fermoy, a town nearly forty kilometres outside of Cork City, but also Blackrock, a suburb.

Nearly two decades later he remains at large and I miss my family like phantom limbs. Their absence in my life, the tragedy of their fates and the pain they must have suffered is a constant ringing in my ears, a taste in my mouth, an itch on my skin. It's everywhere, always, and I can't make it go away. Time hasn't healed this wound but made it worse, turned the skin around the original cut necrotic. I understand much more about what I lost now, at thirty, than I did when I actually lost it at twelve. And the monster responsible is still out there, still free, still unidentified. Maybe he's even spent all this time with *his* family. This possibility – this likelihood – fills me with a rage so intense that on the bad days, I can't see through it. On the worst of them, I wish he'd murdered me too.

But you and me, we've just met at a Christmas party. Or a wedding. Or a book launch. And I don't know you but I know that you wouldn't know what to do if I said any of this out loud, now, in response to your question. *So am I the girl who ...?* I feign confusion. *The girl who what? Just how many of those drinks have you had, anyway?*

I'm good at this. I've had lots of practice. You will think you're mistaken. The conversation will move on.

As soon as I can I will, too.

In the aftermath of the attack, my only surviving grandparent – Colette, my father's mother – whisked me away to a place called Spanish Point on Ireland's Atlantic coast. We arrived there in the middle of October, just as the last few seasonal stragglers were packing up, and moved into a tiny, whitewashed cottage that she said had been there since before the Famine. Its bright red door had been newly painted in advance of our arrival and every time I looked at it, all I could see was fresh blood dripping down pale bedroom walls.

We were there three weeks before I realised there must have been funerals.

The cottage was squeezed on to a narrow slip of land between the coast road and the yawning expanse of the seemingly endless sea, churning and wild, the winds angry to meet their first obstacle for thousands of miles. Our position felt precarious. Lying in bed at night, I'd listen to the roar of the waves and worry that the next one would rise up, crash down on to the cottage and carry away what was left of us with the force of its retreat.

It didn't help that Spanish Point was so called because two ships of the Spanish Armada were wrecked against the headland there in 1588. According to local folklore, the sailors that didn't drown were executed and buried in a mass grave in a spot called *Tuama na Spainneach*, the Spanish Tomb. Sometimes, in the winter months, when night arrived early, I stood on the beach as it darkened and imagined the ghosts of these men emerging from the sea. They always looked like a cross between Egyptian mummies and Hollywood pirates, and they were always walking directly towards me.

Our life in Spanish Point was painfully simple. We had no TV and no computer, and I don't remember there ever being newspapers in the house. My grandmother, who I called Nannie, listened to the radio for a couple of hours in the morning but only ever stations that played traditional Irish music and never anything with news bulletins in between. We had a landline, which occasionally rang, but whenever it did I'd be shooed into another room or, weather permitting, sent outside while Nannie spoke to whoever was on the other end in hushed tones. The phone rang often in those first few weeks and months but afterwards, almost never. Eventually calls became so rare that the sudden shrill of the ringer would make us both jump and turn to one another, panicked, as if a fire alarm had just gone off and we hadn't known there was a fire or even an alarm.

That first year almost every day was the same, our tasks expanding to fill however many hours we had like an emotional sealant, preventing the grief from bubbling up to the surface and breaking through. Each meal had a preparation, consumption and clean-up phase. Even a simple breakfast of toast and eggs could be stretched to an hour if we put our minds to it. Mid-morning we did what Nannie called the jobs, tasks like housekeeping and laundry. After lunch, we'd take a long walk down the beach and back, returning with an appetite for dinner. In the evenings, Nannie would light a fire and we'd sit in silence, reading our books, until the flames were reduced to embers. Then we would double-check the doors were locked, together, and go to bed.

It was only then, when I was under the covers, alone in my room in the dark, that I could finally give in. Let it in. The sadness, the grief, the confusion. I would yield and it would rush in and engulf me, a mile-high drowning wave. I knew no matter what happened during the day, whatever the effectiveness of Nannie's distractions, this was what awaited me at the end of it. I cried myself to sleep every single night and dreamed of decomposing corpses writhing around in muddy graves. Anna's, mostly. Trying to get out. Trying to get back to me.

We never, ever, talked about what had happened. Nannie didn't even say their names. But sometimes I heard her whimpering softly in her sleep, and once I walked in on her looking through one of my mother's boxes of old photos, her lined cheeks wet with tears. I had so many questions about what had happened, and *why* it had, to *us*, but I didn't dare ask them. I didn't want to upset Nannie. I presumed that her and I being holed up in that cottage meant that the man who had murdered the rest of my family was still out there somewhere and that, by now, he knew that he'd missed one of us. Sometimes, in the twilight moments between sleep and wakefulness, I'd see him standing at the end of my bed. He looked like a killer from a horror movie: crazed, blood-splattered, wild. Sometimes the knife was in me before I'd wake up and realise it wasn't real.

Once a week we'd go into the nearest town to exchange our library books and do our food shopping (or to *get the messages*, as Nannie called it – and as I did too until I realised, at college, that not everyone did). She wouldn't let me out of her sight on these excursions and told me that, if anyone ever asked, I was to say my first name in full, Evelyn instead of Eve. Afterwards, when I started secondary school one year late, the forms had Nannie's maiden name on them and I had been issued a further instruction. I was to say my parents had died in a car crash and that I was an only child, but only if I was asked. Never volunteer information, Nannie said. That was the golden rule and one I still follow now.

I didn't question this. I just wanted to be normal, to fit in with the other girls in my year. I assumed that how I felt – like my insides were one big, raw, open wound and that my body was just a thin shell built to hide this – was a permanent state that would only be made worse by acknowledging it. I got really good at pretending that I was fine, that everything was, but it was a delicate surface tension that threatened to break at any time.

I pretended my way all through school, through my Leaving Cert exams and through four years of college at NUI Galway, where I chose to study a business course purely because it was a known quantity. I loved reading and writing, and the night I applied, I sat for a long time with the cursor blinking over options with 'Arts' and 'Literature' and 'Creative Writing' in their title. But I couldn't chance being trapped in a seminar room discussing things like trauma, or grief, or violence, especially not while strangers stared at my face. I'd be undone. Databases and mathematics seemed safer and they proved to be.

I didn't dream of reanimated corpses or knife-wielding killers any more, but I had started tormenting myself by searching crowds for my sister's face, looking for her proxy, for someone who matched what I thought she might look like now – which was what I looked like when I was sixteen, because that was my only data point. I never found any candidates.

'Is it any good?'

Jim snapped the book shut, releasing a sound that seemed as loud as a thunderclap.

Steve O'Reilly, the store manager, was standing beside him. Leaning against the shelves with his arms folded, wearing his trademark expression of bemused superiority.

The inside of Jim's head was an echo chamber of screams. *I was twelve years old … A man broke into our home … murdered my mother, father and younger sister … The lock was flimsy … But for some reason, he didn't.* He mentally beat them back until he found the words, 'Not really my thing,' and returned the book to the shelf, taking the opportunity to pull in a deep breath and moisten his lips.

His fingers had left misty smudges on the book's glossy black cover.

'Oh yeah?' Steve raised his eyebrows. 'Could've fooled me, Jim. You looked like you were *well* into it.'

Steve was twenty-six and wore shiny suits and came to work every day with globules of gel hardening in his (receding) hairline, yet somehow had the idea that he was a somebody and Jim was a nobody. The greatest challenge of working for him was resisting the urge to correct him about that.

Jim turned to face Steve dead-on. He mirrored his stance, folding his arms and leaning lightly against the shelves, a simple trick that always seemed to make other people uneasy. His settled his face into a perfectly neutral expression and looked Steve right in the eye.

'Did you need something, Steve?'

The younger man shifted his weight.

'Yeah. I need you to remember that you're here to work. This isn't a library.' He reached out and took down the same copy of *The Nothing Man* that Jim had just returned to the shelf. '*The Nothing Man*? What were you doing, Jim? Reliving your glory days? Oh wait, no – you were sitting at a desk somewhere, weren't you? They didn't let you chase after the actual criminals.'

Steve cracked open the book right in the middle, where the pages were different: bright white, thick and glossy, and displaying photographs.

On the page to Steve's left was an image of a large detached house and a family of young children posing by a Christmas tree.

On the opposite one, a pencil sketch.

The pencil sketch.

Steve tapped the page. 'Yeah, yeah. I've heard of this.'

Jim was looking at the sketch upside down but he didn't need to look at it at all to recall it perfectly. It was of a man with small, hooded eyes set deep into a round, fleshy face. Wearing what looked like a thick-knit hat pulled low enough to cover his eyebrows. The angle was slightly off,

21

the head turned a few degrees to the left, as if the man had just heard the artist call his name and was still in the process of turning to respond to it.

In the book, the sketch took up two-thirds of the page above a small paragraph. Presumably the text said something about it being based on the testimony of a witness who had happened to drive past the house owned by the O'Sullivan family of Bally's Lane, near Carrigaline, Co. Cork, in the early hours of 14 January 2000, and caught this man walking along the side of the road with her headlights. *Walking furtively*, she'd said. It was the only glimpse of the killer they called the Nothing Man that anyone had ever got.

Jim had made sure of it.

That night, while he waited in the darkness, he thought he'd have some warning if a car approached, that he'd hear the rumble of the engine long before its lights lit up the road. But the car driven by Claire Bardin, an Irishwoman living in France but home for Christmas, seemed to come out of nowhere. She'd surprised him, coming suddenly around a bend, and, unthinking, he'd looked directly into the light. Recalling it now, Jim thought he felt a cold breeze, and for a split second he was back in the dark on the side of the road, tense and determined, his body fizzing with adrenalin.

It would have been impressively accurate even if Bardin had driven straight to the nearest Garda station to meet with a sketch artist that very night. But she'd done it six months later when, on a trip to Cork for her sister's wedding, she happened to read a news report about the attack and realised that the date and place matched her odd sighting, which made its accuracy remarkable. The morning after Jim first saw it in a paper, he'd started swimming lengths of the local pool every day until the flesh on his face began to tighten and cling, revealing a harsher jawline and hollows beneath his cheekbones.

But the eyes and ears. They didn't change with weight or age – the eyes especially. Even if you opted for surgery you couldn't change where they sat in the bone structure of the face, the distances between them and your other features.

And Claire Bardin had got them exactly right.

Back in the present, Steve was frowning at the sketch.

'Get back to work, Jim.' He snapped the book shut and tucked it under his arm. 'I'm off on my break. Don't let me see you still slacking when I get back.'

Once he knew the book existed, Jim could think of nothing else. It was a ring of fire around him, drawing nearer with each passing moment, threatening to torch every layer of him one by one. His clothes. His skin. His life. If it reached him it would leave nothing but ash and all his secrets, totally exposed.

He had to put it out. Now.

But what was *it*, really? What was this book? Why had she written it? Why now? Nothing had changed. No one had come for him. If it really was about her search for him then he already knew the ending: spoiler alert, she hadn't found him.

But that wasn't enough. Jim needed to know what Eve Black had filled all those pages with, what she'd been doing since he saw her eighteen years ago standing at the top of the stairs, what she was telling the world about that night.

When one of the checkout girls asked Jim if he was feeling okay – he looked flushed and sweaty, she said, was he coming down with something? – he saw an opportunity. He radioed Steve to tell him he was going home sick, then turned the radio off before Steve could come squawking back. He punched his time-card and hurried to his car in the shopping centre's staff car park.

But Jim didn't drive home. He drove straight into the city.

There was a branch of Waterstones on Patrick Street. He'd only been inside once or twice, a long time ago, but he remembered that it was big and that it ran all the way back to Paul Street on its other side.

Jim didn't think he was in any danger but still, there was no need to draw attention. He wasn't going to buy the book from the store where he worked, and neither was he going to get it from some tiny shop where the clerk would likely remember every customer and what they purchased. Buying it online would leave a digital trail and take too long.

Jim needed a copy now.

He parked in the multi-storey on Paul Street and walked to the bookshop's rear entrance. He had put his coat on, hiding his uniform. As the doors swung shut behind him, the buzz from outside died and he was cocooned in the hush of the bookshop.

There were three, four other customers that he could see, plus a guy in a T-shirt in the corner stacking shelves. Way too quiet altogether. There wasn't even a radio playing.

Jim slowly but purposefully made his way to the front of the shop at the other end. He made sure to look like a typical customer. Picking up the odd book here, there, admiring it, reading the back, putting it down again. Stopping to inspect special offers. Having a cursory flip through the books in a bargain box marked LAST CHANCE TO BUY.

He found *The Nothing Man* just inside the main doors.

It had its own table. There were stacks of it on there, each one several books high, arranged in a semicircle. One copy was standing upright in the middle, resting on a little Perspex mount. A handwritten card promised, *The story of Cork's most famous crime, told by a survivor.*

Jim picked one up and placed a palm flat on the cover, as if he could feel what the pages inside held for him, for his future.

Was it all in here, every bad thing he had done, all the things he had packed away since? *The Nothing Man* was a threat, yes, but the idea of reading it, of reliving his glory days ...

It also brought the giddy promise of a treat.

'Just came in today, that one did.' A smiling man was now on the other side of the table, three feet in front of Jim. Mid-forties, dressed casually, wearing a name-tag that identified him as Kevin. 'Great read, by the way. If you can stomach it. Crazy to think it all happened right here.'

'You've read it?' Jim asked.

'A couple of months ago. We get sent advance copies.'

'And *did* she? Find him?'

'No. Well, yes and no. You see, it's hard to say ...'

No, it wasn't. Because here Jim was, still free, still unidentified. He considered asking Kevin to explain himself, but he'd already had more of a conversation than was probably wise. Two teenage girls in school uniform came pushing through the doors, laughing and talking loudly, distracting Kevin, and Jim took the opportunity to snatch up a copy of the book and walk away.

The cash desk was in the middle of the shop. En route, Jim picked up another book the same size as *The Nothing Man*. Its cover was mostly baby-blue sky above a row of multicoloured beach-huts. He also lifted the first greeting card he saw that said HAPPY BIRTHDAY from the selection by the register.

The cashier was female. A young, artsy, college-student type who considered each title with great interest as she scanned its barcode.

'Bit of a random selection,' she said wryly.

Mind your own business, Jim wanted to roar.

He said, 'Well, I'm not sure what she likes. My wife. It's her birthday.'

'And so you're …' The cashier looked at the two contrasting covers in front of her. 'Hedging your bets?'

'Something like that.'

'If you like, I can help you pick—'

'I'll just stick with these, thanks.'

He had planned to leave the store the way he'd come in, but Kevin was down that end of the shop now, straightening shelves, so he turned on his heel and made for the main doors instead.

As he pushed through them, he saw that the entire front window was filled with copies of *The Nothing Man*.

Behind them, pinned to a red felt board, was a collage of old newspaper clippings.

Horror attack in Blackrock.

Special Garda Operation To Chase 'Nothing Man'.

Family of 4 Dead in Murder Spree in Passage West.

The last one was factually incorrect, a misprint the morning after when the exact details from inside the house on Bally's Lane were still as messy as the scene itself.

Only *three* people had died in that house.

That, now, was the problem.

Back in the car park, he sat in his car and locked the doors. He had purposefully parked in a far corner, away from elevators and the pay machines and so, passing foot traffic. He took the second book, the one with the beach-huts on the cover, out of the bag and slipped off its dust jacket. Then he did the same with his copy of *The Nothing Man* and swapped the two over, so now each book was wearing the 'wrong' cover, disguising its true content.

Just in case.

Jim opened his own copy of *The Nothing Man* and flicked through the opening pages until he found the spot where Steve had interrupted him.

Then he shifted in his seat, getting comfortable, and read on.

Every weekend, holiday and summer break I returned to Spanish Point and fell back into life with Nannie the way you fall into your own bed at the end of a long day. I took her greying skin, her shrinking size, the tremors that had crept into her voice, and I put them away with everything else I was determined not to think about.

Nannie died in her sleep on the Feast of the Assumption in 2010, aged eighty-four. I remember finding her in the morning, the temperature of the skin on her forearm telling me that it was already too late to call for help. Then nothing except blurry, fragmented images for weeks after that.

I had never really grieved for my parents and my sister, not actively, not in the way that helps a person process their pain and find a way to move forward, around it, alongside it. Now I was grieving for them all. It was as if the tectonic plates beneath my life had shifted, yawning apart, creating a deep and treacherous chasm into which every steady thing suddenly slid. I was the only thing still standing now, the only one of us left, and my feet were slipping. The problem was that, by then, I'd got so good at pretending, no one could tell.

I finished my degree, graduating with a first. A college friend was now a boyfriend, even though I could never quite trace the threads of our backstory and he knew practically nothing of mine. I sat through what felt like endless meetings in over-lit offices with dusty vertical blinds while document after document was slid across a table to me so I could sign my name by the colourful little stickers that seemed far too jaunty for the task at hand: taking ownership of things that didn't belong to me because now I was the only one left.

I pushed everything down, down, down, until it was safely locked away beneath the numbness.

I was twenty-one years old.

When college ended, I was set adrift. Studying was a series of small tasks that, once completed, were instantly replaced with another, like a game of whack-a-mole. *Get to class. Get that project completed. Study for that exam.* All I'd had to do during those four years was keep moving forward, keep putting one foot in front of the other, start on the next thing. Now there was nothing to do except think of things to do, and I found that I couldn't do that at all. Over the course of six dark months I unravelled, melting into a dull puddle of the person I had been – or had pretended to be. I lost the boyfriend, my few friends and too much weight, in that order. I was a compass needle that couldn't find true north. The truth was I wasn't *trying* to find it, not really. It was so much easier to stop looking, to let go, to sink. And besides, where on this earth were you supposed to point towards when you had no family left?

The quick sale of Nannie's home in Cork meant that I was under no immediate pressure financially, so while my classmates took up exciting jobs abroad and postgraduate places, I rented a crappy bedsit off Mountjoy Square and bedded down. I made my life so small that not even my neighbours knew me. At night I lay awake and during the day I sleepwalked. I don't even know how I passed the hours, only that the time passed and afterwards I had nothing at all to show for it, not even memories.

After months of this, when I could no longer deny that something greater than my own grief was pulling the circuits apart in my brain, I managed to drag myself to a doctor who pushed me on to a therapist, but I couldn't bring myself to tell her the real reason I was there, who I really was and what I'd suffered. Each week I said just enough to keep her writing me prescriptions. I wasn't even sure the pills were doing anything for me but at the same time I was absolutely terrified that they were. I didn't want to find out if what felt like rock bottom was merely halfway down. So I kept going to therapy, kept taking the pills, waiting to feel something different, differently.

And then, finally, things began to change.

I started to sleep at night, bringing my days back into focus. That made me feel restless and jittery in the flat during the day, but there was nothing I *had* to do, no one to see and nowhere to go. So I started to walk. For miles and miles, on paths that hugged the edges of Dublin Bay. Usually heading off around eight o'clock in the morning, pushing against the workers striding into the city until I was out of it and free of them, and *feeling* free as the rising sun broke into shards of light on the water, feet away from me. My go-to route was north out of town and along the water as far as Clontarf, but sometimes I pushed on to Howth Head, and once I walked south across the river and kept going until I found myself in Dun Laoghaire hours later, where I collapsed into a seat on the 46A and slept all the way back.

But it wasn't the same on dull days and I had no interest in doing it on the wet ones. I started searching for an alternative rainy-day activity, something that would get me out of the flat but into another dry, warm place. I chose the library, the largest one I could find, right in the heart of the city centre. There was a steady stream of people into and out of it so I could be anonymous, moving among them unnoticed if not unseen. I started hiding in corners, eyes skimming the same page for the umpteenth time as rain drummed against the windows and our collective breath turned them misty and opaque. Eventually I began to forget myself, falling into whatever book I'd selected as a prop. I found I had an attention span again. Soon after that I was borrowing, bringing books home to read into the evening or even take with me on my walks. Then came cooking: simple, wholesome meals from scratch. Taking care of the rooms in which I lived. Taking care of myself. I didn't recognise it as such at the time, but I was doing for myself what Nannie had once done for me: keeping a simple, quiet life that would help to heal me. I had always assumed we were merely hiding.

I can't say exactly when the last wisps of my fog disappeared, but they did. When they did, I bought a notebook and a pack of sharp pencils, because I knew what it was that I was going to do next: take a chance.

If you think you've read some of these words before, you may have. *If* you have, you already know what I did next.

In September 2014, I began a Masters in Creative Writing at St John's College in Dublin. I choose St John's partly because they were willing to choose me, but also because the campus was already associated with horrific crimes. Several years before, five female first-years had been snatched from the paths that ran along the Grand Canal, their route back to their halls of residence after a night out in the city's pubs and clubs. Each one was left unconscious beneath the black waters to drown, and drown they did. The Nothing Man may have been a headline for a time, but the Canal Killer was an *industry*, spawning documentaries and blogs and — the latest thing — podcasts, even then, years after the fact. (Unbeknownst to anyone but the Canal Killer himself, the story would soon be continuing. There were three new murders connected to St John's and one attempted one while I was writing this book.) I figured this was the only university in Ireland that already had its own monster and he was even more notorious than mine. I might go unnoticed. I might get not to be the girl who in the place where.

I wanted to write. Had always wanted to. What or how or for whom, I didn't know, but since I had dragged myself out from under the darkness, I had been thinking about it more and more and now, finally, I'd made a decision. I would learn how and then I would do it. I had notions of writing a novel, something dark and twisty into which I could – anonymously – pour all of my pain. This path was fraught with danger but I was stronger now and once again ready to pretend. That's what fiction was, wasn't it? Pretending?

Not according to our course director, the renowned novelist Jonathan Eglin, whose debut novel *The Essentialists* was longlisted for the Booker Prize. He told us this in our very first class. He said that fiction only really worked if it was built like a lattice through which you were repeatedly offered glimpses of absolute truth. That was our aim, regardless of what form our writing took. He then proceeded, over the course of those first few weeks and months, to systematically sandpaper away all of our armour, our masks, our carefully constructed personhoods, until we were left naked and bleeding directly on to the page.

I resisted as long as I could. I was sure, I was absolutely *certain*, that if I as much as put the words *when I was twelve years old a man broke into our home and murdered my mother, father and younger sister, Anna,* seven years old then and for ever on to a virtual page or dared write them in ink on a real one, what little ground I'd secured to stand on would collapse beneath my feet. There'd be no coming back from the depths of *that* abyss. So I wrote short stories about happy families who loved each other. The act of creating them comforted me. Whenever I wrote, I got to go back and see them, and find out what had happened to them since. The time I spent at my laptop were my visiting hours.

Then came the day of the forgotten deadline. It dawned on me one afternoon like a bullet of stone-cold dread to the chest: I had to submit two thousand new words first thing the following morning, for a grade, and I had completely forgotten about it until that moment. I holed up in the library late into the night, but found myself paralysed by the blinking cursor. No matter what I tried, the words just wouldn't come. I walked home on dark, wet streets and sat in my bedroom, staring helplessly at the still-blank white space on screen.

The clock ticked past midnight, bringing a new date to the display on my computer: 21 March. Anna's birthday. That one would've been her twenty-first.

The words began to bubble up inside me, unbidden. I would write about her, I decided, and change the names once I was done. It wasn't a good idea but, in that moment, all I was really concerned about was getting myself out of this jam, away from the blank page and its awful emptiness. I started typing. *When I was twelve years old a man broke into our home and murdered my mother, father and younger sister, Anna, seven years old then and for ever* ...

Eglin wasn't fooled. The piece had a quality to it, a scalpel-grade sharpness, that none of my previous work had even hinted at the promise of. Half an hour after I emailed him the piece in the grey light of the early hours, Eglin emailed back to ask me to come to his office first thing. I steeled myself as I walked down his corridor of the Arts building, ready to deny all, but he didn't even bother asking me if it was true. He already knew it was.

Instead, he urged me to publish it.

I remember not knowing what to say, not knowing where to begin with why that could never happen. And then him saying, very softly, 'But, Eve, you might catch him with it.'

And that, then, changed everything.

It felt like flinging myself off a cliff. The night before I knew the piece was due to go live, I dreamed of Anna, crawling out of the sea like the Spanish sailors had when I was a child. She looked like a banshee. She came clawing at me with rotting fingers, her blonde hair wild and tangled with seaweed, screaming at me for failing to protect myself. But I was beginning to realise that protecting myself was also protecting *him*. I couldn't get them back. But I could, maybe, make him pay for their taking.

My piece went live on the *Irish Times* website at 4:00 a.m. on the last day of May 2015 and appeared in their print edition later that morning. By close of business, I had officially gone viral. It started on social media, where a few influential accounts shared a link, and then the people following *them* started to share it. It was picked up by a broadsheet in the UK, then a monthly magazine in the US. Everyone, it seemed, had always wondered what had happened to that girl who'd survived the Nothing Man's worst and final attack. Now they knew some, they wanted more and more.

Intrepid reporters found my contact details via the St John's College student portal and invitations to appear on radio and TV shows started to stream in. I couldn't possibly talk about what had happened in real time – I wasn't physically able to do that yet – but I wanted to do *something*. Eglin put me in touch with his editor at Iveagh Press (pronounced like *ivy*), who encouraged me to expand the article into a book. She said if I did, she would publish it. This is the book you hold in your hands now.

Just a few weeks earlier, agreeing to write a book about what had happened to my family would've been utterly unthinkable. But when 'The Girl Who' went viral, something else important had happened to me too.

Within hours, articles about my article began to pop up online. Classmates of mine kept sending me links to them, excited that one of us was making such a splash with our written words, seemingly oblivious to the pain behind my story. At first I ignored them. I'd never read anything about the Nothing Man case. I had steadfastly avoided doing so. In the years since that night, I'd never learned anything more than the broad strokes of what he had done to my family, and they were bad enough. I didn't want the blurry shapes to come into focus. I knew I'd never be able to unsee them again.

But eventually, curiosity got the better of me. I started clicking on the links, scanning rather than reading the articles they led to, keeping the text moving ever upwards on the screen.

In the fourth or fifth one I looked at, I was stopped cold by a phrase. *rope and knife beneath one of her sofa cushions*

I went back to read the sentence from the beginning. *Gardaí had already been to the apartment complex two weeks before, when another tenant, a single woman living alone, discovered a rope and a knife beneath one of her sofa cushions. She hoovered there on the same day every week and was certain the items had not been there the week before, and to her knowledge, no one else had been in the apartment since. She immediately reported the find to her local station. Gardaí would come to believe that the Nothing Man had planted them there on a preparatory visit, ready to use on his return.*

My pulse pounded in my ears. Because I, too, had once found a rope and a knife beneath a couch cushion.

But I'd never told anyone about it.

It was shortly before the attack, maybe mere days. I was watching Anna for half an hour while our mother popped to the shops, and she'd convinced me to play a game that, for some reason lost to me now, necessitated that every cushion from every chair in the living room be tossed on to the floor in a pile. When I lifted the last remaining cushion from the couch, the action revealed two items lying amid the biscuit crumbs, lost hair-ties and sticky copper coins: a rope and a knife. The rope was braided and blue, and was still looped neatly inside the glossy band that served as its packaging. The knife was about the length of a hardback book, with a thick yellow plastic handle that reminded me of Fisher Price toys. The blade had little jags along the edge and it looked very, very clean, if not brand new. Shiny.

I didn't wonder what they were doing there. My mother had a habit of storing things under couch cushions – the post mostly, the bills she wanted to hide from my father, but also the odd magazine or knitting pattern – so although I thought these were strange items to find there, it didn't strike me as particularly odd. I knew enough to know the knife was a potential danger, so I put the cushion back and told Anna the game was over.

Later, when I saw that same blue rope tied around my father's wrists and ankles as he lay broken and contorted at the bottom of our stairs, the connection my brain made was that *that man used my dad's rope*. It never occurred to me that the Nothing Man had been to our house in advance of the attack, that *he'd* put the items under the cushion. That doing so was part of his preparation, that he was going to come back and use them. After the attack I had had one Garda interview, during which I cried endlessly and choked out one-word answers. The rope had never come up. I was numb and in shock and twelve years old; it never crossed my mind to connect the two events. At some point I'd forgotten about it altogether.

The sudden realisation that I may have been able to stop it, to prevent it – the idea that if I had just told someone about the rope and the knife I might have *saved my family* – was too much to bear. It was a pressure that pushed down on me, crushing my lungs, smashing my heart into sharp pieces all over again. It is still the most intense pain I have ever experienced. Even worse, somehow, than the original loss, because now I saw that it didn't have to happen.

But mixed in with this was another, more welcome revelation: after all this time, the Nothing Man investigation might have a new lead.

The night he came and killed my family wasn't the first time he'd been in our house. He'd been there before, perhaps more than once. Could someone have seen him on those occasions? I could describe the knife. What if it was an especially distinctive one, only available to buy from certain places? Would that help find him? Could it, now, even though nearly twenty years had passed?

What else did I know? Could I have other useful information, hidden in plain sight in my memories? Could the other survivors, the other victims? And what about things like DNA, forensic science? They were better now than they'd been then, and were getting better all the time. What if we went back and looked for the Nothing Man again, now?

What if, this time, we found him?

What if *I* did?

So ask me again. *Am I the girl who …?* Because this time – these days – I'll tell you the truth: no, but I *was*.

I was the girl who survived the Nothing Man.

Now I am the woman who is going to catch him.

— I —

FROM THE DARK

– I –

True Life

Before the events of 4 October 2001, crime came regularly into our home, but only on twin spools of glossy black tape encased in shells of hard plastic – and it was me who carried it inside.

That last Christmas, I got a portable television with a built-in VCR player for my room. My mother had reluctantly agreed to this on the basis that it would never be connected to any TV channels, that I could only use it to watch videotapes. (I'm sure another deciding factor was that if I was in my room watching *that* TV, I couldn't also be whinging and moaning about whatever my mother was trying to watch on the one downstairs, in the living room.) In a house where technology meant a cumbersome Compaq Presario that took half an hour to come to life, a sluggish dial-up connection and the fax machine my father had for work, the novelty of there suddenly being a TV screen in my bedroom was on a par with there being an alien spaceship in the back garden. Whenever I turned it on, its power spread out beyond the set itself, electrifying the entire room with its hum, bringing every molecule in the air alive with the excitement of endless possibility. Sitting on my bed, facing it, with the remote in one hand and something sugary within reach of the other, was my happiest place – until I ran out of things to watch.

We had a typical home library of VHS tapes for the time: Disney movies, things recorded off the TV, a few random series of Friends that we'd got on sale. Having quickly exhausted these offerings, I negotiated a deal with my dad: I would be allowed to use my parents' account at our local video rental shop provided I paid for the tapes and assumed responsibility for returning them on time. I soon figured out that in order to maximise my weekly budget – three of my five pocket-money pounds – I needed to avoid the New Releases and instead dig around at the back of the shop where a handwritten sign threatened 'TRUE LIFE'. Here, the cover designs were predominately a palette of bruising, all black and dark blues, and the ominous red titles on them dripped blood for effect.

These were made-for-TV American movies based on infamous American crimes, for some reason available to rent on VHS in Ireland. They had low production values, cheesy dialogue and at best a tenuous relationship with the truth. When I first encountered them in spring 2001, the vast majority were already at least a decade old, covering cases that had happened even further back. But you could rent two for a week for the same price as a new movie for one night, so I started working my way through them. I quickly became obsessed.

A Killing in Beverly Hills told the story of the Menendez brothers, who shot their parents dead so they could either escape their father's abuse, as they claimed, or start spending their inheritance, as the prosecution did. Ambush in Waco re-enacted the siege in Texas sparked by a bungled government raid that resulted in the deaths of four federal agents and seventy-six members of a cult called the Branch Davidians. In Small Sacrifices, Diane Downs, played by Farrah Fawcett's hair, stops her car on a dark country road so she can shoot her three young children, before driving slowly to the nearest hospital and claiming that a bushy-haired stranger did it instead. A flame-haired, teenage Drew Barrymore played the title role in The Amy Fisher Story, in which a sixteen-year-old girl dubbed the Long Island Lolita, a moniker completely lost on me at the time, had an affair with thirty-five-year-old Joey Buttafuoco and then attempted to murder his wife by shooting her in the head.

If I had a 'favourite', though, it was Victim of Beauty: The Dawn Smith Story. Dawn's seventeen-year-old sister, Shari, was kidnapped in broad daylight from the end of her own driveway by Larry Gene Bell in May 1985, then murdered by him. The made-for-TV version of events, starring Star Trek: Voyager's Jeri Ryan, focused on Bell's obsession with Dawn – a blonde, blue-eyed beauty pageant contestant – in the twenty-eight-day period between Shari's disappearance and Bell's capture.

These VHS movies weren't *all* crime. I vaguely remember one about a young couple with a baby whose car got snowed in on a mountainside and who then had to take cover in a cave in order to survive, and another about a pair of blonde girls who'd been accidentally switched at birth and then, as teens, found that out. But they were *mostly* crime, and it was the crime ones that I liked the most.

They were hardly appropriate viewing for a twelve-year-old, but the bored teenager manning the counter at the video shop didn't care and my parents, I have to assume, didn't know. The general rule in our house was that so long as you were being quiet, whatever else you were being wouldn't be queried. These days I can easily minimise it by drawing comparisons to what children might watch now, when they can go to bed with a device small enough to hide under the covers that can effectively show them anything at all. In any case, to pontificate about what effect my true-crime habit might have had on me is very much a moot point seeing as I was, unknowingly, in line for a ticket to the live show. But the truth is I don't think they had any effect on me at all.

I knew the events I saw re-enacted on my little TV screen were real on some level, but they weren't *my* reality. This was Ireland at the turn of the millennium. Our police force didn't carry guns. We'd never had a confirmed serial killer, defined by the FBI as a person who commits at least three murders over the span of a month or more, allowing time for a distinct 'cooling off' period between them. When murder made the news here, it was nearly always terrorism or gangland related. Your risk of being the random target of a murderous stranger was exceptionally low, if not practically non-existent. (In the popular podcast West Cork, which centres around one of Ireland's most famous unsolved murders, the death in 1996 of Frenchwoman Sophie Toscan du Plantier, hosts Jennifer Forde and Sam Bungey describe how the locals refer to it as '*the* murder' because there hasn't been another one in the area since.) Besides, I knew how to avoid the bad men. The same lessons were repeated in every movie. Don't walk home alone in the dark. Don't accept lifts from strangers. Be a good girl.

I *was* a good girl and I was at home with my family. The doors were locked and the curtains were closed. I was safe.

How do you know what you know about your parents? Lately, I've been putting this question to friends of mine. Their answers generally fit into one of two categories: either they found out things from other people, like relatives or their parents' friends, or their parents shared stories with them directly. The second one happened more and more as time went on, as in, they were told more the older they got. I should also say that these friends have adult siblings, uncles and aunts and, like all good Irish Catholic families, cousins to spare. They've been collecting friends all their lives and so too have their parents, dotting their social orbits with figures like the girl who lived next door to their childhood home and the guy they worked with in that place that time. One friend told me that, after thinking about it, most of what she knows about her parents' initial meeting and pre-married life comes from snide comments her maternal grandmother, who never liked her father, would make during family get-togethers when she'd had one too many G&Ts.

But both of my parents were only children, and they and my only sibling died when I was twelve, an age when you have zero interest in who your parents are or ever were outside of their being your parents. After that I was left with just one familial link, Nannie, and in our remaining years together I didn't dare question her about them. The sad truth is I know very little about who my parents were as people.

My mother's name was Deirdre. She was short and slight; physically, Anna took after her. She had worn her hair the same way since before she'd got married, in a bob that stopped just above her shoulders in her natural light brown. She worked as an illustrator, adding images to a series of French and German textbooks aimed at the Junior Cert cycle and also, during term time, as a waitress in a café in Carrigaline. She would drive us to school on her way to work and pick us up on our way back, by which time a box of something from the café – creamy cakes, demi baguettes, fruit scones – would have appeared in the passenger-side footwell. She worshipped the sun and would be out the back garden on a sunlounger, oiled up and skin bare, at the merest suggestion of light peeking out from behind the clouds. She'd been born in a town called Killorglin in Co. Kerry, hadn't been to college and spoke little of her own parents, who had died when she was just a teen. In secondary school she had been a competitive rower and was always saying she was going to get back into it, somehow, just for exercise, but we all knew the talking about it was the start and end of her efforts.

My mother was very easy-going, relaxed and unfussy. If Anna or I acted up, she would award us a bemused expression and then leave us to burn ourselves out – which, without a reaction to fuel our temper-tantrum or an audience to perform it to, we would quickly do. Her best friend was a woman called Joan who she'd known since secondary school. Joan owned the café where Mam worked. I don't really remember her spending time with people without my dad. When they left us on an odd Saturday night in the care of Nannie, it was to go somewhere together, usually to another couple's house for dinner or out to a work do.

She could be very funny, always there with a witty remark or devastating comeback, which made her an odd match for my serious dad. She took a lot of photographs and got them developed but stopped there, her grand plans to organise them into volumes of albums remaining just that. She left me with boxes and boxes of bulging envelopes thick with glossy 4x6 prints, none of which have names or dates or places to go along with them, and now *my* plans to do something with them are so far failing to materialise too. Nearly all the photos are of Anna or me or the two of us together.

My father's name was Ross. He was from a place called Sunday's

Well on the north side of Cork City, where large houses backed on to the river and the families who owned them were well-to-do. After he'd moved out and got married, Nannie had sold up and moved to Blackrock. His father had died of heart failure before I was born and had been, as Nannie muttered occasionally, 'fond of the drink'. My father had met my mother in a pub in the city and within eighteen months they were married. They'd only ever lived together in the house in Passage West.

My father was tall, over six foot, and, according to my mam's photos, had been balding since his twenties. I understood little about his job, which involved chemicals and a big factory in Ringaskiddy. He worked long hours and was missing from most of our home life. The one rule both Anna and I knew to observe was to never go into his office on the ground floor of our house. When I think of my dad I think of the cards Hallmark make and the unimaginative gift guides department stores put out at Christmas. He could've been their model for A Typical Dad. He took a briefcase to work. He carried handkerchiefs with his initials on them. He liked whiskey and watched golf and kept classical music CDs in the car, and everything he wore came from the same palette of dull brown tweeds and knit navy blues.

A few weeks after my article came out, I received an email from a woman I'll call Michelle, who said she had worked with my father for many years and that they had been great friends. She spent nearly a thousand words sharing her memories of a man I had never met, a version of my father who was funny and spontaneous and good at giving advice, who gave Michelle carefully chosen books as gifts and left journal articles on her desk that he thought she'd find interesting. Michelle still missed him terribly and wanted to meet me. Starved of information on my parents, I should've jumped at the chance. But there was something lingering between the lines of her email, something delicate and treacherous, that I didn't dare unpack. I had never heard her name. I ignored the message and she didn't contact me again, but she left my father standing in a light I'd never seen him in before, and I didn't know what to make of it.

From what I witnessed, my parents' marriage was a solid partnership. They bickered but never fought, although this might have been because my mother just couldn't get herself worked up enough over anything to have an argument. Before it could get heated, she'd shrug her shoulders and back down. They didn't act like the couples you saw on TV, the ones who were always kissing and hugging and flirting like teenagers, but when I grew up I would discover that hardly anyone did. My father did hold my mother's hand when they'd walk together in public, and I often heard them talking softly to each other late into the night through the wall our bedrooms shared.

When you're twelve years old, adult life seems like an endless adventure – or rather, *your* adult life feels like it will be. In those last few months I had a thick hardback notebook in which I recorded my private thoughts, observations, secrets, hopes and dreams. I had covered it in a leftover scrap of the wallpaper my mother had hung in the living room, a dense toile pattern in duck-egg blue and white, and kept it covered in a series of multicoloured rubber bands arranged in an order only I knew, so I would know if anyone had interfered with it in my absence. I think I got that idea from a Judy Blume book. Flicking through its pages now, I find a girl who is planning on living several lives.

I wanted a great love affair like in (Baz Luhrmann's) Romeo + Juliet. I wanted to live in New York and London and Paris. I wanted my teenage years to be like the American shows I watched on TV, full of proms and cheerleading and wearing your own cool clothes to school. I wanted to be a professional dancer, and also a scientist who got to work in the Antarctic, and also a hairdresser on a cruise ship because my friend's mum had done that when she was younger and was always talking about how much fun it was. So when I looked at my parents – living in the city they grew up in, doing normal jobs, being normal people – I couldn't help but feel unimpressed. Why had they done nothing with this, their one wild and precious life? Why didn't they desperately *want* anything? Why didn't they have dreams and adventures and wishes and goals?

I didn't know anything about their *desires*, that was the problem. Without that missing piece, it was hard for my parents to live as fully formed people in my mind. But recently I've started to wonder if they wanted nothing because they already had it, if our family life *was* their dream. I like to think so. I've decided that from now on, I will.

What really strikes me about that diary is what is missing from it. I only mention my parents to complain about them and I barely mention Anna at all.

I have very few distinct memories of my sister that I can play back in my mind. There are flashes and my mother's photographs, but few moving images. When you're a child, and especially when you're a child on the cusp of adolescence, a gap of five years is a chasm. Anna was an annoyance to me, mostly, buzzing around on the periphery of my days, demanding things: help, a loan of something, my attention. When she'd ask for these things she'd come to me quietly, hands clasped behind her back, head bowed, knowing the odds weren't on her side but wishing that this time would be different, that *I* would be different.

I can see her now, blonde hair held back by a pink band, a spill of freckles across her nose, wearing those Velcro-strap trainers with lights in the soles. One leg is bent behind the other and she's looking up at me with naked hope. I am desperate to go back and tell her she can have anything she wants, that she can have all of me, that I'll forgo all others and spend every moment of the rest of her life with her doing whatever she wants, that I love her and love being her sister.

Actually, no, scratch that. If we're getting to go back, I'd scoop her up and run away with her, and we'd stay safe and grow up and reach that place where, as adults, we can be friends. But I was just a child, we both were, and neither of us knew what was coming.

Here's what I do remember: when Anna played, it was at being a grown-up. While I was into Barbie dolls, casting them in elaborate soap opera-worthy storylines involving adulterous Kens and kidnapped Skippers, Anna liked the life-size baby kind that came with prams and pushchairs and, one memorable Christmas, the ability to make a little brown smudge in a nappy. We had a waist-high shelving unit in the living room that Anna would drag away from the wall and stand in behind, and then we'd all be forced to queue up to visit whatever business she was conducting that day, be it the bank, post office or coffee shop. One summer we got a barbeque and Anna hired my dad to be the chef in her restaurant, which only seated three around a somewhat battered patio table but had printed menus and a very attentive waitress, from what I recall. (The chef, meanwhile, burnt all our burgers and clearly needed retraining.) Her lands of make-believe never seemed to involve princesses or mermaids or superheroes, but air stewards and office workers and librarians. She was so eager to play in the adult world she couldn't wait to stop being a child. Her pretending, as it turned out, was all she would ever get to experience of it.

That last summer, two things happened that I can recall quite clearly. The first was that, in June, Anna had an accident. She was riding a friend's bike down a steep hill near our house when the front wheel caught in the lip of a pothole and vaulted Anna up and over the handlebars. She was wearing a helmet but ended up covered in bloody grazes, and with her awkward landing managed to dislocate the ring finger on her right hand. Resetting it had to be done under general anaesthetic, which meant that Anna had to stay in hospital for two nights. She was a small child anyway, but seeing her lying on a hospital bed, barely troubling it, looking tiny and lost, shocked me. I spent hours with her over those two or three days, reading to her, playing card games, painting glitter on the little nails that peeked out from her cast. When she came home, I granted her control over my TV – *temporarily*, I warned her several times – so she could watch her favourite Disney movie, The Emperor's New Groove, and then Toy Story 2, which Dad had just bought her as a get-well-soon treat. She asked me to stay and watch them with her and, with that image of her in the hospital bed still fresh in my mind, I agreed, although with some eye-rolling and sighing just to save face. Mam delivered us popcorn and cans of fizzing Coke on a tray, entering the room carefully and stealthily, as if we were wild animals in our natural habitat whose equilibrium was at great risk of being disturbed.

I was less well behaved at Anna's party, my other clear memory from that time. For some reason my mother had agreed to take Anna and five or six of her friends to our local McDonald's as an end-of-school-year treat, which Anna promptly took to calling a party. There was a special designated area in the restaurant for children's parties, with toadstool chairs and sunflower tables, and although I had been enlisted by our mother to attend in a sort of chaperone-slash-child-wrangler capacity, there was no way in hell I was going to be caught sitting in that section and I made that quite clear. Repeatedly. This made Anna anxious. I can see it now, when I look back: the way her mouth would get small and tight and her eyes wide whenever I brought it up, each time I complained that I had better things to do on a Saturday afternoon in the summer than go to a *child's so-called party*. She desperately wanted me there and was clearly worried I wouldn't come. I did, in the end, but I sat a few tables away, picking at fries, repeatedly checking my watch and doing my very best to look pathologically bored.

Anna, from what I could tell, had a great time. She was just starting to knit together her own circle of friends outside of school, and when I see her in my mind's eye at that party I see her in the centre of it, smiling and laughing and reaching to dip a chicken nugget in one of those little ketchup containers. I know she was pleased with how it went; I overheard her proudly telling my mother that the reports from the girls who'd attended were good. But I wish I had just sat with her, sat right next to her, been her big sister.

What I really want to tell you about Anna is the teenage girl she turned into and the woman she became after that. I want to know what she looks like and how she is, *who* she is, and where she went and what she did. I want to know what she studied in college and where it led her. I want to meet her partner and her children, to see how she dresses and decorates her house, to visit at Christmastime with a bottle of wine for us and presents for her kids, for all of us to go on holidays together. I want to sit with her late into the night and reminisce about playing bank, bike accidents and birthday parties. I want to hear her say that she's okay, that she's happy, that she's had a good life. I want to hear her adult voice.

But because of *him*, I can't.

– 2 –

Let's Play a Game

In the final minutes of 31 December 1999, in a nation abuzz with a mix of uncharacteristic optimism about the dawn of a new millennium and a Y2K-induced fear that planes were about to fall out of the sky, I was sitting on the couch in our living room with a sleeping Anna on one side of me and a softly snoring Nannie on the other. My parents had gone out to a party in the Carrigaline Court Hotel; I wouldn't see them until I woke up the following morning. On the TV, a concert was broadcasting live from Dublin City. Fireworks were imminent. My eyelids were heavy but I was determined to stay awake long enough to see them. I may have reached for a sip of Coke, or maybe even got up and made myself a cup of tea.

At about the same time, in another living room about twelve minutes' drive away and only a couple of minutes' drive from the Carrigaline Court Hotel, sixteen-year-old Tommy O'Sullivan was looking at the same thing on his family's television screen.

Then the phone in the kitchen started ringing.

At first Tommy thought he wasn't hearing anything on the line because the speaker was being drowned out by the noise of the television, or perhaps that of his charges: his siblings David, aged twelve, Nancy, ten, and Emer, seven. They were hopping around the floor in front of the TV screen, dancing and clapping and occasionally play-fighting, hyper on the last of the Christmas sweets and fizzy drinks. The O'Sullivans' landline was fixed to the wall next to the fridge in the kitchen. Tommy shushed the children, pulled the door connecting the two rooms shut and said, 'Hello?' into the phone for the second time.

He heard what he would later describe as a crackling sound, followed by a long, slow sigh. Someone was blowing hard into the mouthpiece on the other end, generating a strange, creepy sound. The voice Tommy was about to hear was male and raspy, somewhere between a hoarse whisper and the damaged vocal cords of a chronic chain-smoker. It said, *'Let's play a game ...'*

The words carried no discernible accent, but the way the caller spoke had a kind of theatrical menace about it. It reminded Tommy of the teen horror movie Scream. In its opening sequence, Drew Barrymore's character is home alone when she receives a phone call that at first seems like a playful prank. But the caller is soon revealed to be a masked murderer who gains entry to the house and kills her. This was fresh in Tommy's mind because he and his friends had watched the movie on Halloween night. Now it was New Year's Eve and Tommy was the only member of that same group who wasn't at Mike Hickey's free gaff, drinking spirits smuggled out of parents' cabinets and listening to music at a volume that, on any other night, would have guaranteed a visit from the guards. Instead, Tommy was stuck with babysitting duties, his parents at the same New Year Eve's party as mine.

He had never been happy about this arrangement but was even less so now, with the clock ticking down to midnight and the wrenching feeling of missing out, of being *left* out, approaching its most acute. Convinced that this phone call was one or more of his friends taunting him about this situation, Tommy muttered something like, 'Oh fuck off, dickheads,' and hung up. The following day, his friends would deny that they had made the call.

A fortnight later, on the morning of 14 January 2000, Tommy was woken by the piano-key ringtone of his mobile phone. It was his first but second-hand, a hand-me-down from his father with a new pay-as-you-go SIM card inside. Tommy had had a Saturday job in the SuperValu in Carrigaline since the summer, restocking shelves and packing bags, and, each week, he set aside ten pounds of his earnings to spend on phone credit. That was more than enough because he only used the device to exchange text messages with the friends of his who also had mobile phones, names he could count on the fingers of one hand. His mother didn't have one and his father only used his for work, which was why it was confusing that, according to the little green, square screen glowing in the dark of his bedroom, it was 'DAD' that was calling him now. When Tommy saw the time, he was even more confused: it was 5:02 a.m.

'Tommy?' His father's voice sounded far away even though he was, presumably, just on the other side of the wall. 'Is your door locked?'

It felt like the middle of the night and he had just been jerked awake from a deep level of sleep; Tommy's first thought was that his father was losing his mind. He asked him to repeat the question.

'Is your bedroom door locked? Go check.'

'Dad, what the f—' Tommy caught the swear word he used so easily with his friends and bit down on his lip to stop it from slipping out. 'What's going on?'

'Just do it.'

His father sounded weird. The weight of teenage tiredness was clawing at Tommy's eyelids, pulling him towards his pillow, making his limbs heavy and slow. All he wanted to do was go back to sleep as soon as possible. He got out of bed with a groan and trudged to his bedroom door – which was, indeed, locked.

When Tommy bent down to look through the keyhole, he could only see light: the key was missing.

'Ours is locked too,' his father said. 'And your mother isn't in here.'

'What did she lock the doors for? Where is she?'

His father didn't answer either question. Tommy held the phone to his chest and called out, 'Mam?' No answer. Again, louder. '*Mam?*' Still nothing. He banged on his door a couple of times. Then he went to the wall he shared with his brother David and thumped on that.

'I'm going outside,' his father said. 'Through the window. I'll let myself in with the spare key.'

They ended the call.

The next thing Tommy heard was a groan of protest through the shared wall: David had finally woken up. Tommy coaxed his younger brother out of bed and got him to check *his* door. Same deal: locked, key missing.

Tommy went to the window. It was pitch black outside. The houses on Bally's Lane had generous plots and there were no streetlights. He was pretty sure he could make out the shapes of two cars, though, meaning his mother must be in the house. But doing what? He thought of Christmas – Christmas Eve, specifically. There'd been a couple of years there where Nancy and Emer's excitement over the imminent arrival of Santa Claus had become a kind of mania, each one amplifying the other's, leaving both children wide-awake, wired, for nearly the whole night, and taking it in turns to tiptoe down the hall to the living room to see if their presents had been delivered yet. Exhausted and exasperated, his mother had eventually resorted to locking them into their rooms. Is that what *this* was? Was she planning some kind of surprise for them that she didn't want them to discover until the morning? But if so, why take the keys? Why lock her own bedroom door too? Why not respond to his calls?

As Tommy watched, a shaft of yellow light fell on to the gravel drive, followed by the dull *thunk* of a window opening. His father was climbing outside. It took the man a minute but then gravel was crunching underfoot and a shape was hurrying past Tommy's own window, a shadow moving in the night. He listened for the sound of a key in the front door, but it never came.

Instead, he heard his father shouting.

He was telling Tommy to ring the Gardaí.

The ring-tone on Jim's mobile phone suddenly annihilated the silence of the car, startling him. Still in the fog of memory the book's pages had generated, he answered it without thinking.

'Oh,' he heard Noreen say. 'I didn't expect you to pick up. I was just going to leave a message. Aren't you at work?'

'What is it, Nor?'

'Katie's coming for dinner.' Even though their daughter had allegedly moved out, into student digs near the university on College Road, she seemed to be around their house as much as ever. 'So I need you to grab a few things from Centra on the way home.'

Jim looked at the book on his lap. 'And why can't you walk up there and get them?'

'Money,' Noreen said quietly.

'But I gave you plenty on Friday. Where did it all go?'

'On the *bills*, Jim. And the food we've eaten so far this week. I can't just—'

'Text me a list.'

Jim ended the call and threw the phone back on to the passenger seat. He refused to listen to her when she was hysterical. It gave him a headache.

And he wanted to get back to the book.

Eve Black had found the knife and the rope, then. That was news to him. They'd still been there when he went to collect them on the night of the attack, so there was no way he could've known. That was an interesting revelation, even if it changed nothing. And Spanish Point. He'd never been there, but he knew where it was. That was a question answered. He'd always wondered where she'd disappeared to after the attack. Childhood memories: boring. He didn't care who any of these people had been.

The lie was interesting, though.

Or, to give Eve the benefit of the doubt for now, the *misremembering*.

Would she describe the events of that night in detail, of *the* night? What would she say? He was very tempted to skip ahead and see.

But he also wanted to savour it.

Reading it was stirring something. A feeling. *The* feeling. It was just like the voice of a great friend you'd lost touch with: you couldn't remember it at all but once you were reminded of it, you couldn't believe you'd ever forgotten it.

He would have to, though. He was nearly sixty-three years old. He couldn't move as fast as he used to.

He didn't have the energy any more for all ... *that*.

It was half past one. He normally got home from work around three fifteen, so allowing for him to get out to the suburbs in after-school traffic and stop at the shop, he figured he was safe for another forty-five minutes or so.

Jim's phone beeped: a text from Noreen.

Chicken breasts, oven chips, mushrooms, bottle of white wine.

No *please* or *thank you.* And she could forget about the white wine. Jim wasn't about to serve his own eighteen-year-old daughter alcohol on a Tuesday night and anyway, Katie wouldn't want it. She got up at the crack of dawn every morning to hit the gym.

And did Noreen think he was *made* of money?

Jim set a timer on his phone and went back to his book.

Instead, he heard his father shouting.

He was telling Tommy to ring the Gardaí.

From the outside, the O'Sullivan house was aggressively unremarkable. It was a bungalow, typical of the kind that littered the Irish countryside but made no effort to connect with it: a squat, rectangular box built of dirty grey brick, set back from the road. The windows looked both too short and too wide, as if they were being uncomfortably compressed by the pressure of the pitched roof, heavy with dirty slate tiles. *Aurora* – the name was etched into a brass plaque by the front door – had been built from a book of plans in 1978. Since then, its only update had been a conservatory built on to the back by a cowboy builder who'd disappeared before the job was done, leaving a room too cold to sit in for ten months of the year and a set of French doors that didn't lock properly.

Tommy's parents, Alice and Shane O'Sullivan, had met at a birthday party in Blarney when they were both nineteen. She was originally from Clonakilty, he from Bandon; on that first evening they'd drawn vocal maps of mutual friends and common places and marvelled at how they had never crossed paths before. Since then, their shared life had moved easily along the path it was supposed to. They'd dated for three years, then married and bought the house. Alice was pregnant with Tommy within twelve months. Shane got into the bank and began working his way up. Three more kids arrived, one more than Alice had imagined having.

It'd been tough there for a while, manic even, but now the kids were growing up and Alice felt she had some space to breathe again.

Shane had been appointed branch manager in Douglas three months ago, so there was not only time to think but a little money to spend, too. Alice had started saving her Children's Allowance when, not that long ago, she had relied on it. And she'd started making plans. A family holiday abroad, ideally in France. A new extension that would give them the extra bedroom they needed to give each child their own. Knocking down that God-awful conservatory.

It was Alice who met him first.

In the early hours of 14 January 2000, she awoke to find herself blinded by a bright, white light. It was all she could see. When she closed her eyes, it seemed to barely dim. It crossed her mind that she might be having a stroke or some kind of brain haemorrhage. That headache she'd had the other day – should she have gone to the doctor about it? Was it too late now? Frantic, Alice patted the bed beside her, searching for the warm shape of Shane's body, trying to alert him that something was terribly, terribly wrong, but something – *someone* – grabbed her before she could. The light changed, its epicentre swinging away from her, replaced with a heavy weight on her body, pressing her down, pushing something sharp into the soft flesh of her neck.

It all came together in one horrific flash of understanding. The light was a head torch strapped to the forehead of a masked man who shouldn't be in her home but who was, who was now *climbing on top of her*, his right arm pinning her left to the bed just inches from the fabric of Shane's T-shirt and his left pressing something sharp into her neck. He smelled like wet leaves and earth and there was something on his breath, familiar but mildly unpleasant. Was that ... *coffee?*

A gloved hand clamped down so hard on her mouth that Alice tasted metal. The force of it had made her gums bleed.

'Don't make a sound,' the intruder whispered. 'I'll slit your throat. Then I'll slit everyone else's, one by one. Nod if you understand.'

Alice did.

Her whole body was shaking so badly, she couldn't understand why Shane hadn't already woken up. But then Shane *did* stir. She felt the movement beneath her own body, heard the creak of the springs in the mattress as he rearranged his limbs. But then there was the sigh of her husband's breath as he settled back to sleep.

The weight disappeared off her body and the light in the room changed, returning to the state she would've expected: dark, with a sliver of weak light from the bulb further down the hall pushing through the few inches of open door. It happened so fast, Alice thought for a moment that she had only *now* woken up and that everything in the last ten seconds had been the tail-end of a dream, a horribly vivid nightmare, like those ones where you think you're late only to wake up and discover that you still have plenty of time. Relief was flooding her veins when, under the covers, a hand came at her from the wrong side and yanked hard on her foot.

He was under the bed, or crouched on the floor beside it. Holding her ankle now with a gloved hand. Tracing the tip of the knife's blade down the back of her leg, lingering at the heel, making a figure-8 motion with the tip. Then back up the leg, inside her thigh, pricking at the lace trim of her underwear. Alice was trembling with fear, a phrase she'd heard and read many times but had never actually experienced, and she was worried that the involuntary movements of her own body would push her skin into the knife. Now the masked man was tugging on her other leg, then her arm too, pulling her out of the bed, and whispering in her ear. '*We're going to play a game.*'

With the knife pressed against her neck, the intruder pushed Alice out of the bedroom and down the hall, towards the front door. She made no effort to escape him. She didn't think she could. She thought, *He's taking me from here. He's going to kill me.* As they passed the doors to her children's bedrooms – Tommy's, David's, the one Nancy and Emer shared – Alice felt as if this masked man had already driven the knife into her chest. They passed the front door and went on into the living room. Why was he bringing her here, to the opposite end of the house from where everyone was sleeping? She thought he was about to rape her.

If she had a hope at this point, it was that that was all that was about to happen. She could at least physically survive that, she reasoned, and learn to live with the memories, somehow, in time. She said a silent prayer that everyone else in the house remained asleep – that everyone else *was* asleep, that this monster had started whatever this was by coming to her in her bed. The alternative was just too horrific to contemplate.

The house had two bathrooms: the family one by the bedrooms and a smaller one off the kitchen. It was tiny, barely five foot by six, but they'd managed to squeeze in a toilet, a sink and a shower a tad too tight for the adults but sufficient for the kids, enough to ease the stress of school mornings. The masked man opened the door to it with a soft kick and shoved Alice inside. He told her to get on the floor, pointing the knife to the wedge of space between the foot of the toilet bowl and the shower door. Alice dropped to her knees, leaving him standing directly behind her.

There was a blur of movement and a burst of red hot pain: he'd smacked her head, face-first, into the porcelain. Alice, stunned, let out a yelp and toppled over. She felt something slick and soft on her lip – blood – and thought her nose might be broken.

Blankness.

When she opened her eyes, she was half-lying on the floor, looking at the tiles. Her brain felt like it was trying to break free of her skull. Her vision had turned pink: blood was running from the gash in her forehead down into her eyes. Cautiously she raised a hand to assess the damage, but only got halfway. While she'd been stunned by the blow, the intruder had used a length of rope to secure her to the pipe behind the toilet. It was looped around her wrists several times and had been tied off in a series of neat, tight knots.

He was standing in the doorway, making shadows of the hall light. He bent down so he could whisper in her ear, his breath a warm tickle on her skin.

'*Tommy. David. Nancy. Emer.*'

Alice got the message. She would behave.

Thinking the real attack was about to start, she braced herself for it. But instead the intruder stepped outside, back into the hall, and closed the door gently behind him. There was a tinkling sound as the key turned in the lock.

It was dark in the bathroom now and she was alone. Was he leaving? How long would she have to stay quiet? What would he do while she did that? How did she know he *wouldn't* hurt the kids? Should she cry out now, to alert them? Or would that guarantee that they'd get hurt? What should she do?

Over the next few minutes, the silence in the house grew steadily louder, like the electronic hum of a speaker system set at full volume but playing no music. It mixed with her own beating pulse, the thumping pain in her head. The pain was taking on a shape in her vision, a glow that she was struggling to see around. Or maybe that was because her eyes were swelling. Or maybe it was her nose that was. Alice heard sounds but she wasn't sure if they were real or, if they were, what had made them. The gentle creak of a door hinge. The brush of a foot on the carpet. A distant clink of glass against something different, maybe wood.

Alice closed her eyes and prayed for the lives of her children.

Shane would tell the Gardaí it was possible he'd been woken by a noise but couldn't say for sure. What struck him when he did wake was not necessarily the absence of his wife in the bed – she could've got up to go to the bathroom as she often did during the night – but the closed bedroom door. Ever since they'd brought a wailing Tommy home from the hospital, it had been left ajar. Shane had lain awake for a minute or two, listening and waiting, before his confusion became concern and forced him out of bed. He discovered the bedroom door locked, the key removed from it. That didn't make any sense. Part of him wanted to call out for Alice, to find out what the hell was going on, even if he woke the whole house up. Part of him thought doing this would be a comical overreaction.

He remembered Tommy's mobile phone, and called it with his own which had been charging on his bedside table. When his son told him that *his* bedroom door was locked too, Shane knew something was terribly wrong. He put on shoes, awkwardly climbed out of his bedroom window and hurried around to the front door of the house. He was planning to let himself in with the spare key they kept under one of the terracotta planters, but he didn't need it. The front door was open, pulled right back.

Had Alice left the house? Shane scanned the garden, the gravel drive, the road, but there was little to see in the inky blackness. He should get a torch, he thought. There was one in the junk drawer next to the fridge. He went inside and started towards the kitchen, flicking light switches as he went. The air smelled like someone had been making coffee and, indeed, there was a cooling mug of black coffee on the kitchen counter.

Everything about this was odd. Alice took her coffee with milk, only ever drank one cup of it first thing in the morning and would never have used that mug. It was part of a set of four they'd received as a Christmas present, expensive ones, handcrafted by a famous Irish homeware designer, which his wife had classified as 'too good to use'. They normally sat in one of the glass-fronted cabinets, on display, brought out only for special visitors. Now one was sitting on the kitchen counter, splotchy with coffee stains, still warm in the middle of the night.

But there was something even stranger on the kitchen table: five silver keys, long and slim and simple. The keys for their internal doors. The sight of them set a cold fear coiling like a snake in Shane's stomach, because he knew what was happening now, he was sure. He called out for Tommy to ring the Gardaí, not caring any more who else he woke.

It was all starting to add up: the front door open, the doors locked from the outside, Alice gone … and Shane a bank manager. He'd been briefed about this. Tiger kidnappings, they called them. A threat to his family, a warning not to contact the Gardaí. No doubt there'd be a phone call any minute, or maybe they'd left him a note with further instructions. Alice was probably in the back of a van somewhere, terrified but physically okay. He'd go into work as normal later in the morning and walk out again with tens of thousands of pounds in cash. Or they'd instruct him to go into work now, before anyone else did, disarm the alarms and clear out the safe for them. Later he'd give the money to a member of the gang and then, soon after, Alice would be returned to their home.

That was what was supposed to happen, at least in the minds of the criminal gang. His employer, the country's largest commercial bank, had been crystal clear on what to do if such an event occurred: disobey them. This was not, after all, an armed robbery. These guys were thieves, yes, but murderers? No. The Gardaí had special officers trained to deal with these situations, who would help him fake compliance until they could swoop in and snatch Alice back.

Shane scooped the keys up with one hand and went looking for their matches, trying key after key until one turned in the lock. Nancy and Emer were asleep in their beds. David was sitting up in his, his face a question. The room he shared with his wife was as he had left it. Tommy was standing on the other side of his door, waiting, holding out his phone: the 999 dispatcher was asking what was wrong. Shane quickly summarised the situation. The woman on the other end of the line assured him that a car was already on its way from Carrigaline station. He handed the phone back to Tommy and then realised that there was something in his left hand, pricking the skin of his palm: a key. Five keys, four bedrooms. Somewhere, a door was still locked.

When he opened the bathroom door, his foot hit his wife's leg before he could turn on the light. Alice was woozy and incoherent; her face was a mess of swelling and blood. She had suffered a broken nose and a shallow head-wound, both of which she'd recover from quickly and completely, but that night her face was an unrecognisable pulp.

The first Garda car arrived five minutes later. There would be an investigation, but into what? There were no witnesses aside from Alice, who hadn't seen the man's face. He'd left no trace of himself inside the house. There'd been no sightings of a vehicle in the area in or around the time of the attack and, due to the location, there was no CCTV footage to check. No one could even say how the intruder had entered the home. He may as well have been a ghost.

Privately, Gardaí wondered if there'd even been an intruder at all. It would be months before a woman named Claire Bardin would report what she'd seen while driving along Bally's Lane around the time of an attack: a man wearing dark clothing, who she'd surprised with her headlights. Bardin lived abroad and hadn't realised the significance of her sighting until she'd heard a report about the case on a return visit to Cork. She worked with a police artist to create a sketch which was released to the public, but it failed to generate any new leads.

Meanwhile, the O'Sullivans installed new locks, security lights, electronic gates. They waited for news, for updates, for an arrest. None ever came. There were a handful of reports in the paper and on the local radio, all of which framed the incident as a tiger kidnapping gone wrong. Alice told family and friends that she was fine, that she just wanted to forget about it, but six months later she was still spending most nights wide awake on the sofa, looking at the flickering blue light of a TV screen but not seeing it at all. Doors and locks had lost all meaning. She now felt as at risk in her own home as she did on the side of a dark, deserted street. Eventually a FOR SALE sign went up on *Aurora* and Shane put in for a transfer to a branch in another part of the country, any part.

The children heard different versions of what had happened that night. Nancy and Emer were told almost nothing and for several more years would think that their mother had got up to go to the bathroom and tripped over something in the dark. David was told she'd disturbed a burglar, who wouldn't be able to get in now thanks to all the new security measures. Tommy was told the truth but not the details. He didn't know that the man who'd entered their home that night had said something to his mother about playing a game, just like the prank caller had said to him on New Year's Eve. He had no reason to connect the two events at all.

The telephone in the O'Sullivans' kitchen was a payphone: an angular boxy chunk of charcoal-grey plastic with big blue buttons and a slot for coins that looked utterly out of place on the wall of a private residential home. In Ireland in the 90s, this was a smart way for parents of teenagers to control their phone bills. A classmate of mine, Danielle, had one in her home, but she'd discovered where her mother kept the key for it. Whenever she needed to make a call, she'd simply wait for the opportunity to surreptitiously open the coin box, lift out a handful of pound coins and fifty-pence pieces and run them through the phone another time. Her mother never noticed because she herself often did the same thing.

I sometimes picture that phone, so incongruous in the O'Sullivans' kitchen, on the night of 31 December 1999. I'm helped by the photographs I've seen of a country-style kitchen where crystal glasses and china plates are displayed neatly in glass-fronted cabinets above countertops cluttered with the detritus of family life. The phone is next to the fridge, which has a parish newsletter clipped to its door with a magnet, the paper folded to show Mass times. Everything is still and dark and inanimate, the only signs of life the sounds of them, muffled music and the yelps of hyperactive children coming from another room.

In this moment, we are all alive and safe, we still feel safe, and live in a world where when we enter our homes at night and close the door behind us, we believe that we have slid into place a barrier that divides everything warm and secure and familiar, and everything cold and dangerous and unknown.

And then in the next, a phone begins to ring.

Its shrill cuts through the air. Perhaps there is something on its little LCD screen or a light that indicates a live incoming call. Perhaps this intrusion is only aural. Either way, a monster waits on the other end, his whisper at the ready.

For years I have kept a mental list of things to ask the man who murdered my family if I ever get the chance, and third from the top (underneath *why?* and *why us?*) is *why that night?* There had never been a midnight so full of promise, this dawning of the year two thousand. A date that, even when it was finally here, still seemed so of the future that it was foreign on our tongues. What was it about that moment that made him make his move? What was he thinking that night when he decided to emerge from the shadows and call the O'Sullivan home? Had something happened to him that had finally flicked a switch? Or had he planned it for months in advance? And why call at all? What was the point of it?

But mostly I wonder what would've happened if Tommy O'Sullivan had known the combination of buttons to press that would call back the last incoming number. I wonder where, if he had, a phone would have rung. In a telephone booth, already deserted, on the side of a lonely country road? Somewhere unexpected, like a university, hospital or Garda station? Or in a house just like the O'Sullivans', filled with music and children's voices and fizzy celebrations, readying itself to join the rest of an entire nation in an historic countdown?

I know which scenario scares me the most. It's also the most likely one.

The first thing Jim saw after he'd pulled the car into the drive was the big lump of sloppy dog shit sitting right in the middle of the front garden. The sight of it flash-boiled his blood. He stormed out the gate, along the path and up the driveway of the house next door. Where there was no dog shite in *their* garden. Funny that.

When he rang the bell, Karen came to the door.

Karen and Derek were in their early thirties. She was sallow-skinned with tumbling dark curls and a small, hard body that she wrapped in tight, stretchy fabrics. He was skinny and pale and didn't make any sense standing beside her. They'd no kids and had mostly been inoffensive neighbours – until they 'rescued' some stupid, ageing dog, who had some kind of irreversible stomach problem that had him constantly evacuating his bowels in other people's gardens.

'Jim,' she said, smiling tightly. 'What can I do for you?'

They both knew why he was there. He had been there for the same reason on two previous occasions in the last month.

'It's happened again,' Jim said anyway.

Karen pursed her lips. 'Well, I'm sorry to hear that. But he's a dog. I'm not sure what it is you want us to do.'

'It's very simple: keep him out of my garden.'

Another tight smile. 'We'll do our best.'

'If it happens again, we'll have no choice but to take things further.'

Karen glanced over her shoulder, back into the hall. At first Jim thought she was checking to see if Derek was in there, if he could come and back her up. But then he caught the tiny lift at the corner of her mouth, and the way her lips were pressed together when she turned back to face him, and he realised that what she was actually doing was covering up a laugh.

Jim felt his face grow hot.

He was the man who had let himself into the house on Bally's Lane and pulled a sleeping woman from her bed. Who'd tied her up and whispered the names of her children into her ear. Who'd smashed her head into the side of a toilet bowl.

And since then, so much worse than that.

But what Karen saw standing in front of her was her pensioner neighbour. A man with only tufts of white hair left on either side of his head. Brown spots on the back of his hands. Strong and fit, yes, but with a qualifier: *for his age*. She saw a man who had already had his (unremarkable) life, who had given all he was going to give (not much), who couldn't change things now (because it was too late). He'd made a point of telling them when they'd first moved in that he used to be a member of An Garda Síochána, but even that didn't seem to have the same effect as it once had. People just had no respect these days.

Some day soon, when age finally rendered him completely invisible, Karen wouldn't see anyone standing there at all.

But if she knew the truth, she wouldn't be smirking at him.

She'd be screaming and running away.

'It won't happen again,' Karen said. She wasn't even trying to sound convincing. 'I better go, I've something in the oven.' She started pulling the door towards her.

'If you don't get rid of that dog,' Jim said, '*I* will.'

It sounded like a threat and he meant for it to. Normally he wouldn't have pushed things that far, but perhaps reading about that night on Bally's Lane had warmed up something he'd let grow cold.

He'd needed reminding of who he really was.

All that he was.

But Karen wasn't fazed. She just said, 'Have a good evening, Jim,' and closed the door in his face.

Jim had left *The Nothing Man* on the passenger seat of his car. It looked like some light-hearted summer beach thing, but in *his* car that seemed even more suspicious. It was obvious now: this was a mistake. He'd have been better off with a cover stolen from a sports biography or something about astronauts. He whipped off the 'wrong' cover, ripped it to shreds and dumped it in the bin round the side of the house, along with the book it'd originally belonged to. He did the same with *The Nothing Man*'s dust jacket and the birthday card he'd bought. Now, of his bookshop purchases, he was only left with *The Nothing Man* book itself, naked, a plain black linen cover with its title embossed in gold on the spine. He locked it into the glove box and took Noreen's groceries into the house.

She was in the kitchen, chopping vegetables at the counter. The table was neatly laid for three with place mats, good cutlery and napkins. Noreen was in short sleeves, a floaty thing whose cheap, sheer material only served to highlight the drooping outlines of the excess fat on her back. Jim hit the OFF button on the thermostat by the kitchen door.

'Where were you?' Noreen said without looking up.

Jim dumped the bag of groceries on the table as heavily as he could by way of an answer.

'I meant just now. I heard you pull in five minutes ago.'

'Next door,' Jim said. 'That damn dog did it again.'

Noreen set down the knife and turned to him, wiping her hands on her apron.

Her eyes lingered on his face and he wondered if she could see it on him, somehow. His other self. His true one. Had his reading about what happened back then made it more obvious? Summoned it closer to the surface? Was he more at risk of being exposed than he had been this morning, yesterday, for the past eighteen years?

Almost certainly not. Noreen was unfailingly oblivious.

'I hope you didn't cause a scene,' she said. Her eyes dropped to the bag, whose contents were mostly identifiable through the shape of the thin plastic. 'Where's the wine?'

'In the shop. You don't need it.'

'I *do* need it, that's why I asked you to get it.'

'Katie has no interest in drinking alcohol on a weeknight and *you* certainly don't need to be doing it.'

'It wasn't *for* Katie. Or me. It was for our dinner. To put *in* our dinner. I needed it for—' Noreen stopped, took a breath. Then, calmly, 'It's an ingredient in the dish I'm making.'

'Then make something else.'

Jim pulled open the fridge door. As ever, it seemed full of food. He pointed at it, but Noreen was rooting in the bag.

'Oh, for God's sake,' she said. 'I said *oven chips*.'

'They're all the same, Nor.'

'No, they're not.'

'That's just a marketing ploy. Jesus, you'd fall for anything.'

Noreen glared at him.

'What time's Katie coming?' Jim asked.

'She's already here.' Noreen pulled open a drawer, took out a baking tray and slammed it down on to the countertop. This was the kind of childish temper-tantrum Jim refused to acknowledge. 'She's upstairs having a shower. Because I suppose it's cheaper for her to do that here, in the house where she doesn't have to pay the electricity bill.'

'*You* don't pay one anywhere, Nor.'

If there was a response to that, Jim didn't wait to hear it. He went back into the hall and paused at the end of the stairs to see if he could hear the shower running. He could. So long as Katie was in the bathroom and Noreen was in the kitchen, now was as good a time as any to transfer the book to a safer place.

Jim retrieved the book from the car and walked quickly around the side of the house with it held low by his side. Tucked into the east corner of the rear garden was the shed. *His* shed. He kept the door locked with an industrial-sized padlock that only he had the combination for.

The space was small, eight by ten, and wholly unremarkable, but it was the only space Jim had entirely to himself. There was a tall, steel tool cabinet in one corner with another, smaller padlock securing its doors. A folding picnic table with an old transistor radio sitting on top. A battered armchair, its upholstery bleached and torn, saved from the rest of the suite they'd dumped from the house a few years back. The shed only had one small window that Jim kept permanently covered with a blackout blind. A paint-splattered desk lamp sat on an upturned plastic milk crate next to a small, open shelving unit that held the standard garden-shed paraphernalia: old tins of paint, fertiliser, rat poison, a tub of bird feed, a neatly wound-up garden hose.

There was no need to go overboard here: it was just a book and the shed was secure. He could leave it sitting in the open if he wanted to. No one came into the shed but him. In the end, he lifted the seat cushion of the armchair and slid the book underneath.

For old time's sake.

Jim was turning to leave when his eyes landed on something on the open shelves.

The rat poison.

Jim lay awake in the dark, hands crossed on his chest, waiting. All around him the house was silent and still. Since the clock on the bedside table had ticked past midnight, he'd been struggling to stay awake. Exhaustion was pulling on his limbs, weighting his eyelids, slowing his breath. His curiosity was the only thing keeping him from slipping into slumber. The hours of darkness were his best opportunity to read more of *The Nothing Man*. He had to stay awake.

Dinner had been about as tasteless as he'd come to expect. The only highlight was the little tub of shortbread biscuits Katie had brought: her roommate had made them. She'd talked animatedly about college, which she seemed to be enjoying. Katie had always been active, but now things had kicked up a notch. She had joined a rowing team and a daily running group. When Jim hugged her goodbye, he felt the sharpness of her shoulder blades through her clothes. That was new but also showed that she was working hard.

Of course, Noreen had had to mention it as soon as the door was closed. How thin Katie had got, how she should start eating properly and resting more, wondering why she hadn't eaten the biscuits herself. Jim told Noreen she could stand to learn a thing or two from their disciplined daughter and that had been the end of that.

Noreen was sleeping beside him now. Her breaths were deep and regular, her body settled. She slept on her back and made wet nasal sounds in her throat. One hand was over the covers and even in this almost-dark, Jim could see the ripples of mottled, ageing skin loosening itself from the back of her hands. The crêpe-like surface of her fingers. The swollen flesh threatening to swallow the gold band of her wedding ring. Noreen was so much younger than him and yet, due to her complete refusal to take care of herself, these days she looked like the older one.

At 1:00 a.m., she hadn't stirred in half an hour. Slowly and stealthily, Jim extricated himself from their bed.

They had lived in this house all their married life, so Jim knew the exact location of every creaky stair and whining door hinge. As he moved silently through the dark house, he couldn't help but marvel at the weirdness of the situation. How many nights had he done this very thing on his way out into the dark? How many times had he slid the front door lock open, silently, expertly, wondering if tonight would be one of *those* nights, if he would find circumstances to be just right? And now here he was, years later, making the very same journey so he could sit and read a book someone else had written about what he'd done. It was weird. It was thrilling. By the time he got outside, he didn't need the shock of the cold to make him feel awake.

Jim was in his pyjamas and slippers and a coat he'd lifted from the rack in the hall. He would be an odd sight if anyone happened to see him. He paused by the front door and scanned the street. Theirs was the second-last house in a row of identical pairs of semi-Ds, which faced another row of houses that looked just like it. He scanned their windows but found only drawn curtains and darkness. A couple of porch lights had been left on but that was it. This was a housing estate of young kids, nine-to-fivers and mature couples like him and Noreen. At this time of the night, everyone was already asleep in their beds.

Satisfied, he walked around the side of the house and let himself into the shed. He checked the blackout blind was covering the entire window before switching on the lamp. He pulled the book out from under the armchair's cushion and then sat down.

It seemed colder in the shed than it had outside and he thought maybe he should invest in a little heater or bring a blanket from the house. A cup of tea wouldn't go amiss either, but kettles were noisy. Maybe he'd get a flask he could fill earlier in the day.

Jim opened *The Nothing Man*, found where he'd left off and read on.

– 3 –

Dreamcatcher

In the summer of 2000, Christine Kiernan was twenty-three years old and living alone for the first time in her life. She had inherited a property from her grandmother, a two-bed unit in a complex called Covent Court, off the Blackrock Road in the suburbs of Cork City. It would have been called a mid-terrace house were it not for the fact that Covent Court was famous. The development had been designed by a Northern Irish architect named Paul Berry and was considered an especially fine example of 1960s modernist design. Groups of college students still travelled from abroad to behold it, sketching its elevations while sitting cross-legged in the central courtyard, while curtains twitched and residents rolled their eyes, long bored by the attention if not secretly still pleased about their residence's hallowed status. A little plaque by the vehicle entrance even noted that Covent Court had won the RIAI Silver Medal for Housing in 1972. Whenever any of its number came up for sale, the listing would invariably describe it as a 'townhouse' and the assigned estate agent would quickly tire of correcting prospective buyers on the name. *Actually, it's cov-ent. Yes. No, there's no 'n' in it.*

Christine hated the place. When I visited there on a dreary April day, it wasn't difficult for me to see why. Many of the features that had made Covent Court a cutting-edge construction six decades before – flat roofs, aluminium sliding doors, cedar-clad ceilings and exterior sliding – now looked decrepit and crumbling, a poor choice of materials left to be weather-beaten by the rain. If the complex reminded me of anything, it was of the swathes of social housing built elsewhere in the city around the same time, where costs were cut at every opportunity and things had started to fall apart before they were even complete.

Inside, Covent Court had more in common with the set of an old James Bond movie or a *Life* magazine photospread of astronaut wives. The interiors were a series of strangely shaped rooms hostile to modern furniture that I imagined must be dim on even the brightest days. The exposed brick, the cladding on the ceilings, the huge slabs of polished concrete that made features like fireplaces, kitchen counters and stairs – they all snatched at the daylight and swallowed it down whole.

The estate agent who showed me around the unit for sale near the entrance suggested painting everything white and hanging mirrors. It was the middle of the day but I noticed he'd turned on every lamp and ceiling light.

Christine's unit at Covent Court was hers to sell, but it was also the last connection between her and her grandmother, and between her grandmother and the rest of the wider family. Mary Malloy had died suddenly and unexpectedly at the age of sixty-four, the pedestrian fatality in a car accident, and the entire Kiernan clan was still reeling. It seemed cruel to dispose of what had been the woman's home so quickly, to obliterate this house of memories, to sell it on to strangers. Christine didn't want to be responsible for doing that and, anyway, she suspected that her mother, Mary's eldest daughter, wouldn't let her.

So she redecorated. She put photos of faraway places in brightly coloured picture frames and hung them around the house in little galleries. She changed the couch, opting for a modern design in emerald velvet that she snapped up in an ex-display sale. She put a hanging basket of petunias just outside the front door and a dreamcatcher outside the rear one, the one that led through her little back garden to the alley that offered a shortcut to the main road. The dreamcatcher had wind chimes and whenever they caught in a breeze, it made a soothing, tinkling sound, soft and gentle enough not to get on anyone's nerves. In the hope that it would let in more light, she wondered about taking down the net curtains.

Covent Court is all windows. They had been one of its most innovative features: floor-to-ceiling panes, more window than wall. The buildings are arranged in a tight, angular U-shape around the courtyard and although Christine knew from looking out of her own windows that the people directly across from her couldn't *really* see into her home, she still felt exposed. Not least because despite the PRIVATE PROPERTY signs littered throughout the complex, there was no gate or barrier – although, after a recent burglary in the neighbourhood, there was chatter among the residents that perhaps there should be. Technically, anyone could come walking in.

Early one morning in the first week of July, most likely the fourth but no later than the sixth, Christine removed the net curtains from her ground-floor windows. The effect on the light was dramatic, and she was pleased. A little uncomfortable, perhaps, but pleased. It would take some getting used to, but the pay-off was a much brighter room. Christine was intent on getting used to it and keeping the curtains down.

Then she saw the handprints.

Jim set the book aside and hoisted himself out of the chair with a groan before remembering that it was the middle of the night and he was striving to be silent. He opened the tool cabinet and scanned its contents for something to write with. There was a stubby pencil in a jar of loose screws and Allen keys. Barely a nib on it, but it would do for tonight. Tomorrow, he'd come to his reading room better prepared.

There was an old compact hoover sitting on the bottom shelf of the cabinet. Just the unit itself – its hose and other attachments were missing. It was turquoise green and said GOBLIN on the front. Jim had taken it from a skip parked near the entrance to the estate years before. He bent down and went to lift the cover off it, but then changed his mind and stood up again.

Not yet. Not now.

Reading the book was one thing, but opening that was quite another.

He locked up the tool cabinet and sat back into his chair. He flipped to the inside cover of *The Nothing Man* and wrote:

Eglin – who/where now?
Irish Times article – May 2015
Knife/rope – neighbour new report?
'recent burglary' – more??? Check!

with the stubby pencil. It made his letters thick and smudged.

Then Jim returned to where he'd left off and, pencil in hand now, read on.

They were on the living room's window the following morning, the largest one to the front. She was certain they hadn't been there the day before. Two large impressions, a little more than halfway up and side by side, as if someone had been standing with two hands pressed flat against the glass, looking in. Christine went outdoors to examine them more closely. They were smears rather than prints, as if the leaver had touched something greasy first. The fingers were unnaturally splayed, like children's finger-paintings.

It was as if the matching hands had been *trying* to leave evidence there, Christine thought. She cleaned them off and, later that day, put the net curtains back up.

One night, when I was nine or ten, I woke up to the sound of footsteps coming up the stairs, a steady rhythm of distinct, alternative creaks. *Left foot, right foot. Left foot, right foot. Left foot, right foot.* I knew instantly that something was very wrong, because I could also hear the soft snoring that meant my father was asleep in the bedroom next door and, as my eyes adjusted, see the little mound of blankets in the bed across from mine that was Anna, still asleep too. The timbre of the footsteps sounded nothing like my mother's light tread, so who was coming up the stairs in our house in the middle of the night? And why were they taking so long?

I held my breath and lay stiff with fear for what felt like an eternity, but was probably closer to several seconds in reality. Then, happily, I realised my mistake. What I was actually hearing was my own bedroom door, trapped in the draught of some forgotten open window, repeatedly opening half an inch, closing half an inch, the hinges protesting every time.

On the night of 14 July 2000, Christine Kiernan had a similar experience, in that she woke up to the sound of footsteps coming up her stairs and felt her limbs freeze up with fear. But this was no aural illusion. The sound drew closer and closer. It changed as the steps left the bare wood of the stairs and crossed the carpeted floor of the landing. And then a shadow detached itself from the darkness and moved towards her until it became a masked man standing at the end of her bed.

None of her neighbours would recall hearing it, but Christine managed to let out a short, piercing scream before a gloved hand was clamped over her mouth and the sharp tip of what she knew must be a knife was pressed against the skin of her neck. In a strange, almost theatrical whisper, her attacker told her that if she stayed quiet, he would 'only' rape her. If she made a noise or tried to escape, she would die. Then he rolled her on to her stomach so he could bind her wrists behind her back, and after that there was only pain.

Christine was five-foot-six and weighed less than eight stone. Physically, she was no match for this broad, tall, heavy man on top of her – and he had a weapon. So while he violated her body, she did the only thing she could and rolled down steel shutters around her mind. She tried to detach herself from what was happening now and focus instead on what she was already determined to make happen next: she'd make sure he was caught, tried and locked up.

She mentally catalogued what she knew about him. She could picture him standing in the doorway, so she'd be able to tell them how tall he was. There'd been no real accent to his weird whispering, but that in itself told a story: he was Irish, probably from around here. She had seen the skin around his eyes: he was white. She got the impression he was in his thirties or forties. There was a strange, earthy smell off him. Wet leaves and mud. She told herself that, if she got the opportunity, she would rake her nails across his skin. She knew from TV that she would end up with pieces of him beneath her fingernails and that the Gardaí could scrape it out and test it for things. But with her hands tied behind her back, Christine never got the chance. When he was done, her rapist turned her over and roughly stuffed some woolly material – a balled-up sock – deep into her mouth. She couldn't breathe and began to gag.

She tried to pull herself into a kind of sitting position, hoping that would help. It didn't. She began to feel faint. Her attacker didn't react. He was sitting on the edge of the bed, watching her choking and spluttering. All she could feel was pain, as if a sustained electrical shock was cursing through her skeleton. And now there was the burning in her chest too, the panic of not being able to breathe. At the very last moment, just when Christine thought she'd have to give in, to give up, her rapist held the knife in front of her face, then pointed the tip off to the side. It was a question and Christine nodded the answer desperately. She wouldn't scream. He pulled the sock from her mouth and she immediately vomited, sending the spray all over his sleeves, the T-shirt she slept in and the sheets.

He recoiled as if the substance was radioactive. He scrambled off the bed and stood at the end of it, regarding her. Then he abruptly turned around and left.

For Christine, one of the most horrific aspects of this most horrific experience was that she didn't know how long she would have to suffer it or what might happen next. Would it get worse? What else would he do? Would she be able to take the pain? What kind of injuries would she have? Wouldn't he just kill her anyway? As long as he was in her bedroom, there was a terror much worse than the violation of her body: the not knowing just how bad this might get. His sudden leaving, the end point, already here – it allowed her to think about what had happened as *what had happened*, past tense, to know the parameters of what had to be dealt with, moving forward. And it was so unexpected, Christine didn't know quite what to do. She listened as he hurried down the stairs and slammed a door closed behind him. Then she sat still in the silence that followed. She cried and hurt and bled.

And, as the sky lightened, she went in search of help.

Christine was an only child. Her father owned a chain of fast-food restaurants and her mother ran a public relations agency, well known around the city for its embarrassingly lavish product launches and D-list celebrity photo-calls. The Kiernan family home was an architect-designed glass-fronted mansion overlooking the estuary on the Rochestown Road. Built on a rise for the views, their friends said, or so everyone could see how much money they had, their enemies muttered. It was known locally as the house with the swimming pool. Christine had attended a school in the city which educated similarly moneyed daughters for generations, but even there she had stood out as being separate and *other*, a tier up and a world apart, because her family put their money on display. When she'd enrolled in University College Cork, she'd found herself at sea, so disconnected from the worlds of her classmates, what with their part-time jobs, their fiery political views and their dingy student digs, that it was as if she had arrived from another planet speaking another language. She had few friends and didn't share her feelings with the ones she did have. Three months before the attack, Christine sat her final exams and left campus without looking back.

She took a job as an executive assistant in a firm of solicitors that bore her father's best friend's name and quickly grew close to another new hire, the son of one of the partners. There'd been a few summer weekends spent with him, his family and his friends, including one where the two of them had decided, on a whim, to fly to Paris for the day. Christine had been close with one of her first cousins, Emma, growing up and had traded letters with her ever since Emma and her family had emigrated to Dubai in 1996. These days they exchanged emails and in them, earlier that summer, Christine had told Emma she was happy or at least getting there.

Christine had had every privilege in life. She'd been heading for a future that would be easy, comfortable and financially successful. But then a man came walking up her stairs in the middle of the night. When it came to what was needed to recover from it, it quickly became apparent that, in that area, Christine was poor to the point of poverty. She wasn't close with her parents, had no siblings and few, if any, close friends. Her relationship ended, instantly crushed under the weight of what had happened to her body. She didn't want to be touched, which was understandable, but neither did he want to touch her, which seemed cruel. Meanwhile, her neighbours in Covent Court seemed more concerned with the inconvenience of the Garda presence and the bad publicity than they were with Christine's welfare. In a decision that was inexplicable to many, Christine returned to Covent Court and continued living there, alone, after the attack. She did have an alarm system and new locks installed, but still.

Nothing like this had ever happened in the area before and in the immediate aftermath, the story dominated the headlines. None of these reports included Christine's name but locally everyone knew who she was. There was seemingly a long line of former classmates lining up to add colour to the various threads of local gossip. Like how she'd driven a Land Rover to school in fifth and sixth year, her *own* Land Rover, and how her father had arranged special permission for her to park it in a staff space. How she'd worn labels to school and carried her textbooks in a designer handbag. How her mother had purchased an apartment in the Elysian for her to live in while she was at college so she could avoid the thirty-minute commute to and from the family home. No one dared come out and say it, but it was there in the subtext: *everyone has to suffer something*. Christine had never suffered, so it made a kind of sense that her first serving came in such a devastating portion. And hey, it wasn't like she'd died.

Seven weeks after the attack, Detective Garda Geraldine Roche, the lead officer on Christine's case, arrived at Covent Court for a pre-arranged visit. When Christine didn't answer the door or her phone, Roche became concerned and forced her way into the property. She found Christine unconscious on her bed. She had ingested a lethal dose of painkillers and would pass away in hospital two days later.

The victim of a violent crime had been found unconscious at the scene of it so, once again, the house at Covent Court was processed by Gardaí as part of a criminal investigation. Every inch of it was explored, photographed and catalogued – perhaps even more thoroughly than before as, this time, Christine wasn't able to tell the story of what had happened there.

During this, a civilian forensic technician noticed that there was an active landline installed but, due to the lack of a telephone, apparently not in use. The unit was found packed away in a cupboard, its corresponding cable wound around the receiver. It was a large, beige rotary model that had most likely belonged to Christine's grandmother and probably never been used by Christine herself. Still, the Gardaí needed to make sure.

The civilian technician knew there was a quick way to find out. She plugged in the phone and dialled the three-digit number that, in the summer of 2000, accessed Eircom's built-in voicemail service. The access code had never been changed from the default 1-2-3-4 and she was able to listen to the messages.

The first thing the technician heard was a robotic voice warning her that the mailbox was full. The second was the first of a number of near identical voicemails, distinguishable only by the various times and dates they had been left. Each lasted between one and two minutes and featured the same male, raspy voice whispering, 'Here I am, Christine. Come down and let me in,' over and over again while, in the background, the tinkling sound of wind chimes could be heard loud and clear. Christine's wind chimes.

The date on the first voicemail was 20 July, six days after the attack. The most recent one had been left two weeks before, on 19 August. Christine's attacker had been returning to Covent Court.

There were thirteen voicemails in all.

The day of my second visit to Covent Court was a much better one: blue skies, light breeze, warm sun. I had been trading emails with Margaret Barry, the neighbour who had found the knife and rope beneath her couch cushion two weeks before Christine's attack, and after weeks of tentative correspondence she had finally agreed to meet me.

As I crossed the courtyard, I passed a huddle of what looked like college students. I felt their eyes follow me as I walked by. I assumed they were here for the architecture but when I mentioned them to Margaret, she said that since my article had come out, it was hard to know. The Nothing Man was back in the news and bringing a different kind of enthusiast to Covent Court: the true-crime tourist.

Margaret is in her sixties now with short, steel-grey hair. She goes by Maggie. A first-generation Irish-American, she grew up in Berkeley, California, with her Cork-born parents, and came to live in Ireland at the age of twenty-six. In the summer of 2000, she was working in University College Cork's International Office. She had bought the house in Covent Court less than a year earlier, when a long-term relationship that she'd thought was heading for marriage had instead fallen apart. She'd seen Christine's grandmother, Mary Malloy, around but had never spoken to her; they lived on opposite ends of the complex. She didn't know Christine existed until the morning after the attack, when Maggie opened her curtains to find a fleet of Garda vehicles parked outside and two uniformed members about to knock on her front door.

The day we met she was wearing a long, flowing summer dress in a bold print and glittery sandals. When I remarked on them, she told me she was going to a friend's birthday barbeque later that afternoon. Her American accent was still intact. We sat in the slice of sun that bisected her rear garden and drank strong, bitter coffee from delicate little cups. She told me she'd read my article but wasn't sure if she'd have the stomach to read this book.

Maggie had been hoovering her living room when she'd found the knife and rope. It was a Saturday morning; she 'blitzed' the place at the same time every week. At first she didn't do anything, didn't react at all. She just stood there, unmoving, staring, with the hoover humming loudly at her feet. Waiting for what she was seeing to start making sense. After a beat she turned the hoover off with a stab of her foot and stared at the items some more. How could they be there? They weren't hers. She was sure she had done this same thing seven days ago and they hadn't been there then. No one but her had been in the house since.

She'd called 999, waiting outside her front door until the car came because for some reason it felt safer out there. Eventually two uniformed Gardaí arrived, both female. They took a statement from Maggie, had a look around and took the knife and rope away with them. They advised her to keep her windows and doors locked and left a card with a number she could call if there were any other incidents. 'They did take me seriously,' Maggie said, 'but there just wasn't anything else they could do.'

This wasn't a world in which masked men broke into suburban homes in Cork City in the middle of the night to attack the women who lived alone there. Not yet. For close to two weeks, what tormented Maggie about the discovery was not so much its threat as its mystery. She tried on all sorts of explanations, canvassed her friends and even called the company who had manufactured the sofa to ask about what tools they used, but nothing she could come up with quite fit. It didn't feel plausible that someone had broken into her home to leave something beneath a couch cushion, left again without taking anything and made sure not to damage any window or door coming or going. Why would anyone do such at thing? It just didn't make any sense.

Then Christine was attacked and everything took on a new, horrible meaning. The knife had reminded Maggie of DIY stores but now it made her think of stabbing motions. The rope had seemed like something climbers might use but in her mind's eye, Maggie could see it wrapped tightly around delicate wrists and ankles. She went to Togher Garda Station to make a statement. She noticed that the Garda she spoke to spent a lot of time asking her to describe in minute detail what the rope and knife had looked like.

'Don't you have them?' she asked. 'Can't you just go look?'

'We're having trouble locating them,' he eventually admitted. 'Looks like they might have been labelled wrong. We're sure they'll turn up eventually.'

I asked Maggie about the moment she connected what had happened to Christine with the items under her cushion, when she realised that they belonged to the rapist and that, at some point, *she* had likely been his intended target.

I wanted her to say that she felt like she had done all she could, because even though she had reported the find it hadn't prevented Christine's attack from happening. I wanted her to say this to absolve me of my failure to do the same. Perhaps I could relieve myself of some of my own guilt about saying nothing if I knew that saying something wouldn't have changed anything anyway.

Maggie didn't answer immediately. I took a sip of my coffee to give her a chance to think. When I looked at her again, I saw that her eyes had filled with tears.

'Relief,' she said quietly. 'What I felt was relief.'

Jim could still smell it, that vomit. The acrid sourness of it. And the confusing, foreign heat of it against his skin. It had been yellow-green and stringy, flecked with orange bits. It hadn't just soiled the sheets but the entire affair. He knew he'd never be able to replay the memory of that night without recalling the smell too. It was forever ruined. There seemed no point in continuing so he'd just got up and left.

Even though he could've killed her.

Should've, seeing as she was going to end up doing it herself anyway.

If only that other stupid woman, her neighbour, hadn't found the knife and rope hours before he was planning to return to her house and use them on her.

At least he'd learned something that night: no socks. A neck tie across the jaw and knotted at the back of the head, forcing the mouth to remain open, was better at keeping them quiet and also removed the gagging risk. The penultimate time, at the house in Westpark, he'd used the man's own tie. He hadn't killed anybody yet and no one even knew that the Nothing Man existed – that was all to come, still. The couple probably thought he was a burglar. He needed to let them know that he wasn't; that this was going to be something much, much worse. He wanted to see the terror in their eyes, feel it in their shaking limbs.

So he stood in their bedroom door and pulled a tie from his pocket, a distinctive one whose design was made up of little cartoons of brand-name chocolate bars. It belonged to the man. They knew as soon as they saw it that this couldn't be the first time he'd been in their house. The crying and shaking had started immediately.

He'd always been especially proud of that.

– 4 –

Night Terrors

I will never find the house on my own, I'm warned, so Patricia Kearns suggests we meet in Fermoy town so she can drive us there. She tells me to park outside the Aldi and look for a red coat and short blonde hair. I see her as soon as I pull in, standing near the entrance, holding a cardboard tray with two takeaway coffee cups. After introductions and me thanking her, again, for doing this, she steers me towards her car, a Dacia Duster the colour of glazed terracotta. 'It takes the whole team,' she tells me, patting the chassis fondly. Patricia has three kids, ranging in age from eleven to seventeen. She apologises for the state of the car and I wave a hand, telling her I'll take no notice, but when I pull open the door I see an interior covered in crumbs and empty food packets, and pulling my seatbelt across my chest leaves my fingers feeling sticky.

Patricia drives fast and in a couple of minutes we've cleared Fermoy and are hurtling down narrow country roads lined with hedgerows that twist relentlessly. At first, I try to keep up with the turns, mentally drawing a map of the route, ready to assure myself that actually I could have found the house myself if only she'd let me try. But soon I realise that even if I were to come back a second time, I'd have no hope. I lose track after the third left turn and we still have a crossroads and two forks to navigate. There are no street signs out here and every stretch of road looks like the one before. I give up and look out the window at the fields rushing by.

It takes ten minutes to get to the house. It's on a stretch of road that dead-ends where five detached houses sit in a row – Patricia says the land all belonged to one farmer who chopped it into plots and sold them off – but she doesn't need to tell me it's the last one. Only it has the look of a sprawling American McMansion, with multiple roof levels and a double-height window at its centre through which you can see the smooth curve of spiral stairs. There are no cars parked outside and all the window blinds are down. 'They're in Florida,' Patricia says as she cuts the engine. She's parked right outside the gates. 'But Jean said we're okay to have a walk around.' She means outside, around the perimeter.

Gravel crunches underfoot as we walk up the drive. The sun is behind the house and I have to shield my eyes to look up at it. I ask Patricia if she had ever been here before the day she was sent here.

'No,' she says. 'I'd only driven past it.'

She's looking up too. Her lips are pressed together and turned down at the ends, as if she can taste something sour.

'Awful,' she says. 'Probably the worse thing I've ever seen.'

There's no need for her to clarify that she's not talking about the house.

The Criminal Assets Bureau, the CAB, was founded in October 1996, at a time when organised crime in Ireland was at epidemic levels. That June, *Sunday Independent* journalist Veronica Guerin had been assassinated in her car while stopped at a red light on the Naas Road just outside of Dublin City. Two men had pulled up alongside her on a motorbike; one of them had pulled a trigger six times. Both were known associates of a convicted criminal named John Gilligan. Guerin had been publicly asking how a man like Gilligan could enjoy a millionaire's lifestyle despite being one of the country's long-term unemployed. In the national outcry that followed her death, the Irish people were demanding answers to the same question.

The formation of the CAB and the power given to it by the Proceeds of Crime Act enabled authorities to seize any and all assets they believed had been bankrolled by illegal activity, even if their registered owner wasn't the one who'd committed the criminal act. Property, cars, cash – in the first fifteen years of existence, the CAB took control of more than €70 million worth of them. Contributing €250,000 to the pot was a six-bedroom detached house ten minutes' drive outside the town of Fermoy, in north Cork.

The deeds were in the name of Barry Pike. Pike's father, Richard, was a perennially suntanned millionaire who told friends he was in overseas property development when what he was actually in was the counterfeit cigarette trade. After the elder Pike was forced to move into Mountjoy Jail in late 1999, the house in Fermoy was put on the market. It languished there for months. Viewings were brisk with the nosy but it seemed that no one wanted to live in a house that'd been on the nine o'clock news for all the wrong reasons. The asking price dropped three times. Eventually Conor and Linda O'Neill, thirty-somethings returning to Ireland after a ten-year stint in San Francisco, put in a rock-bottom bid which was, to their surprise, immediately accepted. They took possession of the keys on the last day of February 2001.

Linda had no qualms about living in a house that a criminal had built, but she wasn't impressed with where he'd chosen to build it. Back in San Francisco, her and Conor had lived in a one-bed apartment in Pacific Heights with other people above, below and beside them. The soundtrack to their lives had been always-on televisions and constant car horns. Here in Fermoy, there was nothing but the birds and the odd rumble of a tractor engine. Their closest neighbour was far away enough to be rendered silent. There were no passing cars even, because the house was at the end of a lane that didn't take you anywhere else.

The town of Fermoy was a ten-minute drive away, and it had to be a drive as walking or cycling along the surrounding country roads was too dangerous, and there was no public transport. But it was hardly worth the effort. Linda told friends back in San Francisco that Fermoy was one street offering the bare essentials – bank, supermarket, hairdresser, hardware store, five pubs – and that you couldn't go there without meeting someone you knew or someone who knew you. Like one of their new neighbours. Or a relative of Conor's, who'd grown up in the area. Or one of the tradesmen who was working on the house. They were all nice people, but Linda pined for her lost anonymity. 'So let me get this straight,' Conor would tease her. 'You don't like that there's no one here and then when you go into town, you don't like that there is?'

It wasn't that Linda had grown up in a bustling metropolis. She was from Shanamore, a 'glorified crossroads' by the sea in East Cork, population 538 until she'd left to go to college in Dublin, where she'd met Conor in a queue for a nightclub during Freshers' Week. But the ten years they'd spent in San Fran had been her happiest and now, marooned in the Irish countryside, it felt like that was because Linda was a city gal at heart. The fact that this was a preference she'd acquired didn't change the fact that that's how she felt.

But there was nothing she could do now but get used to it. This was the first step in the plan her and Conor had agreed. Their American life had been far from perfect, what with its long hours, extortionate rent and constant pressure. They'd both yearned for a change of pace and eventually settled on the idea of returning to Ireland, to the township where Conor had grown up, where most of his family still lived and where the money they'd saved would go much further, maybe all the way to a forever home and having kids.

It didn't help that Conor had stayed working for the same company that had brought him to America in the first place, transferring to their European headquarters in Cork City, while Linda had had to leave her job behind. She'd initially looked at this as an opportunity, a quiet pause in which she could decide what she really wanted to do. She had vague notions of writing a novel or starting her own consulting business or maybe opening a yoga retreat on one of the empty acres behind the house, but for the moment, she'd be spending most of her time dealing with tradesmen, overseeing the renovation of the house. The man who'd built it had doused it in his *nouveau riche* tastes and personal safety paranoia, installing bullet-proof windows, an elaborate CCTV system with a closet-sized 'control room', solid gold bathroom fittings, an elevator (that went up one floor) and a printed mural of a tropical beachscape that took up three walls of the master bedroom. Linda couldn't wait for it to start looking like theirs.

When Conor announced that he'd been recalled to San Francisco to steer an important project towards completion, Linda declined to go with him. It was only for three weeks, but she used the work on the house as an excuse. The real reason, the one Linda didn't want to say, was that she feared it would be too wrenching a heartbreak to leave the city she loved for the second time in six months, this time with the knowledge of exactly what she was leaving it for. So she chose to stay at home, in Fermoy, alone.

When the incidents first began, Linda took little notice of them. So much so that, later, it would be impossible to discern exactly when they had started, or the order in which they'd occurred. She could only say that it had been after Conor left for San Francisco and that she could clearly remember:

– Swearing that she had left the hall light on when she went upstairs to bed the night before, only to come down and discover it off in the morning. It wasn't that the bulb had gone, a quick flick of the switch proved that. Linda had shrugged it off, presuming she had misremembered.

– The television in the living room coming on by itself. It had happened early one evening when Linda was in the kitchen stacking the dishwasher. She'd been frightened by the sudden voices, then confused when she'd realised they were coming from the TV in the next room. It didn't occur to her to worry that someone was in there and had turned it on – at that time, that was outside her realm of what was possible. She found the remote control wedged between two sofa cushions and told herself that, somehow, a pressure change on the red power button was what had made this happen. Failing that, an electronic malfunction. She'd turned the set off, put the remote on the TV stand and gone back to the dishes. It had never happened again.

- Finding a sopping-wet towel in the bathroom with no apparent explanation for why it was wet. A hand towel, in the upstairs bathroom. Linda thought she remembered using it the night before, just before she'd gone to bed. She'd dried her hands with it. Even for it to be damp all these hours later would be a bit of a stretch, but when Linda shuffled into the bathroom just after waking up around 7:00 a.m., the towel was so wet it was dripping on to the tiled floor below. There was no leak she could see and, even if she'd found one, what kind of leak dripped directly on to a hand towel hung on a rail directly below a medicine cabinet that itself wasn't wet at all? It didn't make any sense. But again, Linda told herself that her own memory was the problem, and that one of the builders had used the towel the day before to surreptitiously mop something up, and that's how it had got wet. She didn't ask any of them about it.

- A number of items going missing or being moved. Little things, like a lipstick Linda thought she'd dropped into a bowl on her dressing table that later reappeared in the living room. A knife that she always put back in the block on the kitchen counter but which, for some reason, was now in a junk drawer. One evening she'd settled down to watch the movie *Gladiator* on DVD only to discover that the disc inside the case was actually an instalment of *Jurassic Park*, and in *that* case was another mismatched disc and so on and on for several more of them. Conor was proud of his DVD collection and kept them alphabetised, while Linda liked to have everything in its place. This was no accident. Were the movers messing with their heads? The foreman, Johnnie Murphy, was an old school friend of Conor's; that was *inside* the realm of possibility. On a transatlantic phone call, this was the explanation the couple settled on. They'd laughed about it.

The presence of the builders made all of this relatively easy to explain away. The house wasn't secure. Vehicles pulled up outside and men in heavy boots and hard hats stomped in and out all day, every day. The quantity surveyor, Roisin, had a habit of arriving without warning and leaving without saying goodbye. The front door was rarely closed for very long and the electronic gates at the end of the drive never were. Linda may have been home alone, but she was barely alone in the house. She couldn't demand that things remain where she'd put them, or that other things stay untouched. She was living in a building site. She had to allow for that.

Then her diary disappeared.

Linda kept track of her life in a blue Moleskine diary, about the same size as a DVD case. Stateside, its pages had managed her workdays, each one packed tight with her unusually tiny scrawl, the flap at the back stuffed with business cards, receipts and ticket stubs. By the closing months of each year it would be bloated, refusing to close, and Linda would be eyeing up a new, fresh, unblemished one, which she would christen ceremonially on 1 January with a list of her life goals. When it disappeared that April, the 2001 edition was still practically pristine. This was unusual but, since coming to Fermoy, it had been demoted – there were no workdays now, after all – and its new purpose was to be the holder of pertinent information about the house renovation. Its pages were consulted for things like the plumber's telephone number, the measurements of the kitchen tile and the date the new sectional sofa was due to arrive, but most days it never made it out of the shallow drawer in the hall table where it lived. Then, one day, it disappeared from there and was never seen again.

At first, Linda assumed that one of the men working on the house had taken it to find a phone number and then never put it back. But each of the four men on site at the time denied this. Linda called Johnnie, their foreman, who promised he'd get to the bottom of it but arrived at the house the following morning empty-handed, both figuratively and literally. No one on his crew had taken the diary, he said, and he trusted his men. But Linda was sure she'd put it in the drawer. Where had it gone?

Unlike the other incidents, Linda knows for sure when this one happened. She discovered the diary was missing on 9 April 2001. Johnnie reported that none of his guys had taken it the following morning, 10 April. She knows this because it was late that night, just as the clock ticked into 11 April, that Linda awoke to find a masked man standing at the side of her bed.

She didn't know what woke her up but he was the first thing she saw when she did. A tall, well-built man looming over her. Wearing a black mask with just one slit for his eyes. Holding what she would describe as a 'small' gun that he held over her stomach, pointed straight down. He warned her that he would pull the trigger if she screamed, and that death by bullet wound to the stomach was slow and excruciatingly painful.

She asked him what he wanted. He didn't respond. She pleaded with him to take whatever he liked from the house and to leave her alone. He handed her a blindfold and told her to put it on. When she hesitated, he pressed the muzzle of the gun against her flesh. The blindfold felt like it might be a silk neck tie. Once she'd tied it behind her head, the masked man warned her that if she made a single sound, he would pull the trigger and she would die. Then he raped her.

There was a part of Linda that just refused to believe what was happening. She had lived for ten years in a major American city famously plagued by petty crime. San Francisco could lay claim to the highest rate of vehicle break-ins and burglaries in the whole of the United States. Now here she was in a little Irish country town where the word *crime* only had to stretch to cover incidents of public drunkenness and drink-driving, and she was being raped by a masked man in her own bed. It didn't feel real. It couldn't be real. Was she still asleep? Was she just dreaming this? All her life, Linda had been able to wake herself up from her nightmares. She desperately tried to do it now.

Afterwards, her attacker tied her wrists and ankles with lengths of rope – bright blue and braided – and ordered her off the bed and into the bathroom. He told her to climb into the bath and, once she had done this, he looped another length of rope through the ties on her wrists and then around the safety grip on the side of the bathtub. She was now trapped in there, blind and hurting and naked and terrified. Then the masked man left the bathroom and went downstairs, but remained in the house.

Judging by the distant noise that accompanied his movements, he spent time in the kitchen and the living room. He opened and closed doors, ran a tap, turned on the TV. Then the squeak of a hinge signalled that the back door had been opened and a dull thump suggested it had swung closed again. Had he left? Linda's body temperature had been dropping ever since he'd left her in the bath, bare flesh against cold ceramic, and now her teeth were chattering. The cold was almost all she could think about. It made it increasingly difficult to follow her own thoughts, let alone the sounds from downstairs. She couldn't hear anything now. Was that because there was nothing to hear? Had he left? Was he gone?

Linda thought if she rubbed her head against the tiles on the bathroom wall beside her, she'd push the blindfold up and off. Her movement was limited to a foot or so of rope, but she thought there might be a disposable razor on the side of the bath behind her. If she could reach it, she might be able to fray the rope enough to break it in two.

But she wasn't sure he was gone, so she waited. She clenched her jaw. She tried to ignore the stabbing pain of the cold. She listened as hard as she could. All around her, the house seemed silent and still. She seemed to be the only living, breathing, moving creature inside it. Still, she waited. She thought of the gun and what he could do with it if he caught her trying to escape. Eventually Linda had the sense that a weak grey light was forcing its way around the edges of the blindfold. It seemed like a long time had passed since she'd last heard him make a noise, maybe many hours. It must be if it was getting light outside. He was gone, surely. She waited five more minutes, counting the seconds out in her head. Finally, Linda moved to rub her head against the tile.

There was a noise, a *whoosh*, and then warm breath against her ear.

'You fucking bitch, I *told* you not to move.'

Linda had no idea how long he'd been there, in the room, right beside her. She hadn't even heard him come back up the stairs.

That was the last thing she'd remember. Because then he pushed her head against the tiles with such force that a spider-web of fractures exploded across her skull, one of which cracked so violently that it ejected a tiny shard of bone which lodged itself in the soft tissue of her brain.

Linda would lay in that bath, slowly dying, for the next thirty-five hours.

After four of those hours, Johnnie Murphy and two of his men would arrive at the house just like they did every morning. They had keys and let themselves in. Nothing struck them as being wrong. Linda was there to greet them most mornings but not every one; they just assumed she was out somewhere. When she hadn't appeared by the end of the day, Johnnie left a note on the kitchen table asking her to call him about some light fittings that had failed to arrive.

Twenty-seven hours in, when Johnnie let himself into the house for the second morning in a row, the note was still there but Linda wasn't. Now he did begin to think that something was up. He walked through the house, upstairs and down, calling her name. The door to the master bedroom was open, the curtains still drawn in the room beyond. He poked his head in. The bed was unmade but there was no sign of Linda. The door to the en suite was open too but from where Johnnie was standing he couldn't see Linda's body in the bath. He assumed that *because* the door was open, she wasn't in there. He called Conor's mobile phone but it was after 11:00 p.m. in California and Conor, an early riser, was already asleep in bed. Six more hours would pass before he'd hear Johnnie's voice-message.

Thirty-three hours in, Conor tried calling his wife's phone. It went straight to voicemail. He then called Johnnie, who told him he hadn't seen Linda in a day and a half. Next, Conor tried the numbers he had for friends and relatives who lived locally, who might have seen Linda or even be with her now. No one had or was. Feeling the first ripples of panic, Conor called his parents. They were at a wedding in Gorey, Co. Wexford, at least two and a half hours' drive away from the house in Fermoy, but his father assured him they'd get straight in the car and head to the house now. Before they did, Conor's father called a buddy of his whose son was now a Garda sergeant based out of North Cork's district headquarters, which happened to be in Fermoy. Sergeant Brendan Byrne would later admit that he'd rolled his eyes as he'd listened to his father going on about Conor O'Neill's wife going AWOL while he was off being some big-shot in San Francisco, and had probably said something like, 'What do you want *me* to do about it?' But despite being nearly forty years old and a sergeant, Byrne still felt uneasy about not doing what his father told him to, so he agreed to call out to the house. After he hung up he decided he was too busy to bother with it and directed a junior member of his team, a newly qualified Garda who'd been on the job less than six months, to go there instead.

Thirty-five hours in, having repeatedly got lost on the drive there, Garda Patricia Kearns finally arrived at the O'Neill house. After talking to Johnnie for a few minutes, she commenced a thorough search of the house. She was the one who found Linda in the bathtub.

This delay not only exponentially increased Linda's suffering but also handicapped the investigation into her attack right from the very start. For a day and a half before blue and white Garda tape got tied to the house's front gate, the scene lay unpreserved, getting trampled on, disturbed and repeatedly walked through. Even with elimination samples from everyone working at the house, the collection of DNA and other physical evidence was seriously compromised. And there was only one witness who, having suffered a traumatic brain injury, couldn't speak.

For several weeks, the investigation floundered. Then, in early June, Linda had recovered enough to be able to provide investigators with a short statement. The Gardaí seized upon one detail from it and fixated on it with a laser-like focus: the handgun.

This was Ireland, a nation policed by unarmed officers, in early 2001. South of the border and outside the M50 motorway, which ring-fenced the areas in which Dublin's criminal gangs jostled each other for supremacy, handguns were not commonplace. They were anomalies. Ordinary decent criminals didn't have them. They couldn't get them. Linda's attack was, in fact, the first sexual assault in the county of Cork where the attacker reportedly had one. It was all the Gardaí needed to tie the crime with the original owner of the house.

The coincidence of a crime happening in Richard Pike's former home had never sat well with the detectives assigned to the case, and now it didn't have to sit with them at all. A connection felt logical. Plausible. *Comfortable.* They threw themselves into following it as their primary line of inquiry and, quite quickly, it became their only one. Now the evidence was written in a language they could understand. This wasn't some random monster who was out prowling the Irish countryside looking for women to violate. This was gangland, organised crime, your garden-variety criminal activity. They knew what to do with that.

Several known associates of Richard Pike, including the evidently law-abiding son who'd lived at the house previously, were hauled in for questioning, along with the man himself. None of them gave investigators anything except soon-to-be-dead ends but a rumour that Pike had hidden large amounts of cash in the wall cavities of the house stayed alight for a time, with the Gardaí working on the assumption that someone who knew it was there had been watching the house, waiting for an opportunity to go and get it, but once inside had changed their mind and assaulted Linda instead. No evidence of this was ever found. Two local men with sexual assault and domestic violence convictions were questioned too, but those lines of inquiry eventually fizzled out just like the rest of them. By the time Linda was discharged from a rehabilitation facility six months after the attack, the Gardaí had made no progress except for a list of men they could confidently say *hadn't* entered the house in Fermoy that night.

Conor and Linda were left broken and destroyed. She was dealing with the horrors in her head and the injuries to her body while he was drowning in the guilt of pushing the move to Fermoy and then leaving her there all alone. And they both had to deal with the phone calls.

Linda had waived her right to anonymity after the attack. It seemed pointless to try to preserve it when the entire population of Fermoy and probably most of the surrounding area could tell you it was *Linda O'Neill, Conor's wife, just back from America, you know the two ...* who'd been attacked. Moreover, by the time she returned home from hospital months later, she thought a couple of media interviews was the only way to reignite interest in a case the Gardaí seemed to have given up on. Unfortunately, it just brought out the crazies.

The landline began to ring at all hours of the day and night. A psychic who knew where Linda's attacker lived. Religious nuts who said this wouldn't have happened if Linda and Conor were regular Mass goers. Other men, threatening to do the same. And hang-ups. Mostly hang-ups. Silence or heavy breathing on the line for a second, then an abrupt dial tone. These were the most innocuous and the most likely to be perpetrated by idiot teenagers. Conor wanted to disconnect the line but Linda had herself convinced that someone might call with actionable information. In the meantime, the Gardaí advised them to log all these nuisance calls, but neither of them saw the point of including the silent ones or hang-ups.

One afternoon, Linda happened to pick up the extension just as Conor lifted the phone downstairs. At first, this one sounded like one of the many they'd already received: there was nothing but heavy breathing on the line. Conor muttered something like, 'Fuck off,' and slammed the phone back on the cradle. Linda, still struggling with her hands, wasn't as quick to do the same, giving the breather time to say, 'Linda? Is that you?' And then, after a brief pause, 'Would you like it if we played another game?' There was no doubt in her mind. It was *him*.

The Gardaí were able to trace the call. It was made from a public payphone at Páirc Uí Chaoimh, a Gaelic sports stadium in Cork City, three minutes after the final whistle blew in a Munster hurling quarter-final that had seen Limerick beat Cork. During it, more than 40,000 punters were streaming out of the stadium.

Patricia and I walk slowly around the perimeter of the house. There's not much to see. Different people live here now. Conor and Linda O'Neill were divorced five years after the attack and both have since remarried. Neither of them lives anywhere near Fermoy.

Patricia isn't a guard any more. She hasn't been for years. She tells me that what she saw in the O'Neills' bathroom that day changed her in ways she didn't appreciate at the time. After her first child was born, she didn't want to go back to work at all. She felt afraid to. She didn't want to run the risk of witnessing another scene like that, didn't want to have to bring it home with her. It felt like a threat of contamination. But she liked the area and the friends she'd made there. For the last seventeen years she's raised her family and worked part time at various jobs, most recently at a local garden centre.

When I ask her what she saw when she entered the bathroom, Patricia looks disappointed in me. I tell her that I want people to understand how bad he is, this man, how dangerous and vile and violent, because I want readers to get angry about his continued freedom. She nods, thinks for a bit. Then she says, 'I won't tell you what I saw. That poor woman has suffered enough indignities. But I will tell you this: when I called it in, I said I had a suspicious death. I couldn't feel a pulse, but it was more because of what she looked like. The colour of her, the injuries to her face … When I saw Linda O'Neill in that bath, I thought she'd be going from there straight into a body bag.'

Jim woke up with a start, sending his copy of *The Nothing Man* flying off his lap and on to the floor. He'd been dreaming of the house in Fermoy; of moving through its unfinished rooms; of the woman who'd lived there. Mixed in were his very real memories of standing over her while she tossed and turned in her sleep, breathing on her shower curtain while she stood beneath the stream of hot water on the other side, and listening in the dark to what her husband did to her so that he could do the same, so that she'd know he'd *been* listening. He was desperate to return, to surrender himself to his dream-memories, but the last wisps of sleep had already darted beyond his reach and—

Was that *birdsong*?

It was no longer silent outside the shed's walls. The dawn chorus was warming up. What time was it? Jim pulled the blackout blind away from the window and cursed at the bright sunlight that immediately assaulted his eyes.

His next thought was that his phone was upstairs in the bedroom.

And he'd set an alarm on it.

Jim shoved the book under the seat cushion and left the shed, hurrying around to the front of the house and getting to the front door just as he heard the angry *beep-beep-beep* coming from upstairs.

His alarm, feet from Noreen's head. It was set for seven.

He'd spent the entire night in the shed.

As Jim closed the front door, the beeping stopped. Then came the sounds of Noreen hoisting herself out of bed.

Too late.

He went into the kitchen and took a seat, *his* seat at the head of the dining table. There was a newspaper lying neatly folded on the nearest chair. An issue of the *Echo*, which covered Cork. Jim grabbed it and put it in front of him, opening it up but not looking at it at all. He took a few deep breaths. He worked to still himself, to stop feeling flustered and hurried and caught out.

Upstairs, a toilet flushed.

He wasn't panicked so much as annoyed at himself. He didn't like it when things didn't go to plan. And there was enough noise in his head right now without adding a barrage of Noreen's idiotic questions into the mix as well.

Why was he up already? How long had he been up? Why hadn't he turned off the alarm?

It was enough to drive a man insane.

Everything had been so much easier before, back then. All he had to do was say he was on an operation and that he couldn't say any more than that. He could disappear from the house for days on end and she wouldn't raise a single objection, or ask him where he'd been and what he'd been doing there when he got back. She knew what answer she'd get. But these days, things were very different. He had a job that kept him in one location, the Centrepoint Shopping Mall in Douglas, every weekday between the hours of 8:30 a.m. and 3:00 p.m. Centrepoint was only a fifteen-minute drive from their house. Noreen wasn't the sharpest tool, but she wasn't completely stupid. She knew if Jim wasn't at work, he had nowhere else he needed to be.

Their relatives lived hours away and Jim had no interest in either side of the family; a get-together at Christmastime was all he was willing to suffer through, if even that. He would never meet up with any of his old colleagues because he hated them all intensely, and the last thing he wanted to talk about was his time in the Gardaí. Sometimes he wished he'd put more effort into cultivating friends or hobbies, or even just pretending to, so that he could announce he was off on a golf weekend or going out for a couple of hours to meet someone for coffee. But he hadn't, and it was too late now. He'd never expected there to be a need for it, not at this hour of his life.

But he did need to finish the book. Sooner rather than later. He'd have to think of something.

Heavy steps on the stairs: Noreen on her way down.

She didn't drive. There was that, at least. She'd always been too nervous to, and Jim made sure she'd only ever got more so by telling her in detail about every horrific accident scene he'd heard a colleague describe. Bodies crushed beyond recognition. Skulls split open like eggshells. Brain matter splattered on tarmac. She occasionally took the bus into town, but most of her life outside of their house was confined to the consecrated acres on which sat their local church, community centre and cemetery. She was a Minister of the Eucharist, a member of the Legion of Mary and helped out twice a week with Meals on Wheels. Then there were the events in aid of various things throughout the year. She was friendly with a few of the other women who did the same, but rarely saw them under other circumstances. The first thing Noreen did every morning was go for a walk around the estate, out on to the road, up to the church, around its perimeter and back again, and as far as Jim knew after that she came home and stayed there.

Shuffling slippered feet in the hall.

Noreen could, theoretically, walk to Centrepoint, but Jim didn't think she ever had. She was vocal about hating the place. She complained that half the shops in there were closed down and said she preferred to get her groceries from Tesco and Aldi, neither of which were Centrepoint tenants. He'd be very unlucky if she suddenly decided, six months after he'd started working there and possibly years after her last visit, to suddenly go now.

Noreen arrived in the kitchen.

'I forgot to tell you,' Jim said, 'I'm doing longer days for the rest of this week. Someone's out sick. They need me to stay until five.'

She paused in the doorway and blinked at him.

'Well.' She pulled her grubby robe around her, the one that made her look even fatter than her clothes did, and went to the kettle. 'Good morning to you, too.'

She was behind him now but he could tell what she doing by the sounds.

Taking down two cups. Getting teabags from the tin on the counter. Milk from the fridge.

'You were up early,' she said after a while. 'Why?'

The water in the kettle started to bubble.

'Because I was awake.' Jim turned a page of the newspaper. 'So I said I might as well get up. No point lying there just staring at the ceiling.'

'What time was that?'

'A while ago.'

Jim turned another page. He hadn't been registering anything in front of him except for the shape of the headlines and the size of the photographs, but now the words *NOTHING MAN* suddenly jumped into focus.

For a second he forgot where he was, who he was, that Noreen was there. He leaned over the paper and traced the headline with his finger.

NOTHING MAN CASE REOPENED IN NEW BOOK.

The headline was above a picture of the family in Bally's Lane, one of the front of the house in Fermoy and that goddamn pencil sketch again – and a thumbnail-sized cover of the book itself. Speedily, he scanned the text. *The case that terrorised Corkonians nearly twenty years ago is the focus of a new book ... sole survivor of the Nothing Man's worst attack, Eve Black, who was just twelve years old at the time ... Detective Edward Healy welcomed the book and said he hopes it will reignite interest in the case ...*

'He's still out there, yes, but we're still looking.'

A cup of tea was hovering in the air in front of him.

'Finally,' he said, taking the cup from Noreen so quickly that some of the liquid spilled out and on to the newspaper. He turned another page and leaned over to look with feigned interest at a story about fishing quotas off the Irish coast.

He was waiting for her to move off, to get her tea and go back upstairs with it like she did most mornings.

But she lingered, stayed standing behind him.

'I think that's a couple of days old, that paper,' she said. 'Katie brought it with her last night.'

The shopping centre was busier than it had been the day before, but that still didn't make it busy. Aside from a car that had been abandoned by the loading dock and a handbag that had been reported lost but was quickly found in the Ladies' changing rooms, Jim had nothing much to do except count down the minutes until his shift was over and he could resume reading *The Nothing Man*.

While Noreen was in the shower, he'd moved the book from the shed to his car, where it was now once again locked in the glove compartment. His plan was to drive somewhere after work, maybe down to the Marina, where he could park up and read for a few hours without drawing attention or being disturbed. He could do it because as far as Noreen was concerned, he'd be at the centre until five at least.

In the meantime, he was doomed to be excruciatingly bored. This morning's minutes seemed to be passing by at the speed of sludge.

Until he saw the woman in the trench coat.

Her hair was pulled back today and she was wearing a skirt instead of trousers, but it was the same coat and she was carrying the same bag. He was sure it was her. She must live locally or work nearby or both. She was walking through the fresh produce section of Grocery, holding a wire basket.

All that was in it so far was a bag of apples.

The last time he'd seen her, twenty-four hours ago, she'd been heading for the tills with a copy of *The Nothing Man*. Had she actually bought it? Had she started reading it yet? How much did she know about what he'd done?

How would she feel if she knew the Nothing Man was standing just a few feet away from her right now, watching her, *studying* her?

When she set off in the direction of the frozen food, Jim – on impulse – went too. He kept his distance and made sure to make it look like he was just patrolling the store, but his eyes never left her.

Today the coat was buttoned up, its belt wrapped tightly around her waist, revealing the lines of her body. He watched as she filled her basket with a bottle of wine, two microwavable meals and a four-pack of toilet roll.

Did those choices indicate that she lived alone? Did she ever come in here on her way home *after* work? If she did, could he follow her there? What would he do to her in the dark?

What would he *like* to do?

And would he still be physically able to do it?

'Just the man I was looking for.'

Steve O'Reilly had stepped in front of Jim, blocking his view of the woman. His hair was looking even more thick with sticky gel than usual and standing as he was, with his hands on his hips, exposed the fact that he was wearing cufflinks.

He was the manager in a low-cost department store and he was coming to work with *cufflinks* on. How unbearably pathetic.

Jim almost couldn't stand to look at the man.

'What happened to you yesterday?' Steve asked.

Jim put his hands on his own hips, mirroring Steve's stance.

'Migraine,' he said.

'Migraine,' Steve repeated.

The two men stared at each other hard.

'And what did you do about that?'

Jim feigned confusion. '*Do* about it?'

'Do you have a doctor's note or …?'

'I just went to bed. In a dark room.'

'You just went to bed? In a dark room?'

Repeating everything back but phrased as a question: *An Amateur's Interrogation Technique*, chapter 1. Jim refused to respond to it.

'No painkillers?' Steve raised his eyebrows. 'For a *migraine*?'

His radio beeped. He lifted it off his belt and said into it, 'Steve here, go ahead.' After a squawk of static, a tinny voice said something about a problem with the computer at the customer service desk. 'I'll be right there.' He looked Jim right in the eye and added, deadpan, 'Over.'

The next sound to come from the radio was the sound of a short, sharp laugh and three words that were, in contrast to what had come before, mercilessly distinct.

'Copy that, *Jim.*'

Even tinny from the speaker on the radio, the sarcasm was easily detected.

Steve grinned triumphantly.

Jim felt his cheeks beginning to burn.

True, no one else said that on the radio around here. But Jim did it because a habit formed over thirty years was difficult to break, and because he was right to. It was an established protocol for ensuring clear radio communication. They could make fun of him all they wanted, but who would have the last laugh here: the intelligent man who'd already had an illustrious career as a member of An Garda Síochána or the idiots stuck working in this dump for minimum wage for the rest of their lives?

Steve was holstering the radio, the smirk having spread into an expression of smug satisfaction.

Jim lurched at the younger man, grabbed Steve's throat with one hand and pushed a closed fist into his sneering mouth with the other, forcing open the artificially whitened teeth until his fingers felt Steve's soft palate, and then Jim opened his fingers, flexing and stretching, until he heard the *crack* of a jawbone, the crunch of a tooth, the scream of someone being made to bear unbearable pain. Just at the point where Steve had taken almost as much pain as a human could, when he felt his skull was breaking open from the inside out, Jim yanked out his fist and used it to smash Steve face-first into the nearest glass door of a freezer cabinet, *through* it, repeatedly, until his face was pierced all over with shards of broken glass. Then he pulled him back out by his greasy hair and pushed him down the aisle, door to door, rubbing what was left of his face against them, leaving a long smear of Steve's blood—

'Well, let's hope there's no migraines today, eh?' Steve winked at Jim. 'Or for the rest of this week.'

Back in reality, Jim just glared at Steve's back while he walked away.

Jim turned and faced his reflection in the nearest freezer cabinet, then pressed his forehead to the cool glass.

He felt shaky and light-headed. He needed to calm down. He was letting himself get too worked up.

And the likes of Steve were decidedly unworthy of it.

He started back towards the entrance to the department store. He often positioned himself there for fifteen- or thirty-minute blocks throughout his shift, as that was the most effective place for security personnel to be seen. Standing there made him a deterrent, but also put him within feet of the security sensors. As an added bonus, it was a great place to look like he was working when he wasn't at all.

But Jim didn't make it that far.

At the start of Grocery, just after the flowers and magazines but before the fruit and veg, there was a concession selling hot drinks. It had three high-top tables where people could perch, drink their coffee and crane their necks to stare up at a TV screen hung from the wall. It was permanently muted but sometimes showed subtitles.

This morning, the TV was tuned to one of those shows

where a couple sat on a couch and interviewed people Jim never recognised sitting on another couch alongside. The interviewee was a blonde woman, late twenties or early thirties, pretty despite her attempts not to be. She had white-blonde hair shorn very short, cut with jagged edges, and she had draped her thin frame in some kind of voluminous black thing. She was missing the heavy TV make-up that made everyone's faces look like they belonged on wax dolls but in truth, she could've done with it, because there were purple shadows under her eyes and she was so pale she looked ill. This was all compounded by the fact that she or someone else had swept a bright red colour across her lips but not very neatly, and on a 42-inch high-definition flat-screen TV, you could see it had become smudged and was bleeding past the borders of her lips.

It was Eve Black.

Jim knew this not because he recognised her – he hadn't seen her since she was twelve years old, and only then for a few moments – but because of the words at the bottom of the screen. THE NOTHING MAN MURDERED MY FAMILY: AUTHOR EVE BLACK ON HER NEW TRUE-CRIME MEMOIR.

He watched as it disappeared, then Eve did too.

She was replaced by a floating family photograph, grainy and slightly out of focus: mother, father and two blonde girls holding hands.

Then *they* were gone, replaced by a travelling shot of Eve and another woman walking towards a house, their backs to the cameras. Eve stopped and pointing to something in the middle distance.

The subtitles were off. Jim had no idea what they were saying.

Back to the studio.

A shot of the presenters, their faces pinched with seriousness.

On to Eve.

She nodded and then started talking, moving her hands.

The longer Jim looked at her, the more he could see the face of that little girl in her features.

He should've seen this coming. He'd been so focused on the book, on his reading it, that he'd failed to think about the bigger picture – the far worse, much more pressing problem at hand: *other* people reading it. The story in the newspaper was one thing. It was a Cork newspaper, and anyway who read those any more? This was a TV show. It was *national*.

Now the female presenter was holding up a copy of the book. Jim could guess what she was saying because a graphic had appeared on screen with times and dates.

Tonight, Eve Black was going to be signing copies of her book at a store in Dublin city centre. Tomorrow, she was going to be doing the same at a store here, in Cork.

The very same store where Jim had purchased *his* copy of *The Nothing Man*.

He immediately decided that he would go see her.

– 5 –

Westpark

There are some terrible places where rooms wait ready for children.

The one they took me to that night was small and uncomfortably bright, harshly lit from above by fluorescent strips. There were no windows unless you counted the little pane in the door through which I could see the reflective vest of the Garda who was standing outside, a neon-yellow sentry. The furniture looked like the window display from a charity shop: two saggy couches, a coffee table covered in water rings and a mahogany floor lamp whose shade had a fringe of tassels. Posters hung on the walls, the kind you see at the cinema, all for kids' movies a few years old. A red bin sat in one corner, filled with plastic action figures, dolls with knotted hair and battered board-game boxes that you just knew didn't have all the necessary pieces. For years I thought this room was in a Garda station but I've recently learned it was in Cork University Hospital, a place Corkonians still tend to call by a shortening of its original name, the Regional.

Everything about that room was deeply wrong. The fact that we were there at all, for a start. Nannie was with me, her hair loose around her shoulders, out of its neat bun for the first time in my life. She was mostly staring into space. Another woman was there too, a social worker, who I can remember almost nothing about. She was just a blur of grey in the corner. It was so late it was early, probably around six in the morning. I was wearing borrowed pyjamas with my feet in adult-sized socks. The socks were the heavy wool kind and itchy. No one was talking and there was no noise to distract us from that fact. I wanted to ask what was happening to Anna and my parents – where they were now, how they were, what had happened in our house – but I also didn't want to know the answers. That room was an airlock between my life as I knew it and my life as I feared it would be from now on. So long as I was in there, I could stay suspended between the two. So long as we didn't leave, it hadn't happened. Even if you were already falling, you were technically okay until you hit the ground.

Eventually the door opened and two people came in, a man and a woman. They were in plain clothes and looked like schoolteachers. As they spoke to Nannie about being very sorry and having to ask questions and my well-being being their priority, I began to hear a strange noise, a kind of rushing in my ears. It was as if I was getting slowly submerged in water while they remained standing on the surface. Everyone's voice got muffled, then distant, then became utterly indistinct as I sank. I was drowning and I had no way of raising the alarm.

The man came and crouched down in front of me. He had reddish hair and freckles across his nose. He was so close that when he spoke I could feel the warmth of his breath tickling the skin on my face. But I couldn't make out any of his words.

Detective Garda Sergeant Edward Healy can tell you the exact day, time and place he decided to become a guard. It was 14 August 1980, just after nine o'clock in the evening. He was eight years old and sitting in his parents' living room in Ballysheedy, Co. Limerick. Two uniformed Gardaí were side by side on the couch in identical poses: elbows on knees, hats in hands, buttocks perched right on the edge of their seats. Their black boots were very shiny. His mother was standing by the fireplace, having refused to sit. Tears were streaming down her face. A few minutes earlier, when she'd heard the knock, she'd rolled her eyes and muttered, '*Finally*,' because she thought it was Eddie Senior who was late home for dinner and hadn't called to tell her why. The uniformed men gently explained that there'd been an accident on the quays in Limerick City. One car had careened into another, forcing them both into the river. There'd been no survivors. The driver of the first car was drunk. The driver of the second was Healy's father.

Healy knew he wanted to become a guard, and he knew the wanting had started that terrible night, but he could never quite articulate what one had to do with the other. It would be many years before he'd figure it out. In a world where all the adults were upset and crying and breaking apart, those two men in uniform had remained stoic, solid and in control, everything eight-year-old Healy desperately wished he could be. Really, it had nothing to do with their being guards. They were just the only adults who were there that day who were outside the family's circle of grief. But by the time Healy realised this, it would be too late to turn back.

The day he passed out at Templemore, his pride was like a steel rod in the back of his uniform, pushing his shoulders back, chest out, chin up. He'd always looked to the navy blues for a sign that help was coming, that everything would be all right, and now he was wearing that same uniform. He was proud that he could bring that reassurance to other people. But his graduation day was also the peak of his relationship with An Garda Síochána. Almost as soon as he was on the job, Healy began a slide into bleak disillusionment. He found himself in an organisation bloated by bureaucracy and infected with levels of laziness and corruption that, in his eyes, it had no feasible way to recover from. There was an especially acute heartbreak in having secured the job you'd dreamed of having for more than half your life only to discover that, firstly, it was nothing like you'd imagined it would be and, secondly, it had never really been your dream job at all.

By March 1999, this disappointment had become a corrosive force. There'd been a brief reprieve following Healy's appointment to detective and a move from Ballincollig station in the west of the city to Anglesea Street, the district HQ, before the hope that things would be different for him in plain clothes had died too. Now things felt as dark as ever. His marriage, less than three years old, was one bad argument away from breaking down. Healy worried about the frequency and extent of his drinking, and then drank more so he could stop worrying about it for a while. At night he would lie awake, tormented by the feeling that he was standing at a crossroads and if he didn't move soon – if he didn't make a decision, a drastic change in his life – something would burst out of the shadows and run him over, and after that there'd be no coming back.

Not having anyone to talk to about this made it all the worse. Mental health wasn't something the force even acknowledged back then, let alone prioritised. Members who'd had to deal with horrific scenes and frightening situations worked through what many of them would later come to suspect was PTSD over pints in the pub, and even then ... As one member put it, the prevailing mood at the time was not one of support, but one-upmanship. 'You think *that's* bad? Wait until I tell you what *I* saw today!'

Then one dull Tuesday morning, Healy went to investigate reports of a burglary at a place called Westpark, a housing estate off the Maryborough Road on the southside of Cork City. Or at least it *would* be a housing estate. Then, it was still a building site. Rows of semi-detached houses, smoothly finished and painted cream with the flourish of a red-brick band across their ground floors. The concrete in the driveways was pale and unblemished, but the roads that linked the houses were still loose-gravel tracks. The STOP signs were covered with black refuse bags and the milky plastic film hadn't yet been removed from the houses' windows.

A man in a high-vis vest appeared from the prefab marked SITE OFFICE and introduced himself as David Walsh, project manager at Browne Developments Ltd, the company that was building Westpark. He gave Healy a folded map of the estate. It showed upwards of a hundred houses arranged in rows, their rear gardens nose to nose, feeding into a central roadway that went all the way to the back of the estate. On the map, each house was an empty box about the size of a thumbnail. At least a dozen of them had been marked with a big 'X' in red marker pen.

It had all started six months ago, Walsh explained. Westpark had been built in stages, beginning with the houses closest to the road and then extending on back into the muddy fields beyond. Almost as soon as the first phase was completed, contractors reported odd activity on site. Materials would move during the night, from one room to another or from downstairs to up. Locking mechanisms were discovered missing from internal doors, removed cleanly, leaving nothing but the empty space where the lock had been. Other items – tools, an electric drill, light fixtures – disappeared too. Sometimes things *appeared*, most notably a rolled-up sleeping bag.

Vandalism was a common problem on building sites and usually only a sign that bored teenagers were living nearby, but what was odd about this activity was that it only happened in the finished homes. They were sealed to the elements, their front doors locked, sitting empty and awaiting their buyers to move in. Browne Developments had stepped up their on-site security, employing two full-time security guards to patrol the estate overnight, but this hadn't curtailed the activity and their insurance company had urged them to make a formal report to the Gardaí.

'It was one of the security guards,' Walsh said, 'who found the lair.'

The two men took Healy's car to the back of the estate, where a dense dark wood met a row of empty foundations, patiently awaiting bricks and mortar. Walsh led the way to a break in the treeline.

Once they were standing there, Healy could see that the ground dropped away sharply a few feet further in, leading to a small clearing. The clearing itself was six or eight feet below the level of the estate and this, combined with the fact that it was surrounded by tall, evergreen trees, hid it from view. Sitting in the middle of it was what looked at first glance like the makings of a bonfire. But once Healy had slipped and slid his way down the slope, he saw he was actually looking at a pile of building materials. Sheets of MDF. PVC pipes. Various tools. And, as far as Browne Developments could figure, every single lock that had been removed from the houses' internal doors.

Healy looked from Walsh to the pile and fought the urge to laugh. What *was* this? Why was he here? *Moving things* wasn't punishable by law. If whoever had done this was planning on selling the items, surely they would've done it before now. This was no storage place; it would've been a nightmare to get the loot back up to the road. Since nearly all the items were still in the protective plastic wrapping they'd arrived on site in, even criminal damage was a stretch.

He asked some questions and wrote some things down because that's what people who called the Gardaí to report things liked to see happen. He recommended that the so-called lair be blocked off and that CCTV cameras be installed until the homes were occupied. Browne Developments complied and, when Healy made a follow-up call a few weeks later, they had no new activity to report. After that, there was nothing else to do but occasionally puzzle over it and, over pints, tell a few colleagues the strange story of the thefts in Westpark. One of them said it sounded like the start of some kind of shady insurance claim, and Healy was inclined to agree.

Time passed. Healy and his wife began a period of official separation; under Irish law they'd need to prove four years of it before either one of them could ask for a divorce and she was anxious to get started. Living alone now, Healy's drinking got a little worse before it got a little better. The turn of the millennium came and went. He got promoted to sergeant. He considered resigning from the force. He found himself wondering what it would be like to move away, to go back to college, to become a psychologist. But every morning he got up and went into work and every night he went to bed having done nothing about it.

Alice O'Sullivan was attacked.

And Christine Kiernan.

Linda O'Neill.

And then it was early on a Sunday morning in June 2001 and a colleague of his was calling to ask if he'd heard the news. A young couple had been murdered in their home on the south side of the city the previous night. Initial reports indicated that the woman had also been sexually assaulted. What the Gardaí had found at the scene wasn't making any sense.

'You might be able to help them,' his colleague said. 'It's Westpark.'

Marie Meara and Martin Connolly had met in the summer of 1998, when she was twenty-five and he was twenty-seven. They both worked in confectionery. Martin was an account manager for a well-known chocolate brand and Marie had founded her own artisanal business, which she was hoping to eventually expand into a café. That's how they'd met, first crossing paths at a Bord Bia trade show. When their wedding invites went out two years later, a specially commissioned cartoon depicted the couple as a pair of hand-holding M&Ms, a joke their friends had long been making. The words most often used to describe the couple were *nice* and *generous* and *hardworking*.

At the beginning of June 2001, they had been living at number fifteen Westpark for less than three weeks. The move was so recent, it was still in progress. They hadn't yet received confirmation that the utilities in their rented apartment in Ballincollig had been transferred out of their names, and their landlord, a solicitor named Kevin Prendergast, still hadn't had the chance to return their security deposit. He'd been carrying the cheque around in an envelope for a week, meaning to post it.

As it happened, early on the Sunday of the June Bank Holiday weekend, Prendergast was due to meet friends for a golf game in Frankfield. His route there took him not quite past Westpark, but near enough to it. He could make a little detour and hand-deliver the cheque. He wasn't intending to make contact with Marie and Martin. His plan was to push the envelope through the letterbox and go.

Shortly before 8:00 a.m., he parked on the street outside their house. The morning was warm and muggy, the heat trapped by cloudy skies. As he walked up the drive, he was thinking about the likelihood of rain and hoping that, if it did come, it would wait until after the ninth hole. He registered that Martin's silver Ford Mondeo was parked outside, pointing towards the garage door, but he didn't look too closely at it. The driveway sloped downwards, the house a foot or two below the level of the road.

Prendergast was fond of Marie and Martin – they'd been excellent tenants – and as he approached the front door he was admiring the house and thinking, Haven't they done well for themselves? He was happy they had. In the next moment, he got his first inkling that something was wrong: the front door was open five or six inches and the ceiling light in the hallway beyond was on.

Beep-beep.

The phone lying on the passenger seat suddenly lit up, its screen showing a message that read BATTERY CHARGED. Jim put down the book and picked up the phone, unplugging the connecting cable from the port on the dash with his other hand.

Once his shift had ended, he'd gone to Electric City in the retail park across the road from Centrepoint. He told a clerk there that his wife had dropped her phone in the sink and that he just needed something to hold her over for a few days. Something she could browse the internet on, but not anything that would require a contract. Something cheap.

He needed to watch Eve's interview but he wouldn't do it on the computer at home or his own phone, the one registered to him, and going to an internet café felt like overkill. Instead, he'd bought a burner phone and parked on the Marina after work. It was quiet, with only the occasional passing jogger or dog-walker.

Ever since he'd discovered the existence of *The Nothing Man*, he'd felt himself oscillating between paranoid caution and confident nonchalance. This was him splitting the difference.

Jim booted up the phone and navigated to its internet browser. First, he had to find out what channel the interview with Eve had aired on, and what the name of the show was. That was easy: he had both within seconds thanks to a simple Google search. One of the links that came up in the results deposited him right where he needed to be: on the channel's online catch-up service, a PLAY button partially obscuring Eve's pinched face.

The video was six minutes long. He turned up the phone's volume as high as it would go and tapped PLAY on the screen.

The two presenters were sitting side by side on a bright pink couch and looking earnestly at the camera. The man was in a suit ruined by the floral shirt he was wearing underneath it, the woman in a dress so tight and unyielding that it looked as if it might have been designed primarily for compression.

The woman looked into the camera and smiled, revealing unnaturally white teeth. 'And now,' she said, 'to our next guest. This coming January, it will be twenty years since a faceless killer began to terrorise the city and county of Cork. In October 2001, on the night of his final attack, a masked intruder entered a house in Passage West on the westside of the city and murdered three members of the Black family: Ross, his wife Deirdre and their seven-year-old daughter Anna.' On *seven*, the host intensified her stare into the lens. 'Miraculously, their eldest daughter, Eve, just twelve at the time, survived the attack by hiding in an upstairs bathroom. She joins us this morning to tell us about her new book, her *amazing* book – I'm reading it at the moment and I just cannot put it down – *The Nothing Man*, which she hopes will finally lead authorities to his identity. Eve, good morning. You're very welcome to the show.'

The shot widened, revealing Eve sitting on another, identical couch just a foot away from the one on which the hosts were perched. She was sitting with her knees together and her hands in her lap, managing to look both rigid and fidgety. Clearly nervous. She mumbled, 'Thanks for having me,' just as a graphic appeared at the bottom of the screen.

THE NOTHING MAN MURDERED MY FAMILY: AUTHOR EVE BLACK ON HER NEW TRUE-CRIME MEMOIR.

'This book,' the female host said. She picked up the copy that had been sitting in her lap. 'Wow. I have to tell you, it's a harrowing read but I just can't put it down. It's riveting, it's devastating ... I was up until all hours last night because of it. They had to go thick with the concealer on me this morning.' She flashed a smile, then resumed looking serious. 'Tell me: why write this book? And why now?'

'Well ...' Eve licked her red lips. 'I suppose the simple answer is that, um ... I want to find him. To identify him and find him so he can be caught and punished for what he did. As for why now ...' She paused. 'To be honest, I just wasn't ready until now.'

'It started with an article,' the female host prompted.

'Yes. I wrote a piece, in college – I was doing a masters, in Creative Writing – and it got published, got lots of attention, quite unexpectedly, and then because of that I got the opportunity to write this book, so ...' Eve's voice trailed off and she looked at the female host uncertainly, as if for further instruction.

'It must have been very hard,' the male host said.

'It was,' Eve said.

'Because you don't just write about what happened to your own family, but you write about his other crimes as well. In detail.' He paused. 'Was *that* hard?'

Eve nodded. She was biting her lip and her hands had slipped from her lap to between her thighs. She looked even more nervous now than when they'd started.

This was not the woman Jim had been expecting based on what he'd read of *The Nothing Man* thus far.

'Eve and I,' the female host said, 'visited her childhood home earlier this week and spoke in some detail about that horrific night' – the screen changed to the family photograph – 'and her motivation for writing this book, which, really, is what has stayed with me. Because, Eve, to be honest, I read a lot of true crime, and I watch all the documentaries' – footage now of Eve and a woman Jim realised was the host, walking with their backs to the camera – 'and listen to the podcasts, and I'd never thought about these men, these serial killers, the way you talk about him, about the Nothing Man.' The footage disappeared leaving the screen filled with the female host, looking hopefully at Eve. 'Could you speak about that, for a moment? The "nothing" part?'

'It's just that …Well, we mythologise them, don't we?' Eve stopped to swallow, then started again. 'These men. Ted Bundy. The Golden State Killer. The Canal Killer. We talk about them like they're *others*, a different kind of being. A monster in a human costume. We look at their crimes and we just can't figure out how they did it – but that's only because we don't have all the facts. Take the case of the Golden State Killer, for instance. They used to marvel at how he could get in and out of people's homes without being attacked by their dogs. In fact, there was one occasion where, while he was actually physically attacking someone, the dog was just sitting there watching. It was like he had some kind of superpower, some dark magic that separated him from us. He could control these dogs. That's what they thought, anyway. But when they caught the guy, he had a charge for shoplifting, and one of the items he'd shoplifted was a can of dog repellent. And so that was it. That's *all* it was. He didn't have any special powers. None of these men do.' She was speaking louder now, looking stronger, gesticulating to punctuate her points. 'We know their names because they got *caught*. These men, they're not over-achievers or particularly successful in any other area of their lives. They're boring, unremarkable failures. And that's what I want to prove: that the Nothing Man is too. The Gardaí called him that because they didn't have anything on him, but I call him that because that's what he is: *nothing*. A non-entity. A *loser*. And I want to prove that by identifying him.'

The shot narrowed, cutting Eve out and focusing entirely on the female host, who was blinking. 'Yes, that's … That's so true. Well, I'm afraid that's all we have time for ...' She held up her copy of her book. '*The Nothing Man* is out now in all good bookshops. My full interview with Eve will air on Wednesday night on RTÉ One and trust me, you won't want to miss that. Or this book.'

'And Eve,' the male host piped up as the shot went wide again, showing all three of them, 'will be signing copies of her book in Eason, O'Connell Street ...'

The graphic with the dates and times came up on screen.

The interview was over.

Jim stopped the video and sat staring out the windscreen at the smooth waters of the River Lee. The grey sky was reflected in them. A canoe slid past filled with half a dozen rowers, their oars effortlessly slicing through the water with perfect synchronicity. Idly, Jim wondered if one of them was Katie. The college rowing club was around here somewhere, wasn't it?

He would have to kill her. He'd have to kill Eve. She deserved it, after what she'd said about him. He'd make sure the last thought she ever had in this life was that she'd been wrong.

Because he *was* special. He wasn't one of those ordinary idiots who sleepwalked through the orbits of this earth and called it living. He was smarter. Stronger. Superior. He would emerge from the shadows one last time to kill his most famous survivor, then disappear back into them once again. No one would see him. He wouldn't be caught. He'd force everyone to marvel at him. They'd ask themselves, how could a normal, boring man – what was it Eve had said? – a *loser* do something like that? They couldn't. That was the simple answer. The only answer. Only *he* could.

The Nothing Man.

They'd start to whisper those words again, because they'd fear that saying them out loud would summon him. He'd make sure of it. In the meantime, let Eve Black say whatever she wanted. Let her double-down, dig that hole she'd made deeper and deeper. It would just make the next chapter – the Nothing Man's final one – all the sweeter.

There was much work to do. This wouldn't be like those times before. He'd have to prepare for longer, take greater care.

He'd have to start now.

He already knew the two items at the top of his list: go to her event in the bookshop tomorrow night and, before then, read as much as he could of her book.

Puzzled, Prendergast called out, 'Hello?' two or three times. When he got no response, he rang the doorbell. He thinks he also called out the couple's names. No one answered and, beyond, the house was utterly quiet. No voices, no radio, no television. It didn't seem like anyone was even home.

He thought maybe the couple had walked somewhere local, perhaps to Mass or the shop, and accidentally left the door open on their way out. He reached out and pulled it closed, listening for the *click* of the lock, then pressed the same hand against it and pushed to check that he hadn't made the same mistake. The envelope with the cheque was still in his pants pocket. He posted it through the letterbox. He turned around and, with his back to the door, tapped out a text message to Martin explaining about the door and the cheque, and pressed SEND.

Prendergast hadn't even managed to put the phone back in his pocket before he heard the sound of a text message arriving on a Nokia phone. Three quick beats, two long pulses, three quick beats more. He had a Nokia himself and he looked down at the device in his hand, confused, because he hadn't received a message. The sound had come from another phone. *Martin's* phone, surely, going by the timing. But it had been too loud and clear, Prendergast thought, to have come from inside the house.

He typed another text message, this time consisting of just the word 'TEST', and sent that to Martin too. Just like before, this action was immediately followed by the text alert noise which, paying attention now, he sensed was coming from somewhere on the ground to his right. He scanned the area and quickly found the corresponding phone. It was lying on the ground between a terracotta plant pot and the front wall of the house, inches away from the frame of the garage door and two feet from the front of the Mondeo in the driveway.

When Prendergast bent down to get it, his peripheral vision picked up something monstrously wrong: Martin's eyes, open and staring, in the darkness underneath the car.

The shock made him lose his balance and the fall had the unfortunate consequence of bringing him even closer to Martin's body. And it was, without doubt, a body. Martin was dead. His face was a colour it shouldn't have been and his head was twisted at an angle that didn't make any sense. He had, somehow, been run over by his own car in his own driveway. Prendergast scrambled to his feet and called the emergency services even though he knew there was no emergency here. It was too late.

He went and sat on the low wall that bordered the front garden while he waited for the flashing lights and sirens, for the people in uniforms who would know what to do next. His hands were shaking and one leg was bouncing uncontrollably. All he could see were Martin's wide-open eyes, whether his own were open or closed.

Marie must be out somewhere, he thought, or maybe away overnight. He prayed she wouldn't get here before the ambulance did, so he wouldn't have to be the one to tell her.

Gardaí Elaine Grady and Peter Fine were the first to arrive at the house. They'd been nearby when the call came in and beat the ambulance. Fine stayed with Prendergast while Grady went to make an initial examination of the scene.

Martin's body was wedged beneath the bonnet of the car, in front of the wheels, with the exception of his right hand and right foot, which were trapped underneath one. There wasn't enough room for him under there, which was why his body looked as contorted as it did, and why Grady didn't need the coroner's office to tell her that the cause of death was asphyxiation. Prendergast had told her about the phone and she theorised that Martin had been on the ground looking for the device when the car rolled forward and trapped him underneath. But what had caused the car to roll forward in the first place? Grady snapped on a latex glove and tried the driver's side door. It was unlocked.

The first thing she noticed was that the handbrake was engaged.

The second was that the handle was smeared with blood, which changed everything.

She and Fine locked Prendergast into the back seat of their car and, together, advanced towards the house. There was side access to the rear garden and they found a door at the back unlocked. It deposited them into a small utility room off the kitchen. There were items on the dining table that suggested a meal had been interrupted, but only one person appeared to have been dining. All the curtains on the ground floor were drawn.

They advanced up the stairs. The main bathroom was at the top. When they opened its door they found Marie on the floor. She was wearing only her underwear, her hands and wrists were tied with thin nylon rope and her skin was covered in puncture wounds and slashes. The air was thick with the smell of wet pennies and much of the bathroom was splashed and smeared with blood.

The two Gardaí stood stock still in the threshold, staring and disbelieving, until the wail of approaching sirens reminded them that this was a crime scene and dozens of people were about to descend on it. They retraced their steps to their car. Fine got a roll of Garda tape out of the boot. Grady got on the radio and called absolutely everybody.

Forensic testing would show that the blood in the bathroom and the blood on the handbrake both belonged to Marie. The handbrake sample also contained fibres consistent with the blue nylon rope that had been used to bind her arms and legs, which suggested that the blood in the car had left Marie's body after the attack in the bathroom, when her blood and that rope were both present. Seeing as there were no blood smears or drops in the spaces between the bathroom and the car – the carpeted landing and stairs, the hallway, the front door and first couple of feet of the drive – the Gardaí had to conclude that it wasn't Marie who'd left the blood in the car, but the person or persons unknown who'd attacked her.

That wasn't Martin. He had no blood on his skin or clothing that wasn't his own. The only sequence of events that made forensic sense was that Marie was attacked, her attacker then came downstairs, went outside and got into the car, lifted the handbrake and let the vehicle roll over Martin, who for some reason was already in front of it.

Why any of those things had happened was anyone's guess.

Detective Inspector Graham Harris was to be the lead officer on the case. When Healy went to him and told him about the 1999 burglaries, Harris assigned him a desk in the incident room and tasked him with determining whether or not there was a connection to the murders. Healy was buoyed by the interesting task but not sure where to start with it. Was it even plausible the two things were related? On one hand it would be a staggering coincidence for a double-murder to take place in a home where, when the homes were still mere houses, someone had repeatedly broken in – and in the sphere of criminal investigation, there were no coincidences. But on the other hand, what could some moved tools and removed locks have to do with a woman dead in her own bathroom and a man dead under his own car? One was a petty crime, the other one of the worst crimes imaginable.

Healy made repeated visits to Westpark. He checked security footage, looked into the backgrounds of the men and women who'd worked on the site and tracked down David Walsh, the former project manager. He even looked at the firm of estate agents tasked with selling the finished homes, the shareholders behind Browne Developments and the rest of that first wave of Westpark residents. None of it turned up anything useful.

Despite a month's worth of intensive, round-the-clock work, Operation Optic (a nod to *The Invisible Man*) was, as a whole, having the same problem. The couple at fifteen Westpark had seemingly had no enemies. There were no secrets in their lives. Nothing was missing from the house and there was no apparent motive. In an effort to move things along, DI Harris appeared on Crimecall, the primetime television show where solemn TV presenters sat alongside Gardaí and pleaded for the public's help amid grim reconstructions.

On the night the appeal aired, Healy helped field calls to the dedicated tip-line. He took one from a sales assistant in an electronics store on Oliver Plunkett Street in the city centre who had sold Marie Meara a mobile phone six weeks or so before her death. This sales assistant, Denis Philips, said that when Marie came in to buy the phone, she had mentioned in passing that she was getting rid of her landline because she'd been receiving nuisance calls. He remembered her because there had been a problem with accessing her account and she'd been in the store for so long that Philips had been over an hour late in finishing his shift. He'd heard about the murders on the news previously, but hadn't seen a good picture of Marie until now.

If it were true that Marie and Martin were planning on disconnecting their landline, they'd never got around to doing it. It was still active on the night of the murders and there was no evidence to suggest they had ever made any move to disconnect it. Healy secured records going back three months and pored over them line by line. He found twenty-seven instances of incoming calls that lasted only moments – three seconds here, seven seconds there. They usually came in the evening, in batches of two or three, and they had all been made from public telephone boxes in busy urban areas. One of them had been made on the grounds of Páirc Uí Chaoimh, just minutes after the final whistle blew in the Munster hurling quarter-final between Cork and Limerick – just like the call Linda O'Sullivan in Fermoy had received.

Healy knew about the O'Sullivan case. Everyone did. But everyone also thought of it as an incident of organised criminal activity, most likely former gang members looking for loot left hidden in the bossman's house. The Gardaí thought the subsequent calls had come from cranks. But whatever the chances of a building site that had been plagued with petty thefts coincidentally becoming a crime scene, there was no possible way *this* was a coincidence. It was, undeniably, a connection. And when Healy shared this information with the incident room, another member who'd worked the Christine Kiernan case reminded him of the disturbing voicemails they'd found after her tragic death. Thus, a second connection.

There was one more yet to be made. In light of this new information, DI Harris decided that Healy should do a follow-up segment on the next edition of Crimecall, which aired monthly. On the night of 21 September 2001, Healy sat behind a desk on the Crimecall set, sweating under the lights, and explained to the host about connecting the cases with phone calls. An audio recording of Christine Kiernan's voicemails was played, and a transcript of what Linda O'Neill had heard on the prank call was shown on screen.

Sitting in his student flat in Bishopstown, Tommy O'Sullivan, now a fresher at University College Cork, straightened up when he saw the words on screen. *Would you like it if we played another game?* He called his mother and told her about the prank call he'd received on New Year's Eve two weeks before her attack. She confirmed that her attacker had used similar language. Mother and son would meet at Anglesea Street first thing the next morning to report their revelation to the Gardaí.

The world was still reeling from 9/11, still getting up every morning to turn on the news to see if it had really happened, still seeing inexplicable scenes of smouldering ruins broadcast from the heart of Manhattan. But Healy saw none of it. His world had shrunk to the borders of his desk. He knew now that there was no tiger kidnapping gone wrong. No random rapist. No criminal gang come hunting for loot. Instead, there was a faceless monster who had toyed with his victims, lingered around their homes before and after his attacks, and taunted them with phone calls. Who had started with a knife, then got a gun. Who had begun his horror spree with a physical assault and then moved on to rape before graduating to murder. And for all they knew about him, he may as well be a ghost. When a junior member of the team said as much to a journalist friend, a headline containing the moniker 'The Nothing Man' appeared for the first time in the press the next day.

A few days after the Nothing Man made his first appearance in the press, Healy was walking through Anglesea Street's regional Garda HQ – which happened to be next door to Cork's biggest fire station – when he witnessed members of the fire brigade's Hazardous Materials Unit engaged in a training session outside. A special rig had been built behind the station for this purpose: a narrow, hollow square five or six storeys high with stairs on its exterior, a stand-in for a real office building or apartment block. These training sessions happened regularly and Healy had seen them many times before. But on this occasion, as he stood there watching, a word materialised in his mind: *practising*. That's what the firefighters were doing – and that's what had been going on in the Westpark estate, too. Before anyone had moved into those houses, someone had been practising getting in and out of them. Their killer had used the place as his own personal training ground. Healy had never seen that level of pre-meditation before. It unnerved him. It also motivated him.

Thus Detective Sergeant Edward Healy took four hitherto unconnected, unsolved cases – Alice O'Sullivan, Christine Kiernan, Linda O'Neill and the double murder of Marie Meara and Martin Connolly – and linked them, advancing Operation Optic more than any other single member of the force. He was the one to identify that a serial attacker was at work in Cork city and county. He stopped thinking about resigning, or moving to another city, or going back to college to study something else. He could only think about catching this man.

Detective Sergeant Edward Healy felt alive again. My mother, father and sister only had a week left to live.

Back in that awful room in the hospital on the night of my family's attack, the man with the reddish hair and freckles on his nose was crouched down in front of me, talking.

I looked into his face and willed myself to pay attention. I could still hear that odd rushing noise in my ears. I wanted my mother. I wanted to hear a knock on the door and look up and see her poking her head in, saying, 'Is Eve in— Oh, there you are. Come on!' But instead the door stayed closed and the man kept talking.

Gradually, a few words began to get through.

Remember … Telephone … Anna.

'Where is she?' I said, surfacing suddenly. 'Is she okay?'

Freckled Man looked relieved and moved to sit beside me. When he spoke again it was very quietly, as if he was telling me a secret. He called me Evelyn. He said Anna was very, very sick but she was in hospital and the doctors and nurses were looking after her. It was an explanation for someone much younger than me and I bristled with anger. I was *twelve*. I wasn't a child. I wanted to shout that at him.

He said that after I had some sleep, we'd need to talk about what had happened back at the house. I stayed perfectly still, working to keep my face blank, my whole body tense with terror. Because I *couldn't* talk about it. It was taking all I had to keep it locked away inside my head. Every so often an image would break free – Anna's limp hand hanging off the side of her bed; a spray of red on the wallpaper in my parents' room; the angle of my father's head as he lay at the bottom of the stairs – and I'd physically jolt, whipping my head to the side as if it wasn't a memory but something real right in front of me, and I had the option of shutting my eyes and turning my head away.

Freckled Man said there were two questions he had to ask me now because they were so very important. Just two questions and then Nannie and I could leave and get some sleep. Maybe tomorrow I'd even be able to visit Anna.

'What about my parents?' I asked.

He smiled with his mouth closed. Later, I would look back on this and catch the pity on his face.

'Them too,' he said. 'Maybe.'

I felt a stab of jealousy. 'Are they with Anna?'

'Just two questions, Evelyn.' Freckled Man lightly tapped my knee. 'All right?'

I nodded.

The first question was if I knew anything about prank phone calls, if I could remember anything strange like someone ringing our house lately but then hanging up without saying anything, or maybe I'd heard my parents talking about something like that ...? What I knew about prank calls came from kids' movies. They were funny. They were harmless. They were jokes. In my head, there was no path that could connect such a thing to what had happened in our house. Why was he asking me about that? I thought Freckled Man must be mad. I told him no.

The next question was the most important one, he said. The man who'd been in our house tonight, the stranger who'd hurt my parents and Anna – he wanted to catch him, to stop him hurting anyone else. But he needed my help. Had I seen this stranger? Could I say how tall he was, or what he was wearing? Or perhaps I'd heard his voice? I told him no, I hadn't seen anyone. He asked me if I was sure and I said I was. I could tell he was disappointed, but trying to pretend not to be. He thanked me for answering his questions and said we could go now.

Nannie took my hand and led me out of the room.

I wasn't stupid enough to think that I'd be sleeping in my own bed, but I was surprised when we didn't go to Nannie's house. Instead, she and I were brought to a big, dark hotel. The schoolteacher woman came with us, but not into the room where we'd sleep. I think she said something to Nannie about being right outside.

There were two beds but we both got into the same one. She left the bedside lamps on. I asked what we were going to do in the morning, without clean clothes or my toothbrush, but Nannie didn't answer. She was silent but I knew she was awake because I could feel her body shaking. I slept in fits and starts, and at some point woke up to see that Nannie had turned over, rolled away from me. I touched a hand to the stretch of pillow she'd vacated. It was cold and damp.

The thick curtains were drawn, but there was enough light to see that Nannie was sitting on the chair by the desk, perfectly still, her hand resting on the telephone. I waited, thinking she was about to make a call, but the seconds ticked on and she didn't move.

In actual fact, she had just taken one. It was someone at the hospital ringing to tell her that Anna had died.

It was strange, Jim thought as he made his way home through rush-hour traffic, how Ed Healy was being portrayed in the book. He wondered if Eve Black had really written *The Nothing Man* or if she'd had one of those … What do you call them? Ghostwriters? Because claiming that Healy had done more for Operation Optic than any other member of the force was laying it on a bit thick.

That certainly wasn't how Jim thought of the man. *He* credited Healy with letting this all happen. That day he was called out to Westpark and the dick in a high-vis vest brought him to the so-called 'lair', Jim was there too. Already there, standing only feet away, hidden among the trees. Watching and listening. If Healy had seen him, it would've all been over before it had even begun.

There'd have been no attacks. No murders. No fun.

But Healy hadn't bothered to look.

It was odd too how Eve seemed utterly unable to extrapolate the obvious from the evidence. The Gardaí had had the same problem at the time – especially with Westpark. It was simple. Jim had entered the house while both occupants were sleeping in their beds and proceeded to do what he normally did: wake, threaten, secure. But while he was with the woman, the man managed to escape his binds. He ran downstairs and outside. Jim followed. When he reached him, he saw that the man had grabbed a mobile phone and was trying to use it. Things got physical, which Jim didn't like because that kind of thing left marks – cuts, bruises, swollen knuckles – and he needed to be able to go home to Noreen and into work the next day as normal. So when the man had been reduced to crawling on his stomach in a hopeless attempt to reach the phone that had been kicked well beyond his reach, Jim noticed the incline of the driveway and the car sitting in it and had a better idea. He pulled on the driver's side door: open. He reached into the car, released the handbrake and that was that. He hadn't planned to leave behind a scene so ... *operatic*, but that's how things had worked out. He remembered his colleagues discussing it at the station the next day. *What kind of sick fucker are we dealing with here?* they'd asked one another, while Jim sat among them. As one of them.

It was already dark when he got home. No lights on in the front of the house signalled that Noreen was at the back of it, in the kitchen. Probably watching TV, so she wouldn't have heard the car pull in. Jim took his copy of *The Nothing Man* from the glove box and the Pet World bag from the passenger seat and slipped around the side of the house.

Never having had a dog, he'd been overwhelmed by the choice of food on sale. He'd walked past the pet store in Centrepoint countless times but had never appreciated the sheer size of it, seen just how far back it stretched, until today. It was as large as a supermarket. This hadn't helped

Jim, who had no idea what he was actually looking for. In the end, he'd gone purely by the picture on the box.

He opened the box of dog biscuits and upended its contents on to the floor of the shed. Size-wise, they were perfect. Narrow cylinders, two to three inches in length. Hard on the outside, so they should survive for a while in the soil. But the marrowbone filling wasn't the jelly-like substance Jim had been expecting. It didn't yield as easily as he'd thought it would. In fact, the only way to get the rat poison pellets in there was to force a screwdriver through first and then push the pellet into the hole the screwdriver had left behind.

He made a prototype, a pellet at both ends, and paused to admire his handiwork. The pellets were small and thin and hard, and almost the same colour as the marrowbone.

Perfect.

He made five more.

Later tonight, he'd come back and bury them at the base of the hedge that separated his rear garden from Karen and Derek's.

Since they'd got the dog, they'd reinforced the shared hedge border with metre-high wire fencing on their side, but Derek had installed it himself and done a piss-poor job. The fencing hung loose between the posts, enabling the dog to lift it with his nose, burrow through the base of the hedge and make his way into Jim's garden. That's when the problems with the dog had first begun. His bowels and his leaving home to evacuate them was only the latest and most annoying instalment in the saga.

And Jim had had enough.

He was at the end of the hall, already reaching for the handle of the kitchen door, when he heard the voices. Katie and Noreen. It sounded like they were sitting just on the other side, at the kitchen table. They mustn't have heard him come in. He was about to join them when some instinct, some primal alarm, told him to stop and wait.

Noreen's voice: '... time does it finish?'

Katie's: 'I'd be lucky ... ten o'clock. Please?'

Jim pressed his ear against the door where it met the frame so as to hear better.

'I don't know, love,' Noreen was saying. 'You know I don't like getting the bus home after dark. Can't one of your friends do it?'

'They're either at work or at training with me. Get Dad to drive you.'

'You know your father has absolutely no interest in any of that stuff.'

'He doesn't have to go in, he can just wait outside. And wasn't that stuff his *job*?'

'Exactly.'

'Was he on that case?'

A beat passed.

'No,' Noreen said. 'Your father was never—'

Jim pushed open the door.

The two women jumped. They were sitting at the table, just as he'd thought. It was laid for dinner but they weren't eating yet. Both of them looked up at him in surprise – at first. Then Noreen's expression settled into something more inscrutable.

Katie got up to give him a hug. She was dressed in running gear, her face scrubbed clean and cheeks red. Her hair was damp and smelled like something soapy and floral.

'I just came from the gym,' she said when she saw him looking. 'Cycled here afterwards.'

'Cycled?'

'I have the gear, Dad. Don't worry.'

Noreen stood up and moved behind him, to the stove.

'I came to ask Mum a favour,' Katie said as she and Jim sat down, 'and she made me stay for dinner. You know she's convinced I'm starving myself. She's probably over there melting a stick of butter into that stew as we speak.'

'I can hear you,' Noreen said. 'And it'll be *two* sticks now.'

Jim said to Katie, 'What favour?'

'Oh, well … Yeah.' Katie lifted the jug of water on the table and started filling her glass from it. 'You see, there's this book signing in town tomorrow night. I wanted to go but I just found out Friday night's training's been brought forward to Thursday because there's a game on Friday, and none of the girls are free, so I asked Mum if she'd go in and get a book signed for me but she doesn't want to go on her own. The bus, after dark, etc., etc.' Katie rolled her eyes. 'So I was thinking … Maybe *you* could go with her? Drive her there, I mean. She can just run into the shop, get the book signed and come back out. Five, ten minutes, max.' She smiled hopefully. 'Please, Dad?'

A book signing. Tomorrow night. In town.

Jim's tongue felt swollen, too big for his mouth. His throat was itchy and dry. He wasn't sure words were going to come out but he opened his mouth anyway and said, 'What's the book?' They sounded strangled, like he was speaking and choking at the same time.

'*The Nothing Man.*'

It wasn't Katie who'd answered him but Noreen. She was approaching the table with two steaming plates of food. She set them down just as Katie reached behind her, into the backpack that was hanging off her chair, and pulled out a hardcover book.

Yellow letters on a glossy black background.

'I wouldn't have bought it if I'd known she was about to do a signing in Cork,' Katie said, 'but I presume I can just bring in this one and she'll sign it for me? I mean, I've never actually gone to a book signing but it seems …'

Jim didn't hear the end of the sentence. The rest of the world was falling away, disappearing into the dark, as if his vision was being reduced to a single pinprick of light like a dying television set.

It left only one thing illuminated in front of him.

Something was stuck inside the book, about a third of the way in. Something blue. It could've been a postcard or a folded letter or a piece torn from a cereal box, but it didn't matter what it was. All that mattered was the purpose it was serving.

It was a bookmark.

Katie was reading Eve Black's book.

His own daughter. Reading about the other him.

Jim looked for Katie's face. He found it looking back at him with an odd expression. Expectant, moving towards concerned. Had she asked him something? Her lips were moving. Was she saying something to him right now? He couldn't hear the words. He couldn't hear anything—

A sharp pinch on his shoulder brought him back.

'Here.' Noreen was beside him, leaning over to set a glass of something fizzy beside his plate. She said to Katie, 'Let your father eat his dinner. He's after doing a full day today.' Noreen went to the opposite side of the table to take her own seat. 'Getting up at all hours and then doing *extra* hours ... You need to get a proper night's sleep tonight, Jim. You're not forty any more. Sometimes I think you forget that.'

'*Well*?' Katie said to him. 'Will you bring her?'

He took a sip of his drink to buy time. Its fizziness made his eyes water.

'Why are you reading that?' he asked Katie. 'That book. Why would you want to?'

'I don't know why I bother,' Noreen muttered. 'The food will be stone cold.'

'I heard about it on the radio and I ...' Katie shrugged. 'I don't know. It's interesting. Isn't it? Like, who is this guy? Why did he do these things? How come he was never caught? Is he still alive? It's fascinating. And the book's got good reviews. And she's from here. And it all *happened* here, while you were— Did you work on it, Dad? That case?'

'Katie,' Noreen said warningly. 'This isn't dinner-table talk.'

'I didn't work the case,' Jim said, 'but I was there when it was going on. It wasn't entertainment to us, Katie. People died. And so I have to say, I'm a bit concerned that this is your choice of reading material. Concerned and disappointed.'

'But *everyone's* reading it.'

'Katie,' Noreen warned again.

'But—'

'That's enough,' Jim said.

He looked down at the gloopy mess of stew and mashed potatoes in front of him with determination. When he put a forkful of the food in his mouth, he found he couldn't taste it.

There was a prolonged silence, interrupted only by the scrape of cutlery against ceramic. Then Noreen said something to Katie about exams coming up and Katie started talking about a presentation she had to make and Jim retreated, tuning out just enough to let the voices blend into one humming sound but not so much that he wouldn't notice if they stopped.

Jim wanted to go to the book signing. He had planned to. It was part of his preparation for the next steps. But now so too did his daughter. This was shocking to him, but only because it was Katie. Logically, her wanting to go was *un*surprising. He thought back to the first time he'd seen the book, at work, and then later in the bookshop in town. Numerous copies. Big displays. An entire window of the big bookshop in town devoted to it. And since then it'd been in the paper, and Eve Black had been interviewed on TV, and had Katie said something about hearing her on the radio too? The book was everywhere. And it was true crime. Better yet, *local* true crime. Of course people were interested in it. It was unfortunate that one of them happened to be his own daughter, but why should she be immune?

The problem was her wanting to go to this signing, and not being able to go, and asking her mother to go in her stead. So now Noreen knew what was happening at that time tomorrow evening. That in itself was more of an annoyance than a problem, but what if Jim went and then, at the last minute, Katie's schedule changed and she arrived at the shop? Or what if Noreen decided to go? What if they both walked in there together and saw him?

'We'll go,' he said.

Both women looked at him.

Noreen said, 'Go where?'

'To the bookshop.'

Katie brightened. 'Really?'

'I can just call them in the morning,' Noreen said. 'They can hold a signed copy for her. They do that. I'll go in and collect it Friday morning—'

'But I want *my* copy signed,' Katie said. 'This one.'

'It's fine,' Jim said. 'We'll go.'

'It's Patrick Street, Dad. It starts at seven. You should just be able to pull up outside. There's a loading bay, I think, and at that time—'

'I'll park somewhere. Don't worry.' He looked to Noreen. 'We'll both go in.'

He would have a legitimate reason to be there. Noreen would be by his side, helping to make him look like any other customer. Katie wouldn't be able to pick up her copy until Friday at least, so he could come home afterwards and read it openly. And he liked the idea of it, of all three of them being in the same room less than twenty-four hours from now.

Him.

Noreen.

Eve.

It was poetic really. He was about to walk up to the woman who'd made it her mission to find him and failed at it. Instead, *he* was coming to *her*. But she'd have no clue who she was looking at and Noreen would be utterly oblivious to it all.

'Thanks, Dad,' Katie said, beaming.

Noreen looked down at her food and said nothing at all.

– II –

AMONG THE SHADOWS

− 6 −

Aftermath

I'm obsessed with descriptions of grief. I collect them, literally. I copy them down into a notebook. My motto: no poem, personal essay or misery memoir left behind. 'It is the look of someone who walks from the ophthalmologist's office into the bright daylight with dilated eyes.' Joan Didion in The Year of Magical Thinking. 'Where you used to be, there is a hole in the world, which I find myself constantly walking around in the daytime, and falling in at night.' The poet Edna St Vincent Millay, from Letters. 'That five stages of grief thing is total bullshit because that was ACTUALLY a study into the reaction of people who are given terminal diagnoses, NOT people who've lost loved ones. Grief doesn't follow any pattern. In reality it's MESSY and CONFUSING.' An anonymous commenter on a website happily named TellUsYourGrief.com.

I collect them and try them on, but so far not one of them has fit. Not completely. What *does* it feel like to lose both your parents and your younger sister to a violent crime when you were just twelve years old *and* the first person to come upon the bodies? Who has written about that? Who can give me the words? Because in all these years I've never quite been able to find them. If pushed, I'd say I felt numb. Empty. Alone and lost. I'd drag out all the usual suspects, the standard metaphors, which, I've noticed, are all weirdly meteorological: an earthquake, a fog, rolling waves. I could talk about how, when

eve black

Nannie and I were hiding out in Spanish Point, my grief felt like the effort required to live your entire life with your back pressed against bulging closet doors because if you move from them and they open, everything will come spilling out.

Jim yawned.

He had only just come out to the shed. Noreen had gone to bed early and had been sleeping so soundly when he went upstairs at eleven that he'd chanced coming straight back down. But he was already yawning. Maybe Noreen was right. Maybe he needed to ditch the reading for the evening and get a full night's sleep instead.

Or maybe it was just the reading *material* that was the problem.

Jim scanned the rest of the page, then the two pages overleaf. More grief and loss and feeling sad. Her grandmother feeling sad but pretending not to. Having to lie and say her parents were in a car crash when she started school. Feeling sad about that – and guilty.

He yawned again.

Tonight he'd had the foresight to make a flask of tea before coming outside and he set down the book now so he could swallow a few mouthfuls of it.

Jim was just over halfway through *The Nothing Man*. That wasn't quite far enough to feel confident about what exactly it was he was walking into tomorrow night. He needed to stay awake, to read as much as he could. He needed to get to the part where Eve wrote about what had happened in her family home that night, with Jim. He needed to know what she remembered, or claimed she did.

He picked the book back up, found the page where he'd left off and then flicked ahead.

Enough with the grief already. It didn't interest him and it wasn't important. He could skip it.

Jim found the first page of the next chapter and started to read on.

– 7 –

Blind Witness

In early July 2015, Professor Eglin arranged for me to meet a friend of his named Bernadette O'Brien. She was an editor at Iveagh Press, a publishing house. Since the 'The Girl Who' article had gone viral, I'd been fielding offers for all sorts – books, a primetime television interview, a podcast, something terrifying called *life rights* – but I was at sea in a strange world and had asked Eglin for his help. He'd suggested I meet with Bernadette.

Iveagh Press was a series of small rooms over a café on Dawson Street called Bestseller, a play on its previous incarnation as the headquarters of the National Bible Society of Ireland. I arrived early and was directed to wait in a room with a large bay window that I recognised from outside, a huge conference table and walls lined with books. The air smelled faintly of coffee even before some underling brought me a cup of it. As I sipped, I started to have second thoughts.

Was I really doing this? Seriously considering writing a *book*? How did I expect to be able to do that when writing two thousand words of an article had been such an ordeal? I tried to imagine a world in which my story and *his* were bound together between glossy covers and stacked deep on shelves with price-tags on. I couldn't. I looked through the open door. The reception desk was deserted. I could just get up and leave. I put down my coffee, pushed back my chair. I *should* leave. But then Bernadette came in, eyes bright and arms outstretched, and I decided the polite thing to do was to stay and hear her out.

She had just celebrated her sixtieth birthday but looked five or even ten years younger than that, with a razor-cut bob of jet black hair and thin, delicate gold things dripping from her wrists and ears. That day she was wearing black leggings and a huge knitted jumper that must have been several sizes too big but looked, on her, somehow trendy and fashionable. I was surprised to see that she was walking around the itchy grey office carpet in her bare feet, showing off a shiny gloss of red on her toes that distracted me. Even though she knew exactly who I was and what I'd been through, she didn't tread on eggshells. She talked to me like I was a normal person. I liked her instantly.

If I were to write a book, she explained, it wouldn't be the first about the Nothing Man. There was already a book out there about him, with a title as imaginative as this one: *The Case of the Nothing Man*. It had been written by a journalist named Stephen Ardle and published back in October 2002. I'd never read it but Bernadette had, and she said it offered little in the way of new information. Ardle had been a crime reporter, primarily for the *Irish Examiner,* and the book was essentially a collection of the articles he'd written about the case in real time. (Ardle passed away in 2012.) Since then the genre had moved on. So now, I had the opportunity to write the definitive book on the case woven through with my own story.

My facial expression must have been screaming my misgivings.

'Think of it this way,' Bernadette said. 'Yes, you'll have to open a vein and let whatever comes out dry on the page. You'll have to relive all this. But just once. Then it's done. And writing can be very therapeutic. It may help you. And while you must tell the truth, you don't need to tell us all of it. You can hold back as much or as little as you like, so long as what you do put on the page feels like the whole story to the reader. But here's the kicker: people don't just read true-crime books now, they *study* them. They go looking for more. They listen to podcasts and meet up at conventions and trade theories' – Bernadette mimed typing on a computer keyboard – 'online until all hours of the night. Armies of armchair sleuths. Someone *has* to know who this man is. People change. Relationships end. Consciences grow. A book about the case will renew interest. Jog a few memories. A book about this case by *you* will get *everyone's* attention. It might move things forward. We might very well end up finding out who he is – and *where* he is. This could be what gets the creep arrested. Because at this point, my dear, it's not going to be the Gardaí.'

I don't doubt that our mutual friend had prepped her to say this. Eglin knew that the idea of catching the Nothing Man was what had persuaded me to publish the original essay and now Bernadette was dangling the same hypothetical carrot in order to get me to agree to write a book. But that didn't make what she was saying untrue.

On that day, my parents and Anna had been dead for fourteen years and no one had ever been punished for it. Whenever I thought about that I felt a white-hot rage bubbling up inside of me, and I had to clench my fists and bite down on my lip to stop it from spilling out in tears or words or something worse, and wait for it to pass. But what if I used that rage instead? Channelled it into the courage I'd need to turn and face the past head-on, examine it closely, write this book? And what if I could make it go away entirely? What if I didn't need to feel it any more, because he'd finally been caught, and instead I could think about how he was going to spend the rest of his days locked in a tiny dark cell somewhere where he had nothing to do except think about what he'd done and rot away and die?

'There's a problem, though,' I told Bernadette. 'With the details.' I explained that, all my life, I'd done what I could to avoid them, not just when it came to my own family's attack but the other ones, too. So I knew only the broadest of strokes. What had elbowed its way in, despite my best efforts. What I had found out by accident. And as for the night itself, I'd been locked in a bathroom. I'd heard sounds and I witnessed the aftermath, but beyond that ...

I was saying I wasn't sure I could handle knowing exactly what had happened that night and the four other nights the Nothing Man had struck, but Bernadette misunderstood me. She thought I was asking her how I would go about finding out. She'd reached for the phone on her desk.

'One of our crime writers uses a retired Garda inspector as a consultant,' she said to me, while on the other end of the line, someone's phone rang once, twice, three times. 'She's a friend of mine. She'll ask him who we need to speak to, and we'll get ourselves a meeting with them ASAP.'

All I knew about Edward Healy in advance of our first meeting was that he was a detective and the man I was supposed to talk to if I wanted to know more about the Nothing Man. We arranged to meet in Lafayette's, the café off the lobby of the Imperial Hotel in Cork, early one Tuesday morning. The night before, I googled images of him. The first picture that came up showed him posing proudly with a medal at the end of some race. He had reddish hair and a spray of freckles across his nose. I recognised him instantly: Edward Healy was Freckled Man. This wouldn't be our first meeting. Fourteen years after that, we were having our second.

Ed – that's what I call him now and it feels weird to refer to him as anything else – looks like the kind of airline pilot who comes out from the cockpit to say goodbye to his passengers as they deplane: friendly and approachable, but also confident and authoritative. He is boyishly handsome. Colleagues joke that it's younger he's getting and based on the pictures I've seen, I'd tend to agree. A health scare around his fortieth birthday six years ago forced him to give up drinking, smoking and – in his words – eating things that tasted good. Now he spends his free time hiking, cooking dishes from vegetarian cookbooks and, when he can, sea-swimming in Fountainstown. He does not look like he has danced with darkness. He does not look like the leading authority on the Nothing Man. But he has and he is. And he is more than that. He is the Nothing Man's nemesis.

This wasn't just another case for Ed. It was *the* case, his obsession. The one 'unsolved' all conscientious detectives have that haunts them, that keeps them awake at night. Ed had even stopped his ascent through the ranks because to go any further than sergeant would've taken him away from this case. He had paid for his obsession with his personal life. After sacrificing so much, Ed made a vow to himself that he wouldn't stop until he found the Nothing Man, and he hadn't. But for nearly fifteen years there hadn't been as much as a crumb to add to the case files. Ed had only another ten to go until he'd be forced to retire. Time was running out.

I didn't know all this that morning in the café, but I do remember Ed's eagerness to meet me being a little off-putting. He remembered asking me questions at the hospital and made polite enquiries as to how I'd been since, how my life had been. He'd read my essay and commended me on it. He welcomed the idea of me writing a book and assured me he would help in any way he could. But our conversation was underpinned by an anxiousness, a palpable impatience on his part. He was *desperate* to talk to me about back then, about that night. The hope I might have something for him was coming off him in waves. As soon as I could, I ripped off the Band-Aid: I told him I was here to get information *from* him, that I didn't have any I could give.

'I don't remember it,' I explained. 'What I mean is, I don't have anything to remember. I was in the bathroom. I mostly just heard sounds. And what I saw afterwards … I know very little. That's why I wanted to talk to you: I want to know what happened. In my house and the others. Or at least, I think I do.'

It was mid-morning and only a few tables in the café were occupied. Ed suggested we continue our conversation at Anglesea Street, the Garda district HQ, which was only a few minutes' walk away across the river. He had a small office there, he said, commandeered for his unofficial one-man cold-case unit that only ever looked at the one cold case.

It was a grey, cloudy day and the sky felt heavy with threat. I was warming to Ed but there was a current of doubt running through me that kept me from feeling wholly at ease. Was this a mistake? Was I going to find out something I didn't want to know, that I wouldn't be able to forget? Was I wasting Ed's time? Perhaps sensing my unease, he asked me what my aim was for the book. I could state that clearly: I wanted to catch him with it. I repeated what Bernadette had said about armchair sleuths and he nodded in agreement. Someone *must* know something, I said. If they read the book and took in the extent

of what he had done, the hurt he'd caused, how dangerous he is ...
Well, maybe their conscience would make them pick up the phone
and call the Gardaí.

Ed winced at this and I knew I'd said the wrong thing. He put a hand
out to stop me and we paused by a bench on the quay that looked
across the greenish tinge of the River Lee to the grandeur of the City
Hall on the opposite bank.

'I will tell you now,' he said gently, 'even if we identify him, and find
him, and bring him in, without a confession it will be impossible to
charge him.' The Nothing Man had committed five awful acts and taken
lives during two of them, but he had done it all without leaving any
trace of himself behind. There was no physical evidence to pin anyone
to the crimes. 'TV makes people think that if we have fingerprints we
can just run them through some supercomputer and match them to
the owner, but that's fiction. We need to have collected the match,
too. In this case, we don't even have a set to test. And that's true of
all kinds of evidence in this case. DNA. Fibres. Witness statements.
Vehicle movements, even. Licence plates, tyre tracks, that sort of thing.
Even if someone calls us with a name and we can drive straight to the
guy's house and pick him up, how will we prove that we have the right
guy? What can we check him against? If it wasn't for the phone calls,
we wouldn't even know the same guy had done all five crimes.'

'You're telling me I shouldn't bother,' I said, defeated.

'I'm telling you that if your goal is to find out who this man is, that
may well be achievable. But you might have to make do with that. The
chances of being able to get him convicted and punished for what he
did are about on a par with winning the Lottery. So if it has to be that,
if that's all that would be enough ...' Ed sighed. 'I want you to do this

but I must tell you if that's what you need, you almost certainly won't get it. Not unless he confesses, which, after all these years and no physical evidence, he'd be very unlikely to do. And that's *if* we find him.'

I told him I understood, but my insides were churning. I'd always assumed the problem was that the Gardaí hadn't found him, that finding him would automatically mean he'd get put away. Losing that as the compass point I was striding towards left me rudderless and lost, but I told Ed I wanted to keep moving forward. I didn't know what else to do for now.

I had never been inside the station at Anglesea Street before that day and was surprised by its interior. From the outside, the building looked like a nondescript, squared-off office block. But it was hiding a light-filled atrium and the bare stone on its floor granted it the respectful hush of a grand cathedral. Ed's 'office' was *not* like that. It was clearly a storage room for obsolete computer equipment into which a desk had been shoved. There were spreading stains on the ceiling tiles and a dusty, dried-out water dispenser in one corner. The chairs were plastic and mismatched and uncomfortable. Ed got us more coffee but it was, at best, a distant cousin of the substance we'd drunk back in the café.

He reached into a drawer and plonked a thick manila file down on the desk between us. There was a grubby OP OPTIC label stuck on its front. The room felt charged by it, as if the file was emitting some kind of pulse. In my naivety I thought it was *the* file, the whole thing. In fact, it was just a short summary of the five attacks that Ed kept to hand for easy reference.

Later I would work my way through all the Operation Optic files, boxes and boxes of them, reading through the documents with Ed by my side to explain and contextualise. I would spend endless days in the reference section of the Cork Central Library on the Grand Parade, poring over every published article I could find about the case. I would meet with survivors and listen to them recount their personal horrors in excruciating detail. I would even, eventually, look at some crime-scene photos. But this was the beginning, the first day, and all I could manage was to hold myself together while Ed talked me slowly through sanitised overviews of each of the Nothing Man's five crimes.

He didn't yet have permission to share anything with me beyond what had been reported in the press – that would come later from his superintendent who, like Ed, just wanted the guy caught – so he stuck to bullet points for now. His goal at this point was for me to understand what the Nothing Man was and what he had done before he'd arrived at our house that night. He started by saying that what happened at our house was the worst.

He told me about the O'Sullivans on Bally's Lane in Carrigaline. Christine Kiernan in Covent Court. Linda O'Neill in the house in Fermoy. Marie Meara and Martin Connolly in Westpark. That poor man, trapped under the wheels of his own car, perhaps slowly dying while knowing that, back inside the house, his wife was dying too or was maybe even already dead – when I tried to go to sleep that night, he was all I could think about.

Ed and I had many of the same unanswered questions. *Why these people? These houses? What connected them?* Ed said they had tried every which way to find a link between the victims, painstakingly going through their lives with fine toothcombs looking for some point of overlap, but they'd always come up empty. He believed that if he found the connection, he would find the man. Cork was a city of half a million that felt much smaller; it was notably unusual that the Gardaí had failed to connect any of the victims with each other in any meaningful way. Normally in any random group of Corkonians this size you would find *some* kind of connection, like two people who went to the same school at the same time or even a familial link. None at all was strange.

I mentioned something about our house, the family home in Passage West, and Ed asked me if I'd ever been back there. I said I'd been there that morning, that I was staying there while I was down in Cork. I had never sold it and since the long-term tenants had moved out a couple of years ago, I hadn't replaced them. Instead, I'd started occasionally staying there myself.

'I know it sounds strange,' I said, 'but I kind of like it. It's the place where we were all together. Aside from one night, it's all good memories. I feel close to them when I'm there.'

When I told people this, I invariably got the same reaction: disgust. Staying in the house where my family were *slaughtered*? What kind of sicko would want to do *that*?

But Ed had a different one.

He asked me if we could go there. Together. Now.

Jim was wide awake now.

– 8 –

That Night

Passage West, population: 6,000, is a port town on the west bank of Cork Harbour. Coming from the city, our house forced you to avoid the town altogether, taking a right on to our lane before you'd even reached the WELCOME TO PASSAGE WEST sign erected by the Tidy Towns committee. We lived in a dormer bungalow that had been extended by, essentially, building a facsimile of the original house and them sticking the two of them together, end-to-end but at an angle, giving the building an odd V-shape. We had four acres, with the house sitting right in its centre at the end of a loose-gravel drive.

I had offered to drive us there but Ed said he'd take his car, and then I offered to lead him before realising that he knew very well where it was. We arrived within minutes of each other. He was surprised, I think, to see how untouched it was, how unchanged it had been in all these years. That was unintentional. I wasn't building a mausoleum, I just hadn't got around to changing anything yet.

I surprised myself by saying, 'Let's retrace his steps.'

We started outside, at the back door. It had been unlocked that night and probably every other night before. This whole area was a place of unlocked doors, of keys left in the ignition, of all the neighbours knowing you were away – or at least it had been back then, *until* then. No one knew how the Nothing Man had approached the house, or what direction he had come from, or how he had travelled from his home to here. It was like he simply appeared, materialising out of the blackness. A ghost of a man, made entirely of shadows.

His clothes helped him do this. Ed described what he was probably wearing when he came to our house, based on Alice O'Sullivan, Christine Kiernan and Linda O'Neill's accounts of their attacks: all black clothes, black gloves, black balaclava-style mask. He might have had a torch strapped to his forehead, something not unlike a bike lamp attached to an elastic headband; he had in some of the attacks but not all. Somewhere on his person there was also a knife and perhaps a gun, although if there was a gun he hadn't fired it. Ed pointed out that outside the grounds of our house, beyond the shadows, his Serial Killer Ensemble would've had the opposite effect: it would have made him stand out. This suggested there was a point in his approach where he stopped to put it on. Standing outside our back door, Ed said, 'It was probably here.'

It was daytime, and Ed is fair-skinned, freckled and lean, but for a moment there was a flash of a man in black, pulling down his mask and reaching for the door handle. I shivered even though it wasn't cold.

Ed said to me, 'Ready?' and I nodded even though I wasn't, not at all—

We went inside.

Investigators estimate that the Nothing Man commenced his attack on my family sometime between three and four in the morning. This was predominately based on my calling 999 at 4:10 a.m. And the findings of the pathologist when he came to examine my mother and father's bodies. They also knew from the items they had found in the kitchen that he had spent time there before coming upstairs, but it was impossible to say how much. As ever, he had left no physical evidence, going so far as to spray the rim of the coffee cup he'd drunk from with the bottle of bleach cleaner my mother had kept on the sink. Ed and I walked through there and into the hall.

He paused at the end of the stairs and asked me if I could tell him what I knew before we went up to the bedrooms.

I don't remember the whole thing in sequence, just flashes. But over the years I had managed to piece them together in a linear string. Now I can just about play them through, although the picture is jumpy and the cuts are rough.

It was like making a movie out of a series of photographs, I explained to Ed. All the key moments are there but the connective tissue between them is missing. This memory doesn't unfold, it flickers.

I woke up in the middle of the night needing to go to the bathroom. I never did normally but I had snuck a can of Club Orange up with me to bed. The door to the room Anna and I shared was closed. I know this not because I can remember that the door was closed, but because I remember that the room was dark. I liked it that way. Anna had a little plug-in nightlight that she would fall asleep with but the first thing I did when I went up to bed every night was unplug it. If the door *had* been open, the light from the hall would've lit up the room and I would have noticed that something was different.

Tiptoeing, I moved from my bedroom to the bathroom. This was a journey of mere seconds; it was the next door along. The main light switch was outside but during the night my parents left a smaller light over the mirror on. I closed the bathroom door behind me as softly as I could. The key was in the lock but I didn't turn it because it would make a clicking sound, which I knew from experience would be loud at this time of the night when it had no competitors. I didn't flush the toilet for the same reason.

I had just pulled my underwear back up when I heard a strange noise. My first thought was *asthma attack* because it reminded me of the sounds a girl in school had made when she had an attack in PE class a few months before, a kind of muffled gasping. I thought Anna must be having a bad dream.

I can remember standing in front of the bathroom door, gripping the handle but not depressing it, when footsteps crossed the landing outside. They were moving away from me, left to right, towards my parents' bedroom. They had a rhythm and weight to them that was unfamiliar.

I doubt that at that point it crossed my mind that there was anyone in my house except for members of my own family. It was beyond the realm of my own possible realities that a stranger would be in my home.

And yet, *something* made me stay where I was. A gut instinct. A few moments later, that same feeling made me turn the key in the lock and reach out to pull the string that would turn the light over the mirror off, leaving me hiding in the dark.

There was no screaming or yelling. All I could hear was the low hum of quiet voices and then several minutes, maybe, of a rhythmic whimpering I didn't understand. This was followed by a series of heavy thumps. At one point I thought I heard my father's voice saying *no*, just once, as in *please no*. There might have also been some scuffling, someone moving around on a carpeted floor.

I had no idea what was happening in my parents' bedroom but I also had a profound sense that I *shouldn't* know, that it was something dark and adult and frightening, and that the best plan was for me to wait it out, to stay exactly where I was, and not alert them to my wakeful state.

I can't say if I thought about Anna. If I did it was to presume that she was fast asleep.

Minutes passed. The weird sounds died down and I pushed my ear to the gap between the door and frame, straining to hear. I thought I could hear *something*, muffled and distant, but I didn't understand what activity could match it and, to be honest, I wasn't entirely sure I wasn't just imagining it, that it wasn't merely the kind of pattern in the white noise you hear when you try to listen really, really hard. If I was scared, I mistook it for confusion. Maybe I made that mistake on purpose, to protect myself. But whatever I was thinking, feeling or hearing, I know I stayed in the bathroom. Standing with my nose to the back of the door. My hand on the key. Waiting.

Footsteps, suddenly, on the landing. Crossing it quickly, right to left. Towards the stairs.

I thought they must be my father's. I moved to turn the key.

But then I heard another set of footsteps crossing the landing, and they *also* sounded like my father's.

I froze.

Who was out there? What were they doing?

A yelp. Just the slightest sound, the kind of noise you might make if you slipped on ice and thought your legs were about to go from underneath you. This was followed by a series of thumps and bangs, and for some reason I knew exactly what the corresponding action to that soundtrack was: someone had just gone tumbling down the stairs.

There was one loud painful groan, then nothing else.

I don't know how long I waited for the silence that followed that to end, but when it didn't, I left the bathroom. I remember turning the key in the lock and wincing because the clicking of it seemed as loud as a siren. I remember opening the door. I remember that it was now dark outside, the ceiling light on the landing having been switched off at some point while I'd been in the bathroom.

But there was a light on downstairs. I moved towards it.

When I reached the top step and looked down, I saw a figure lying crumpled at the bottom of the stairs. The light illuminated him mercilessly but kept everything else in shadow. I remember it like a stage spotlight, even though that couldn't have been how it was.

My father's body was spread across the bottom three steps of the stairs. His head was pressed against the wall and his feet seemed tangled in the banisters. Everything seemed strangely angular and broken and wrong. I called out for him but he didn't respond. I started towards him, descending a step or two, but there was something about the positioning of his body, its stillness … I got too scared. I ran back up and into my parents' bedroom to wake my mother instead.

The door to the room I shared with Anna was closed now, I think, but I can't be sure.

The light from downstairs couldn't reach this corner of the landing so once I crossed the threshold of my parents' room, I was in the dark and navigating by memory. I walked forward, knowing that in a few steps I would hit my mother's bedside table and then, a few inches after that, her side of the bed. I think I whispered her name, then said it, then called her. No response. There was a weird smell. Just as I reached the bed, my foot touched something wet and sticky.

I started patting the blankets, trying to find an arm to grip and shake, but stopped when my hands felt the same wet and sticky substance. I reached out to my left, slicing the air in search of the bedside lamp. When I found it, I felt for the switch up under the shade. Pushed. In the sudden light I saw that the blanket was pulled right up to the headboard and there was blood everywhere: on the blanket, on the walls, on the lampshade.

I pushed the switch again, plunging the room back into darkness.

That's it.

After that there's just flashing lights and my grandmother with her hair loose around her shoulders and wrong rooms, and someone carving out a hollow at the core of me with something rusty and blunt, a void that will remain there for ever.

Jim took his pencil and went back over the last few pages, underlining all the sentences that were inaccurate or untrue. Then he circled the words *'That's it'* and wrote, *Is it? Where's the rest???* alongside them.

Did Eve really remember it this way?

Or was this a lie of omission?

I told all this to Ed and then added a disclaimer: you can't trust me. I was only twelve when this happened. Even while I was still in the bathroom, my brain was preparing for my survival, opening the deepest vault in my memory bank so it could send the worst of what I was about to see straight in there. When the vault started to approach capacity, it just dumped some stuff straight out. This is how I've come to understand the effects of trauma on the mind of a child. That night is a jigsaw puzzle missing pieces and some parts of it have clearly been put together wrong.

For example: I called my grandmother from the phone in the kitchen but I have no recollection of going downstairs, a journey that would have involved stepping over my father's body. I don't know what I said to her, and I don't remember calling 999 even though I did. There's a recording of it. I don't remember going back into our bedroom but I do remember seeing Anna's hand, her little nails cut short and painted inexpertly with red polish, hanging out over the side of the bed. How did I see that if I didn't go in? How could there have been no yelling or screaming? How much time passed between these events? Why did the Nothing Man leave me alive?

When I stopped talking, Ed was silent for a very long time. Then he told me what the Gardaí thought had happened that night. We went upstairs so he could show me.

No one could be sure of the exact sequence of events, but it made sense from an investigative standpoint that Anna had died first. The Nothing Man had tried to smother her with her pillow and he'd succeeded, albeit on a delay. She was in a coma when she arrived at the hospital and never woke up.

Our bedroom door was the first one you got to when you reached the top of the stairs, the first one he would have come to. Ed and I paused at its open doorway. There were no beds in the room now but back then, her bed had been directly across from you as you entered the room, pushed against the wall under the window. Mine was opposite it, behind the door.

After I told Ed this he gave me a look I would come to know well, the one that reminds me that he already knows, that he was at the scene, that he's studied the pictures for hours on end. That he probably knows more about what my house was like in October 2001 than I do.

We moved on to my parents' bedroom, stopping again at the threshold. I didn't tend to go into the bedrooms. (When I stayed at the house I slept downstairs, in the room that had been my father's office.) This room was empty but had a garish wallpaper hung by the tenants, pink flowers on green. The radiator was new too but it had been installed in the same place as its predecessor. Ed pointed to it and said it was there my father had been tied up, to the pipe underneath. They knew this because of the shredded blue rope they'd found there.

He'd managed to free himself from it, but his wrists and ankles were still tied. If he had fallen down the stairs, Ed said, this was likely why. It was also why the fall killed him – because he hadn't been able to use his arms to slow his descent. Without the bindings, he might have been bruised and sore or, worst-case scenario, broken an arm or leg. With them, he severed his spinal cord at the neck. There was only one phone in the house at the time, a landline, and it was in our kitchen. Presumably he'd been trying to get to that.

My mother was found in the bed, face down, with the blankets pulled over her head. She had been stabbed fourteen times, mostly in the back and shoulder area. Her wrists and ankles had been bound just like my father's, but the Nothing Man must have used brute force or his knife or maybe even the threat of a gun to keep her on the bed. He had raped her. I can't think about this in any depth. I can't even read back over this paragraph.

Abruptly I left and went back downstairs and into the kitchen. Ed followed me. I drank a glass of tap water and then flicked the kettle on for tea. I wasn't certain I could speak. Those last ten minutes were the longest I'd spent thinking about what had happened in this house since the event itself.

I turned to face Ed, leaning against the countertop because I felt light-headed and hot, and didn't trust my knees to keep me upright. I caught him looking at the phone, hanging from the wall next to the fridge. It wasn't the same one but the newer model had been hung in the same place.

'He never called us,' I said. I looked to Ed. 'Did he?'

Back on the night of the attack I'd said I couldn't remember any prank calls, but that wasn't to say they hadn't happened. I wasn't supposed to answer the phone so it was my mother who would've got them. Or maybe I'd just forgotten.

'He might have,' Ed said. 'Maybe.' He told me that, back in 2001, members of Operation Optic had pored over our phone logs, tracing every incoming call to our house of one minute or less. They had found five to flag as pertinent to the investigation. These had come in at various times of the day but each of them had come from a public telephone box located in or around Cork City. Two of them had come from the same public telephone box on Patrick Street, but beyond that there seemed to be no rhyme or reason to their locations or sequence. None of them were near the GAA stadium from where the Nothing Man had called Christine Kiernan and Linda O'Neill. 'That could've been him,' Ed said, 'but we'll never know.'

We took cups of tea into the living room and sat down, Ed in an armchair and me on the couch.

I asked another question that had just occurred to me.

'If he didn't call us,' I said, 'how do you know it was the Nothing Man who came here that night?'

'The rope,' Ed said. 'Mainly. Plus the nature of the crime, the timing of it and the location. The rope was never described in the media.'

'So he did leave *something* behind ...'

'That brand was widely available. Stocked in more than a hundred and fifty hardware stores all over the country. We visited every one in Cork county and within two hours' drive of it but we had nothing to say to them other than, "Do you remember anyone buying this kind of rope recently, or a lot of it at any time at all?" It wasn't fruitful.'

'And the knife?'

'The knife wasn't *as* widely available but still, we only had a description of it from someone who was never attacked: Christine Kiernan's neighbour. We don't know if he brought the same kind to the other houses. The pathologist said that based on her description it could've been the same one used here, on your mother, but—'

'It was. He did.'

Ed's face changed. 'What do you mean?'

I realised that he didn't know about my finding the rope and the knife – because I hadn't yet told him. I hadn't told anyone. It wasn't in my essay because I hadn't realised its significance until after it'd been published and I'd started reading the other articles. So I told him now.

About playing the game with Anna a few weeks before the attack. About lifting the sofa cushion and seeing the rope and the knife. Unlike the night itself, I could remember them clearly and described them in detail. The blue braid. The yellow handle that put me in mind of Fisher Price toys. The shiny, unsullied blade.

Ed got up, paced a bit, then sat back down. He took out his Garda notebook, flipped up the cover and dug in his shirt pocket for a pen. He asked me to repeat everything I'd said.

At first I was bemused by his reaction. He had just been telling me how the rope and the knife had led nowhere, so why was he so excited that I had seen them once?

But it wasn't the information itself that ignited him, but the fact that, fourteen years later, he was getting it. The *nature* of my information was what excited him. I had known it all this time but I hadn't recognised its significance until recently.

All these years later, things could still come to light.

And so a new phase of the Nothing Man investigation began, years after his last attack, in the very same house where he was last seen. I pictured him in another house, maybe one with a wife busy in the kitchen and children running around, or *grandchildren* at this stage, since his own children, if he had had them, must surely be grown. I imagined him feeling safe, maybe even smug, sure that since he had avoided detection all these years, no one was ever going to come for him now.

But I was coming for him, with Ed by my side.

It was only a matter of time.

In six months, no day at Centrepoint had passed as slowly as Thursday did. Jim was not only bored but exhausted from having barely slept two nights in a row. He killed the minutes of his shift by picturing himself at the book signing, standing inches from Eve Black while she had no idea that Jim was the subject of *The Nothing Man*. Afterwards he used the few hours his white lie about working full days had bought him to park again down by the Marina. This time, he used it to take a nap in his car. He was so exhausted that it was his only option. Finally – *finally* – it was gone six and he and Noreen were on their way into town.

They were driving along the quays when Noreen said something about an interview.

'Interview?'

'Yeah.' Noreen was looking out the passenger's side window. 'She's going to be interviewed first, then she'll sign books after.'

Jim kept his eyes on the road. 'You never said anything about an interview.'

He had been imagining a long queue of people, snaking around the tables and bookshelves of the shop, giving him ample opportunity to look at the woman at the top of it before he got there himself and she saw him. Now he had to throw that out and replace it with rows of folding chairs and her sitting facing them, able to look out into the audience and see every face if she wished. He didn't like last-minute changes. He didn't like feeling blindsided. Details mattered. Preparation was key.

When Jim moved his hands out of the ten-two position on the steering wheel, he saw the black leather shiny with his own sweat. He moved them back.

'Who's interviewing her, then?'

'Some journalist,' Noreen said.

'Which one?'

'I don't know.'

'Look it up.'

'Won't we find out when we get there?'

'*Look it up.*'

She sighed. 'Fine.'

Jim turned the car into the multi-storey car park on Paul Street.

'"Danielle Kennedy",' Noreen read aloud from the screen of her phone. 'It says here she's a reporter for the *Irish Times.*'

They parked near the elevators on Level 1 and got out of the car. The bookshop was only a couple of minutes' walk away now and Jim could feel the weight of what he was doing on his shoulders, hear the little voice at the back of his head telling him that he should stop, that this was a bad idea.

But there was a much louder voice telling him that he *should* go, that she was never going to recognise him in a million years, and that this was necessary reconnaissance.

That was the voice he trusted.

They entered the bookshop via the back entrance, on Paul Street. As soon as Noreen pulled open the door a step ahead of him, Jim felt the muscles in his back release and relax. The shop was packed, the heat and noise and buzzing chatter of what was easily more than a hundred warm bodies hitting them like a wall as they stepped inside.

Noreen had the opposite reaction. She didn't like busy, noisy spaces and so avoided them. But that meant she was ill equipped to deal with them when a situation forced her into one. Jim could see the change in her: suddenly tense, eyes roaming, face pinched with concern.

'Oh,' she said, half-turning back to him. She looked paler than she had a moment ago, although that might be the harsh lighting in the shop. And maybe it was the body heat of the assembled crowd that had forced a few beads of sweat out on to her upper lip, the one she regularly let a line of fine, white hairs grow along. 'I don't know about this. It's much busier than I thought it would be ...'

She looked to him for help.

'We're here now,' Jim said. 'We're not leaving.'

He stepped around Noreen and then away from her, moving deeper into the shop, towards the thickest crush of bodies.

There were rows of folding chairs laid out and each one of them was already taken. That meant he would have to stand, which would make him even more conspicuous once Eve Black had taken her seat in one of the two leather armchairs arranged on either side of a small table at the side of the room, facing the rows of chairs. At least there wasn't a stage or stools; her view of the audience would be from their level. Still. The table had two bottles of water on it, a small vase of flowers and a copy of *The Nothing Man* stood on its end.

Jim kept moving closer to the front of the store, pushing his way past elbows and turned backs. He could see there was another, larger table set up just inside the main doors, half-filled with glasses of wine and water, and next to that an identical one piled high with copies of the book. There was a tiny pocket of clear space just beyond it, near a display of notebooks. If he stood there, he should be close enough to see her but far away enough to make it difficult, if not impossible, for her to see him.

Jim started to push his way towards this spot.

He felt a tap on his shoulder.

He wasn't going to turn around, assuming it was either Noreen or one of the shop workers he'd made the mistake of conversing with, however briefly, the last time he was here.

But then he heard a voice say, 'Jim?'

A male voice. A familiar one.

He turned.

Ed Healy.

The fucking bastard.

'Ed!' Jim stretched a smile across his face and held out a hand. 'Long time, no see.'

'Too long.'

They shook, three solid pumps.

'How's life treating you?' Jim asked.

'Good, good. Can't complain. You?'

'Ah ... you know yourself.'

The two men regarded each other for a beat longer than felt right.

Then Jim said, 'You're still at it, I presume?'

'Ah, actually ... I'm just winding down. Finishing up at Christmas. I thought I'd hang on for the thirty but things changed and I just woke up one morning and realised that I wanted to start living my life instead of waiting to do that, you know?'

Jim nodded, even though he had no idea what the fuck Ed was on about.

'What about you?' Ed asked. 'What are you up to these days?'

'Private security.' That was Jim's stock answer whenever he ran into any of his former colleagues.

That's what the retired ones tended to say to him too, but they meant *bodyguard for some rich eejit*, not security guard in a bloody shopping centre.

'Oh yeah?' Ed said. 'Local?'

'Yeah.'

'Do you miss it at all?'

'Not at all.' Jim made a sound that he hoped sounded like a chuckle. 'So what are you doing here?'

Jim had asked Ed before Ed could ask him.

The younger man lifted his chin, indicating something behind Jim's back.

'I'm with her,' he said.

Jim didn't have to turn around to know who he meant. He could feel her, a cold breath at his back. As he turned to look, everyone else in the room blurred into one long streak of other, indiscernible people.

There was only her.

She must have just appeared in the last few moments, standing near the leather armchairs, chatting with a man and a woman. The man might have been the assistant manager Jim had spoken to briefly and, going by the fact that she was holding two microphones and a sheaf of pages, the other woman must be the journalist.

Eve Black was taller than he'd expected, five-ten he'd say, and in a room full of ordinary people, looked somewhat ethereal. She didn't seem as thin as she had on television, probably because whatever she was wearing – some kind of layered dress or skirt – was swaddling her frame, making it impossible to tell where the black material ended and her actual body began. Her hands were in its pockets, disappearing between the folds of the material halfway up to her forearms. She was wearing more make-up this evening, her skin warm and dewy-looking, the awful red slash of lipstick toned down for something more natural and pink. She was wearing long, dangly gold earrings with lots of little moving pieces that glinted in the overhead lights as she turned her head, and her eyes seemed bigger, somehow, different—

She was staring right at him.

And now, waving.

For a split second he felt the impulse to raise his own hand in response but then he saw, in his peripheral vision, Ed lifting *his* hand.

She was looking at Ed, not him.

Jim said, 'You know her?'

Eve turned back to her conversation.

'Well, yeah …' Ed frowned. 'That's Eve Black.'

'Eve Black?'

Ed's expression was unreadable and Jim wondered if he was pushing this feigned ignorance a bit too far.

'The survivor,' Ed said, 'from the Passage house.' He pointed to the nearby table covered in copies of *The Nothing Man*.

'Oh …' Jim said. '*Oh*. Jesus. Sorry, Ed. I was a bit slow on the uptake there. My wife's dragged me to this, you see. I only realised what the book was on the way in. It wouldn't be my kind of thing.'

Ed raised his eyebrows. 'No?'

'Nah. You know yourself. After thirty years of it, the last thing you want is reading about the ones that got away. Am I right?'

Ed said, 'Hmm,' but he was regarding Jim with something new, something that hadn't been there a few minutes ago.

Scrutiny.

'So you worked on the book, is it?'

Ed nodded. 'You worked on Optic too, didn't you? Back then?'

'Only in the sense that we all did at some point. I think I helped man the phone lines a few times.'

'*There* you are!'

Noreen, a sheen of sweat at her temples, was on Jim's left, looking up at him, radiating annoyance.

She said to Ed, 'Hi. I'm Noreen, Jim's wife.'

Jim glared at her.

He imagined what Ed was seeing, seeing her for the first time. Short, fat and frumpy. She was wearing bright white runners under a dress with a garish pattern on it that, as far as he was concerned, belonged on a tablecloth. She never did anything with her nest of brittle grey hair and, as ever, she wasn't wearing make-up. She was a fucking mess.

Jim wanted to strike her as hard as he could across the face, then smash her headfirst into the nearest hard object. He bit down on his lip to create a point of pain, an anchor to keep him here, in the moment, to stop him from acting on impulse.

Ed introduced himself and shook Noreen's hand.

'You're the one who dragged him here,' Ed said good-naturedly.

Noreen opened her mouth to speak, stopped and looked to Jim for guidance.

'Okay, folks,' a voice called out from the other side of the room. 'Are we ready to go? If you could all just take your seats ...'

Saved by the bell.

Jim took hold of Noreen's elbow, pinching the skin hard.

'We better go find a spot,' he said. 'Can't see a thing from here. Good to see you, Ed. I'll find you after, okay?'

Jim was already turning away, steering Noreen with him.

He pulled her back across the room, through the crowd, until he had found another place for them to stand.

Where they could see Eve, but she couldn't see them.

When not sat in front of a television camera transmitting live to the nation, Eve Black was different. She looked apprehensive, but the fidgeting was gone. While she waited for the journalist – Danielle something – to begin, she sat perfectly still, seemingly confident and relaxed. During the introduction ('… she's an author, survivor and detective') Eve scanned the crowd, smiling at what must have been the faces she recognised, giving a little wave or nod here and there.

'I thought,' Danielle said, 'we might start with a little reading?'

Eve nodded. She leaned down to retrieve a book from the large handbag resting against the leg of her chair. It was *The Nothing Man*, but it also wasn't. It had a soft cover and was completely blank, and black, except for the words 'The Nothing Man' printed in bright white down its spine.

She took a delicate sip of water and cleared her throat.

'Good evening, everyone,' she said. 'Thank you so much for coming. I think what I'll do is read just a little bit from the very start of the book, the introduction. It's safe enough. I don't want anyone to have to listen to … You know.' She paused. 'Any gruesome details.'

Whispers rippled through the crowd. No doubt some of them – *most* of them? – were only here for that.

Jim hoped they were disappointed now. The idea pleased him.

Eve cleared her throat again and then began to read in a strong voice, loud enough to fill the four corners of the room without the need for the microphone, which was still sitting on the table beside her chair, evidently forgotten.

'*When we meet, I probably introduce myself to you as Evelyn and say, "Nice to meet you." I transfer my glass to my other hand so I can shake the one you've offered, but the move is clumsy and I end up spraying us both with droplets of white wine. I apologise, perhaps blush with embarrassment. You wave a hand and protest that no, no, it's fine, really, but I see you snatch a glance at your shirt, the one you probably had dry-cleaned for the occasion, to surreptitiously assess the damage. You ask me what I do and I don't know if I'm disappointed or relieved that this conversation is going to be longer ...*'

Jim tuned out, lost in the strangeness of the situation.

Here he was, standing in a room listening to Eve Black read aloud to him from her book *about him*, while Ed Healy, who'd helped lead the Nothing Man investigation (to nowhere), stood nearby.

And Noreen hovered right beside him.

The feeling he had was what he imagined skydivers felt as they sat in the open door of the plane thousands of feet above the ground, dangled their legs over the side and waited for the Go signal: more alive than ever thanks to the threat of imminent death. But also confident that everything would go as planned, that really there was no threat, that they'd get to feel this way without paying a price for it.

'*This is always my fear,*' Eve continued, '*when I meet someone new, because I am. I am the girl who. I was twelve years old when a man broke into our home and murdered my mother, father and younger sister, Anna, seven years old then and for ever ...*'

Jim surveyed the assembled crowd and wondered what the reaction would be if they somehow suddenly realised that the Nothing Man was here, among them, in this very room.

Would they run?

Or would they turn towards him instead, asking *him* the questions, waiting to hear *his* story?

He was sure he knew the answer. No one was interested in Eve Black. Not really. What all these people wanted to know about was the man who had made her what she was, who had made her *someone*. They wanted to know more about *him*. It had crossed his mind before to go to the press, like the Zodiac Killer and others had done before him, but this wasn't America. Ireland was too small a stage for such antics and, moreover, forensics had moved on.

But still, there was a part of him that wished he could tell *his* story.

Instead of standing here having to listen to this shit.

'*We were the last family this man attacked but not the first. We were his fifth in two years. The media dubbed him the Nothing Man because the Gardaí, they said, had nothing on him ...*'

A man who had been standing directly in front of him – a man who, Jim realised now, was a member of staff – suddenly snapped his head towards the cash register. A distant phone was ringing. He hurried away, presumably to answer it, leaving nothing but clear air between Jim and Eve.

If she looked up now, she could be looking right at him.

'... I understand much more about what I lost now, at thirty, than I did when I actually lost it at twelve. And the monster responsible is still out there, still free, still unidentified. Maybe he's even spent all this time with his family. This possibility – this likelihood – fills with me a rage so intense that on the bad days, I can't see through it. On the worst of them, I wish he'd murdered me too.'

So do I, Jim thought. *So do I.*

But it's never too late to do the right thing.

Eve looked up, into the middle of the crowd.

'Yes, I *was* the girl who survived the Nothing Man,' she said, no longer reading. 'I *am* the woman who is going to catch him.'

Twenty years, Jim reminded himself. It had been, give or take, twenty years since he'd called to the house on Bally's Lane on New Year's Eve night, and in all that time, no one had ever come close to finding him.

Not the full resources of An Garda Síochána, not Ed Fucking Healy, and certainly not a lone woman on a crusade.

Eve turned her head a few degrees to her left.

Scanning.

Searching.

She stopped when her eyes landed on Jim.

'And,' she said, 'trust me: I *will*.'

The room erupted in applause.

Jim reached out to the nearest bookshelf, intending to lean on it for support, but in doing so knocked over a glass of wine that some idiot had left there, on the two inches between the spines of a row of vegetarian cookbooks and the very edge of the shelf. Noreen jumped as the liquid hit the back of her legs and the five or six people nearest to them turned around to see what was going on. A couple of them glanced at Jim's face before turning back.

He felt cold *and* hot. His mouth was so dry his tongue felt swollen and thick. His palms were clammy.

What the hell was that?

Had she *recognised* him?

Eve was mouthing *thank you* to various people in the crowd. Beside her, Danielle beamed and applauded too, then picked up her microphone and said, 'Well. There you go. And that's just the introduction!'

More, harder applause.

Eve picked up her microphone and said, 'Thank you,' into it. 'Thank you very much, everyone. Thanks a lot.' A faint bloom of pink appeared on her cheeks. She was embarrassed.

Or trying to look like she was.

'So let's get down to business,' Danielle said, shuffling her notes. 'I often think books are particularly good at hiding all the messy work that goes into them.' She touched a hand to the copy of *The Nothing Man* standing on the small table between them. 'We have this glossy, finished product here – which, let me say again, is a truly *astonishing* read that will be keeping you all up until the wee hours tonight. But let's talk about how it came to be. Let me take you back, Eve, to the beginning of the process. Many people will be familiar with *The Nothing Man*'s origins as that article we *all* read online. But in fact, it started life as an English essay ...?'

Jim looked around. There was a glass with a little bit of water in the bottom of it and a blush of lipstick on the rim sitting on a shelf nearby. He swigged it back, quickly, before its rightful owner could catch him in the act. It moistened his tongue but the hot, prickly dryness in his throat remained. He was hemmed in by the crowd and didn't want to move, didn't want to draw any more attention to himself. His lower back was soaked by a sudden cold sweat. A dull headache was forming at his temples. He could only take shallow breaths.

He looked to Noreen.

She was twisting around, assessing the damage to the back of her skirt. She turned back to face front, cross and annoyed. Then she looked up and saw Jim, and her face changed.

First, eyes wide with surprise.

Second, features softened with concern.

She whispered, 'Are you all right?'

He looked at her hands. She wasn't holding anything. She hadn't picked up a drink.

Useless to him.

He turned away, ignoring her.

Eve took a sip of water and apologised to Danielle for the momentary delay.

'That's all right,' Danielle said gently. 'Take your time.'

The story of her late essay went on then for some minutes. Eve explained about the impending and, up until then, forgotten deadline, it being Anna's birthday and her professor's reaction to the piece. She called him 'the renowned novelist', the exact same phrase she'd used in the book. She described how the possibility that publishing such a thing might help catch the killer after all these years had helped her overcome the terror of revealing her own identity. She directed her answer at Danielle and waved her hands about while she talked. She spoke clearly and concisely. She had every single person in the room hanging on her every word, enraptured.

Almost every person.

Jim watched her, waiting.

To look at him again, Eve would have to turn her head away from Danielle, to look over her own left shoulder. Had she done that the first time? Turned her head away from her interviewer, away from most of the audience, back towards him?

Or had he just imagined the entire thing?

How could she possibly recognise him? She'd been

standing at the top of the stairs, he'd been in the shadows a floor below it, standing several feet back from the bottom step.

Eighteen years ago.

When she was *twelve*.

'It must have been very difficult,' Danielle was saying now, 'to revisit the past. I have to admit, I found it quite difficult to *read* in parts and you lived this. How did you approach writing about it? Especially that night – although, as you write in the book, it was mostly an aural experience for you. You didn't see anything until … Until after.'

Eve tucked a piece of hair between her left ear, setting off a flash of something on her ring finger as it caught the light. Jim was reminded of the odd phrase Ed had used: *I'm with her.*

'I found it – find it – difficult to explain what I remember about that night. *How* I remember it. It's like a series of flashes. I liken it to – you know stop-motion animation? Like, um, *The Nightmare Before Christmas*?' Danielle nodded and laughed softly, and then a few people in the crowd did too. 'Well, it's kind of like a bad version of that. Not smooth, but jumpy. Jerky. Because some of the frames are missing. Maybe a lot of them are. But I do remember it. But then the other problem is *what* I remember. I was there but I wasn't. I was hiding in the dark in a bathroom. I could hear things but at the time I didn't know what they were. I was scared, yes, but I was probably more confused. And …' Eve swallowed. 'As everyone knows, I saw the aftermath.'

The silence in the room was total.

'But not him,' Danielle said. 'Not the Nothing Man.'

Eve shook her head, *no*. 'I never saw anyone else. Only my family. And I only saw them when ...'

Her voice had started to shake a little and she paused to take a sip of water while Danielle smiled at her sympathetically.

'Let's move on—' she started, deflating the tension in the room like a spike in a balloon. The audience seemed to collectively droop down into their seats, knowing now that they weren't going to get what they'd come for.

Was Eve lying? Or did she genuinely not remember?

After what had just happened, the way she'd looked at him, he was beginning to think she remembered everything perfectly well.

'Afterwards,' Danielle continued, 'you were whisked away west, by your grandmother. How aware were you, initially, about what was going on, about what had happened?'

'Not very,' Eve said. 'My grandmother kept a lot of it from me. Obviously I knew that Mum, Dad and Anna were dead, and I knew that a bad man had come into our house and done things to them, but I don't think I really *understood* it, if that makes sense? Perhaps I didn't want to. And I was so young. I'm not sure I had the capacity.'

Danielle made a *hmm* noise. 'And some journalists tracked you down ...?'

'I think Nannie got word that there were a few hanging around the village, not-very-casually asking questions about us. And one actually came to the cottage.' Eve rolled her eyes. 'Well, two. A photographer and a reporter. Working together. I remember coming back along the path that led to the beach and them waiting by the cottage's gate, a man and a woman, and asking me questions. It was so strange because they knew my name. I thought they must know me. I was about to answer them, but then Nannie came running out of the house, roaring at them and roaring at me to get inside.'

'Did you know there were others?' Danielle asked. 'Did you have any concept of' – she made air quotes – 'the Nothing Man?'

'Not until I was in secondary school. You can imagine how it was. Teenagers whispering. My grandmother had done her best to protect me, but she hadn't counted on the internet. I used to sneak into the library to look up my parents' names online. But I was never quite brave enough to read anything I found. It sounds weird, but it was like there were two universes. The one I was in, and the one in which my parents and sister were in the newspaper because they'd been victims of the Nothing Man. It all felt very … Separate? I don't know. It's hard to explain. But I think I felt very detached from it all during those years in Spanish Point.'

A beat passed.

'Now' – Danielle glanced at her watch – 'I'm conscious of the time and I want to make sure that we can answer a few questions from the audience, but just before we finish up … I think it's fair to say it's not quite a spoiler to reveal that you didn't identify the Nothing Man in the course of your research—'

'No.'

'—but you *have* found out a great deal of new information. Isn't that true?'

Eve nodded. 'We have. And I say "we" because I haven't done this by myself. I am so very grateful to have had the assistance of Ed Healy, who worked on the original investigation. Ed is actually the person who realised there was a serial attacker at work here. He was the one – the first one – to link the cases.' Eve lifted her head and scanned the room. 'Where are you, Ed?'

The crowd turned and twisted to look for him too.

'There he is!' Danielle pointed to the corner of the room Jim had left Ed in. She addressed the room again. 'After you've read the book, I promise you, you'll come to appreciate how dedicated this man has been to this case, to finding this monstrous killer. He still is.'

'I think he deserves a round of applause,' Eve said.

The audience complied.

Jim couldn't see Ed but he could see various members of the audience smiling at the same spot. What were they applauding, exactly? Ed *hadn't* found the Nothing Man and, right now, the man was utterly oblivious to the fact that he was in the same room as him.

Danielle waited a polite amount of time and then said, 'And this new information. What can you tell us? I know that it's probably—'

'We know how he picked them,' Eve announced.

A murmur of interest rippled throughout the room.

Jim's world came to a sudden, screeching stop.

'Wow,' Danielle breathed.

She couldn't. They couldn't. No one could. It wasn't possible.

He became aware of Noreen whispering something to him.

'Jim? Jim, what's wrong? You're shaking your head.'

Eve was smiling. 'I'm pretty pleased about that, I have to admit.'

'You should be,' Danielle said. 'I mean … when I got to that part, it just blew me away. And the way you put it together … I felt like I was reading a thriller!' She turned to the audience. 'We won't say any more on that. I don't want to spoil it for you.'

Jim's heart was beating out of his chest.

Noreen was still looking at him, waiting for an answer.

'One last question,' Danielle said. 'Aren't you at all worried' – she paused, a pathetic attempt to amp up the drama – 'that he'll come for you? I mean … he's still out there, as far as we know. Do you think he's here, in Cork, still? Do you think he knows about the book?'

Eve took a deep breath, considering.

'Here's what I think,' she said. 'If he's still alive, he probably is still here, and if he's still here, he probably knows about the book. But so what if he is, if he does? I'm not afraid of him. He's an old man now. He hasn't done anything in nearly twenty years. And in those twenty years, detection has come on leaps and bounds. I believe if he committed his crimes today, we'd catch him in a few days. If he is still around, he must know that. I think that's why he stopped — because he knew he couldn't continue to get away with it. He was — is — ultimately a coward. But I'm not. And I'm coming for him. My searching didn't stop just because I finished writing the book. I actually think the book — people reading it, reacting to it, remembering the case — will generate new leads. So to answer your question: no. I'm not worried. But I am determined. I *am* going to find him.' Eve paused. 'I know I will — and it will be soon.'

Danielle asked the audience to give Eve a round of applause and in the noise of it, Jim turned to Noreen and said, 'We have to go. *Now.*'

'But I need to get Katie's book signed.'

Katie.

He had completely forgotten she was why they were there.

'Fine,' he said. 'But do it quick. I'll meet you at the back door.'

Noreen looked like she was about to protest. Jim turned away before she had the chance. All around him people were rising from their seats, turning to talk to one another, moving to form a long queue in front of the chair where Eve Black still sat.

Jim moved away from it, in the direction of the rear doors.

The bookshop was long and wide, curving slightly at its middle. Jim passed tables of books; the cash registers; a children's section, strung with colourful bunting. The crowd thinned out more and more the further he got from the front and, by the time he was in Reference, he was alone.

Finally.

He stopped to lean against the nearest bookshelf and take a breath for what felt like the first time in several minutes.

We know how he picked them.

But they couldn't. It just wasn't possible.

He needed to get home, to get back to the book, to read on.

'Jim! There you are.'

Ed Healy's voice. Again. Close. The man must be standing right behind him. Jim arranged his face into an expression of pleasantness and turned around to face—

Eve Black.

So close, there was barely two feet of clear air between them. He could see the fine hairs on the sides of her face. The glittery stuff on her eyelids. The fluttering of her pulse beneath the delicate gold necklace sitting in the little hollow at the base of her throat.

She was staring at him.

And then, smiling at him. Widely. Flashing a neat row of bright white teeth.

'This is Eve,' Ed said. 'Eve, this is Jim Doyle.'

She didn't extend a hand, or move towards him at all. She was standing perfectly still, staring intently at his face.

'I remember you,' she said.

Jim's knees threatened to give way and he found he had to actively instruct them to keep him standing, to consciously dispatch the pertinent messages from his brain. He opened his mouth but no words came out.

There were no words any more, anywhere. His mind was only an emptiness, cleared entirely. He didn't even feel like he was inside his body any more but standing nearby, watching this happen.

'Don't you remember me?' Her eyes were still on his, searching. 'I looked very different back then. My hair was long and dark.'

Jim had never had a heart attack but he thought he might be having one now. A sudden blockade of pain in his chest, an acidic burning in his throat. Being completely unable to take a breath. Panic approaching like a tsunami in the distance.

Eve was looking at him quizzically.

Say something. Say something. SAY SOMETHING.

Jim pushed the words out. 'I don't … I don't remember.'

Eve exchanged the briefest of glances with Ed.

'That's all right,' she said. 'It's not a crime.'

Jim felt as if his entire body might burst into flames. He tried to wet his lips with the tip of his tongue. 'Wh–where …?'

'Togher Garda Station,' Eve said. She waved a hand dismissively, threw him a small smile. 'It was very brief, don't worry. I wouldn't expect you to remember me. I'm just good with faces.'

Like a sudden shock of freezing water, it came back to him. Two, three years ago. He'd been on the reception desk in Togher. She'd come in, looking to speak to a Garda who, it turned out, now worked with the GNBI, the National Bureau of Investigation, out of Harcourt Square in Dublin. Aisling Feeney. It was nothing. Three or four minutes at the most.

The only reason Jim even remembered the interaction was because of Aisling Feeney. She was one of the two Gardaí who had visited the woman at Covent Court and taken the knife and the rope she'd found under her sofa cushion. It was Feeney who'd submitted it into evidence officially; it had been her signature on the bags.

Ever since Jim had taken them from the evidence room and made them disappear, he'd been aware of the name.

But that was years ago, and the Gardaí were involved in all sorts of business, and for all Jim knew the woman asking for her was a relative …

But it had been Eve bloody Black.

'Have you lost Noreen?' Ed asked him. Then, to Eve, 'He got dragged here by his wife tonight. She's probably waiting for you in the signing queue.'

'Oh, really?' Eve said. To Jim, 'Noreen? I'll keep an eye out for her. I'll tell her that her husband helped with the book. To keep an eye out for his name. It's there.'

It's there.

'How are you?' Jim blurted out. He asked it because he thought that's what a normal person in this situation would ask. They would be concerned for Eve. They would feel sorry for her. They would hope that, despite everything, she had found a way to have a good life afterwards. 'I mean—' He cleared his throat. 'How are you now, these days?'

For a moment, Eve seemed bemused.

'I'm—' Before she could say any more, someone tapped her on the shoulder. A staff member, it looked like. They whispered something to her about the queue and she nodded and said she'd be right there. She turned back to Jim. 'I'm in demand, it seems like. I better get over there and start scribbling my name in other people's books. Lovely to meet you, Jim. And please don't feel bad. I was only messing with you. I wouldn't expect you to remember me. Thanks for your help, though. I appreciate it. I'll keep an eye out for Noreen so I can sing your praises.' Now she *did* reach out, but not to offer her hand. Instead, she coiled her fingers around Jim's left wrist, clasping it. She met his eyes. 'Thanks for coming. I hope we meet again soon.'

The voice in Jim's head, the other voice, the one that told him all the risky things were good ideas, scrambled up out of the depths and made the words—

'And I hope you catch him.'

—come out of his mouth.

'Thank you.' Eve smiled. 'Fingers crossed.'

And then she was gone, and Ed was saying goodbye, and Jim was hearing a buzzing inside his head, growing louder, and he moved to go, pushing his way out of the shop, the crowd now dispersed throughout it, most of them holding their copies of the book, and then he was going through the swinging door and now he was outside, on the street, the sky dark and the cobbles glistening with rain, drizzle on his face, trying to steady his breathing, to reset the rhythm of his heart.

She knows.

She *knows* he's the Nothing Man.

But she *couldn't* know. It wasn't possible.

But she'd told him his name was in the book. Why would

she write about someone who'd spoken to her for a couple of minutes three years ago?

And what the fuck was this about them finding the connection? *That* wasn't possible either.

He needed to get home. He needed to read the rest of the book.

The door behind him swung open and Noreen came out.

'Well,' she said, 'thanks for waiting for me.'

Jim mumbled something about it being too stuffy inside.

They started off down the street, Noreen buttoning up her coat against the cold.

'You got the book signed?' Jim asked.

'Yep.'

'Did she say anything to you?'

'Who?'

'The writer.'

'What do you mean?'

Inside, Jim was screaming.

'When you went up to her to get the book signed,' he said, pointedly pronouncing each word individually, 'what did she say to you?'

He could feel Noreen turning to look at him but he kept his eyes front and picked up the pace so she had to hurry to keep beside him.

'She just asked me what name to put on it and said thanks for coming. What else would you expect her to say?'

Katie.

It was Katie's name that had gone on the book. That's why

Eve hadn't said anything to her – because she was waiting for a woman named Noreen.

The drive home was nearly entirely silent. When they got in, Jim asked Noreen for the book. She frowned, but handed it over.

He opened it to the title page. Katie's name and Eve's signature were both scrawled in the same loose, loopy handwriting.

Noreen was looking at it too.

'She'll be delighted,' she said.

It took everything Jim had in him not to rip out the page right then and there and tear it into a thousand tiny pieces.

– 9 –

Connection

I wanted to start work on the book immediately, but I still had to finish my masters. For several months I tried to keep my mind off the Nothing Man, but for the most part I failed miserably. I was itching to get back to Cork and to start our search for him proper. The day after I submitted my final work, I met again with Bernadette and signed the contract for the book. Then I went home to pack a case and prep my apartment to survive an absence that might last weeks or months.

The last thing I did before I left was squeeze in a muted, uneasy dinner with Jo and Rhiannon, the only friends I'd ever managed to keep a hold of for longer than a couple of months. We had met in NUI Galway during a Freshers' Week pub crawl and so they now qualified as my oldest friends, by a very long shot. Our trio was weighted unequally, with them seeing each other far more often than I saw either one. But I didn't want to lose them. Ever since the article had come out, I had felt them slipping away. This dinner was supposed to be celebratory, but they were still adjusting uneasily to my reveal as Famous Crime Victim and none of us felt quite right having a champagne toast to the fact that I was going to spend the next year of my life, at least, excavating the worst thing that had ever happened to my family and four other families as well.

As we parted, I said they should visit me in Cork, come stay with me for a weekend. It was a casual invitation, off the cuff, not thought through.

'Where are you staying?' Jo asked.

My hesitation answered her question and she blanched. Rhiannon looked away, unable to hide her disgust.

I didn't know if our friendship was going to survive this. What was worse was that I didn't really care. The truth was I was itching to get away from them, to get back on the road, to get back to Ed and Cork and the darkest depths of the case. Everything else was a distraction. I had spent all my adult life working hard to hide who I really was and now I wanted nothing else except to be myself entirely.

It was exhilarating. It was terrifying.

First thing the following morning, I drove to Cork.

The only space I had there was the house, and it felt blasphemous to bring any part of writing the book into its rooms. Ed's office was barely that and as a civilian I couldn't simply waltz in and out of Anglesea Street whenever I liked. The sensitive nature of the material meant that we needed somewhere private to work, so coffee shops and libraries were out too. As luck would have it, there was a co-working space on Eglinton Street, not even five minutes' walk away from Ed's so-called office. I rented the smallest private space they had on offer and installed two desks, a bookshelf and three filing cabinets I could lock. I hung a huge whiteboard and bought a little coffee machine. I closed the blinds so we were free to stick whatever we needed to on the walls. I told the building manager that we were working on a book about Irish politics and that we would clean the office ourselves.

On the first Tuesday in November 2015, Ed arrived towing a stack of blue plastic bins behind him on a little cart with wheels. They were stamped 'An Garda Síochána' but he'd stuck masking tape over this so as not to arouse any curiosity among our office neighbours. It was delivery one of eight. Ed's superintendent had agreed to the transfer on the condition that our office remain secure, that we not disclose its location or our activities to anyone who wasn't directly assisting us with the case, and that we not move them again unless it was back to Anglesea Street. Ed joked that the higher-ups were probably glad of it; they had more room for dusty computers and old printer cables now.

For hours we unpacked and organised the files. Ed hung an Ordnance Survey map of Cork city and county on the wall and marked spots on it with a red marker pen. I put my favourite family photo on my desk: Nannie, my parents, Anna and me on our last holiday together in Clare in August 2001. It's also the last photo ever taken of all five of us together.

We made a loose plan: we would give ourselves until the summer to find out as much as we could about the Nothing Man. We made lists of things to check, people to talk to, places to visit. The bulk of the tasks would have to be done by me – Ed would still be working full time, but would spare what hours he could. (This would turn out to be *all* his spare time, for the next eighteen months.) Then, in September, I would start actually writing the book.

The following morning I woke up in my makeshift bedroom long before my alarm was due to go off. Something was different. I started, thinking it was the house, that someone had got inside in the night. But it was me. *I* was different. Lighter, somehow. Energised. Almost …
excited? Yes, that's what it was. I was excited about what Ed and I were about to embark on, which in turn made me feel ashamed.

But I couldn't stay in bed. I couldn't even stay in the house. I wanted to get started. After all this, I *needed* to. I drove into town on dark, deserted roads and was at my desk, halfway down my first cup of coffee, when the alarm set to wake me up went off.

The first thing we did was to simulate a complete review of the case. This involved going through every single piece of paper – statement, report, map, etc., – that had been generated during the course of the original investigation, trying to examine it with fresh eyes. Our progress was hampered by two factors: that I needed Ed to be there for the technical stuff and his time was limited, and the sheer amount of paper involved. More than 5,000 calls had come in to the tip-line, for starters, which made 5,000 one-page summaries of those calls that needed to be looked at again. An old college mate of mine had grown up in Boston where her father worked as a cop and now, as an adult, she had a habit of swearing loudly at anything fictional – TV shows, books or movies – that took liberties with police procedure. 'That's not *realistic*,' she'd shout. 'That's *not* what happens.' Many times over the course of those months in our little office in Eglinton Street, I thought of her, because if any of those things *actually* depicted reality, it would be merely hours and hours of people squinting at pieces of paper, and it would be exceedingly dull.

We started to build a kind of master file into which we put what we thought was the most relevant information. I quickly learned from Ed that it is just as important to rule out things and jettison statements, evidence, etc., as it is to include them. Still, every time I came to decide in which category something belonged, I hesitated, momentarily paralysed by the idea that we were about to dismiss the smoking gun that would finally crack this case. Sometimes I'd lie awake at night, plagued by indecision.

Our goal was to find the needle in a haystack that potentially had the power to blow the entire haystack away: the connection between the Nothing Man's victims. I worried there wasn't one. Wasn't it possible that he just drove around in the dark and targeted people at random? The O'Sullivans were a family of four children and two adults who lived just outside Carrigaline, a commuter town fourteen kilometres from Cork's city limits. Christine Kiernan lived in Cork City's southern suburbs, alone. Linda O'Neill lived thirty-five kilometres away with her husband in Fermoy, a town in the north of the county, but was attacked when her husband wasn't there. With Westpark, the Nothing Man had returned to the city to attack a couple living in a suburban housing estate, and then left it again to attack us in Passage West, ten kilometres away. Three of the homes were detached, one was semi-detached and another was a townhouse with neighbours on either side. The women were in their twenties, thirties and forties and shared no physical attribute aside from being conventionally attractive, and at the Westpark house the Nothing Man had murdered a man. In my house, a man, woman *and* child had died.

But there *were* similarities, Ed pointed out. Despite the seemingly scattered locations, if you plotted them on a map – and we did – all but one fit into a relatively small circle within Cork county. Fermoy was the only anomaly. (Had the Nothing Man lived or worked in that area? Did he operate there because he was familiar with it?) Women were clearly the common denominator. His first three attacks focused on a woman and there was no attack that didn't include one. And then there was the most obvious, glaring connection between the victims, one I hadn't even thought about before because it was *so* obvious: all the victims were attacked in their own homes. He hadn't snatched them from a road or taken them to a second location. Two of them, including my mother, hadn't even been moved from their own beds.

We knew because of my finding the knife and rope under our sofa cushions and Christine's neighbour doing the same that the Nothing Man visited the homes *before* he arrived to attack the occupants, perhaps on more than one occasion. The phone calls told us that he liked to tease and terrorise his victims, and the fact that he knew their telephone numbers meant he had collected information about them. He knew their names. On Bally's Lane, he'd whispered the names of all four children into Alice O'Sullivan's ear as a threat. Ed was convinced that the Nothing Man stalked his victims for weeks, maybe even months, prior to their attacks, and that before Westpark had any residents, he had used the empty but finished houses to practise things like picking locks, breaking windows and moving around in the dark. He was meticulous, never leaving anything behind at his scenes except for trauma, grief and lengths of his favoured blue rope, which had never given up any useful fibres or DNA. There had only been one sighting of him, by Claire Bardin on the road outside the O'Sullivans', and no one had ever come forward to ID the man in her sketch.

All this told us a lot about who the Nothing Man was, how he operated and what was driving him. This was an attacker who studied and prepared, who did his research. He felt superior and was convinced he was smarter than his victims and the Gardaí too. The prior visits to the home suggested a thread of voyeurism in his tendencies – he had probably begun his criminal career as a peeping Tom. It just didn't make sense that, alongside all this, he would choose his victims at random. He was *finding* them, somehow. There was a *why* to this. But the original investigation hadn't found it and now Ed and I, ten months into our unofficial case review, had failed to as well. We were back to square one, stuck.

It was now September 2016. Whatever warm weather constituted the Irish summer could be relied upon to reach its peak the week schools reopened. Ed and I took a rare break to sit in the evening sun outside a bar on Bachelor's Quay. The place was busy with office workers in rolled-up shirtsleeves and bare legs, leaning back in their chairs and tilting their faces to the sun. It was easy to forget why we were there, what Ed and I were doing, and that evening there was a part of me that wanted to. This was all starting to feel hopeless. We had looked at everything and seen nothing new. We distractedly peeled the labels off our sweating beer bottles and took turns saying, 'There must be *something* we haven't thought of,' in between sips.

Then something occurred to me. We hadn't found anything new in the case files, but we were looking at them *because* we'd found something new – my discovery of the rope and knife under the cushion all those years ago. That was a piece of the puzzle I'd had, but until recently I didn't know I had it.

Would it be worth talking to the other survivors to see if maybe *they* unknowingly had such a piece, too?

It wasn't going to be easy. Christine Kiernan had been so traumatised by her visit from the Nothing Man that just weeks later, she'd taken her own life. Linda O'Neill had remarried and was living in San Francisco; she told Ed over the phone that while she sympathised with my need to discover the Nothing Man's identity, she had no interest in revisiting that time in her life. She asked us not to reveal her new married name, apologised and hung up. There were no survivors of the Westpark attack, so that left Alice O'Sullivan, the very first victim of the Nothing Man, who we quickly discovered no longer lived in the house on Bally's Lane. After several phone calls and numerous dead ends, we finally tracked down a number for her in Malahide, Co. Dublin. When we called it we were told that, tragically, Alice had passed away two years before from bone cancer. I was speaking to her daughter, Nancy, now aged twenty-seven.

Nancy was married with two children and living in the house to which the family had moved directly from Bally's Lane. Her father was gone too, having suffered a heart attack five years earlier. But she said the relocation to Malahide had enabled the family to put the events of that night far enough behind them to move forward, and that afterwards her parents had managed to have a good life filled with family, fun and foreign travel. Nancy deeply understood my need for justice and was happy to help, but there wasn't much she could add to our information. She had been in her bedroom, blissfully unaware of the events inside the house and, at ten then, too young to now be able to recall much from that time. But she had a suggestion: I should call Tommy, her older brother. Not only was he likely to remember more, but he had actually spoken to the Nothing Man on the telephone on New Year's Eve 1999.

Tommy was eager to speak with us. As the eldest child in the O'Sullivan family, he had been sitting much closer to the aftermath of the attack. Nancy had been telling the truth when she said her parents had managed to have a happy life but it was *her* truth, her perspective. Being older, Tommy had a different one. He told us that his mother had suffered from bouts of debilitating depression and had been attending a weekly therapy session for Post-Traumatic Stress Disorder until her cancer diagnosis. Even though the Nothing Man had spent less than an hour in their lives, the trauma of it was an incurable infection. They could never feel completely safe again. He was the faceless monster who had crouched in the corner of his mother's mind and it made Tommy angry that the man responsible had never been caught, let alone punished. He welcomed the book and the research Ed and I were doing for it. But he was now living in Abu Dhabi. It would be three long months before he returned home for Christmas and we could speak to him in person, which was our preference. Both Ed and I felt that phone calls and video chats just weren't the same, and we couldn't justify the travel. We busied ourselves with other items on our endless list and settled in to wait.

In mid-December, we travelled to Dublin Airport to meet Tommy off his flight. We waited at Arrivals as people came streaming out of the sliding doors and into the outstretched arms of waiting loved ones. All around us were squeals of delight, tears and even a few handmade WELCOME HOME signs. I was holding a sign that said the name of a man I'd never met and I was waiting to talk to him about a murderer who'd changed the course of both of our lives. This was typical of what being the victim of a violent crime often felt like to me. I looked fine; I looked normal; I could blend in with everyone else. But I had a secret that set me apart, that made me an Other. The lives of the people around me were so different to mine they may as well have been science-fiction. I would never stand in an Arrivals hall to wait for my family. I had lost all the family I'd had. And if I somehow found a way in the future to make a family of my own – something that, when I thought about all the steps I would need to take to make that happen, seemed utterly impossible – I would never let them go anywhere without me. I'd be too scared to. Because even when you were at home, altogether, you still weren't safe. I had seen the proof of this first hand.

Tommy O'Sullivan was thirty-three now and working as an engineer for an aerospace company. His black hair and bushy beard were flecked with grey, and he was dressed casually in jeans with a leather messenger bag slung over one shoulder. He'd flown from Abu Dhabi to London and then from London to here, but his bags had only made the first journey. He wore a wedding ring. His wife, Amanda, had family in England and was spending a few days with them before joining her husband at Nancy's house in Malahide. Tommy was warm and open, easy to chat to and generous with his time, repeatedly reassuring us that he was in no rush to leave. We found a table at the bar on the mezzanine level and ordered a round of coffees. I asked if I could record the conversation on my phone and he agreed.

He told us he'd been waiting a long time for this day. Seventeen years, give or take a few weeks.

The Gardaí had interviewed Tommy at the house, but only for a short time and on the morning after the incident, when Tommy – in his own words – was still half-dazed by the event. Months later, when the *Crimecall* episode had made him realise the prank call was connected, he'd spoken to them again, but that meeting was brief. He'd always believed he knew more than they'd got out of him. Tommy was convinced what happened wasn't a random attack, but that his family had been targeted. *Chosen* was the word he used. Even now, all these years later, he was tormented by *why*. Why them? Why had this man done what he did? And why had he never been caught?

Tommy talked us through the events of that night, which for him had really only begun in the early hours of the morning, after the Nothing Man had left. He described his phone ringing and hearing his father's voice on the other end of the line, despite the early hour and being in the room next door. The locked bedroom door. His father going outside and then calling out for Tommy to ring the Gardaí. A glimpse of his mother's nightgown through a partially open bathroom door. Not seeing her properly until later that day, when she was discharged from hospital, clean and sterile and bandaged up. The Gardaí response. The immediate assumption, by them and his own father, that this was a tiger kidnapping gone wrong.

'But gone wrong *how?*' Tommy said to us, throwing up his hands, the frustration at that assumption still bubbling just below the surface all these years later. 'A tiger kidnapping involves a gang and a vehicle. Where were *they?* There was one guy and no car that we know of. So at what point did it *go wrong*, exactly? It never went right, because it was never a kidnapping. There was zero evidence of that. The only reason that even came up at all was because my dad was a bank manager and made the mistake of telling them that. And they were like, "Oh, great. Mystery solved. Tiger kidnapping it is. Next!"' He backtracked to the phone call two weeks before the attack, the one he'd thought was a friend of his playing a New Year's Eve prank. He described the voice and then did an impression of it. It was raspy, odd and unnatural. A theatrical whisper. *Let's play a game.* He described watching *Crimecall* –

which he'd only happened to catch during a bored channel-surf – and feeling a sudden chill when he realised that the call was part of this, that he'd actually spoken to the Nothing Man.

I asked him if he had ever found anything odd in the house, particularly in the weeks leading up to the attack, and told him about my own discovery of the knife and the rope. But Tommy couldn't remember any similar incident at the house on Bally's Lane.

Ed explained why we'd wanted to meet with Tommy in the first place, why we were hoping to meet with as many survivors as we could. Our priority was finding a connection between the people the Nothing Man had chosen. There *had* to be something, but it was hard to find it when we didn't know exactly what it was we were looking for.

But we had Tommy and me, two eldest children from two Nothing Man targets, who'd lived only miles from each other growing up. Perhaps if we both shared everything we could remember from our families' lives around the time of the attacks, we might hit on something we had in common. It was like a perverse game of Nothing Man Snap, and it was a long shot. But it was all we had.

We started with the basics: schools and teachers, friends, relatives, clubs and other activities. Then we spread out from there. We talked about the restaurants we went to, cinemas we frequented, shopping centres we returned to again and again. Where our mothers did the weekly Big Shop. Where we went on holiday. Where we went if the day was sunny. Where we went if it was not. Bus routes, hairdressers, hospitals. Things that got delivered to the house. Tommy's memory was markedly better than mine, but then he'd been older. He could remember which library his family went to, the name of the piano teacher two of his younger siblings had and where his mother's favourite garden centre was. He could even remember what he liked to order from the café there when she took him along. But we found nothing that connected us.

Tommy had been four years older than me when the Nothing Man came to his house. He had had the beginnings of a life outside his family. He was spending a lot of time with friends. It had widened his world. His family did a lot of things together like go for drives on a Sunday afternoon, go on holiday, go to the beach in good weather to swim in the sea, whereas what counted as activities in my family were going to Nannie's house for lunch or playing outside for a while. If our mother had things to do, she normally dropped us off at our grandmother's on the way there and collected us on her way back. It suited all parties better. I would visit friends' houses on weekends but didn't do much in the way of activities outside of school, and Anna was too young to. Tommy had a large extended family, while both my parents were only children and of our grandparents we only had Nannie left. Thus our universes at the turn of the millennium were two parts of a Venn diagram where his circle was several sizes larger than mine and there was nothing to put in the place where they overlapped.

We clutched at straws until the conversation petered out. Tommy was clearly exhausted, although still reassuring us that he could stay longer. He seemed determined to find the link. We ordered more coffee.

On this section of my recording of the conversation, there's a lot of silence punctuated with the tinkling of teaspoons against the inside of ceramic cups.

Eventually Ed, who had mostly been quiet all this time, spoke up.

'Maybe *he* came to *you*,' he said. 'Maybe this wasn't someone you encountered outside the home. Can you remember any callers to the house around that time? Strangers or perhaps new friends of your parents who you didn't see afterwards? Any sales people, charity collectors, workmen – things like that?'

I was searching my memory for something, anything, that might fit that bill when Tommy said, very quietly, 'There was a guard.'

Ed was instantly alert. 'A guard? *Before* the attack?'

Tommy nodded. 'Yeah. A few months before.' This is what he could remember:

One evening, when it was not yet dark but getting there, the doorbell went. Tommy was watching TV in the living room while his mother ironed school shirts. They were new shirts, coming out of their plastic packing; she was ironing the creases out. This, according to Tommy, sets the event firmly at the start of the school year, so September 1999.

From his perch on the couch, Tommy had a line of sight through the open living-room door, across the hall, to the last six inches or so of the entranceway. When his mother opened the front door, he could see the right arm and shoulder of what was unmistakably a Garda uniform. Curious, Tommy muted the TV so he could eavesdrop. He heard a man's voice say something about a burglary in the area. Gardaí were going door-to-door to make residents aware of this, to encourage them to step up their own home security if need be. At some point, Tommy's father went to the door too.

'And that's why I remember it,' Tommy said. 'Because my mother turned to him and said something like, "I *told* you: we need to get that conservatory door fixed." In front of the guard. She was always on about that bloody door and my dad was always saying he'd get someone out to have a look at it, but it never happened … And then, just a few months later, the Nothing Man got in through that door and I cursed the fact that they hadn't done anything about it, even after the visit from the guard, even after there was a burglary nearby. But now I'm thinking …' Tommy paused. 'Maybe the man wasn't really a guard.'

'Did you see a car?' Ed asked.

Tommy said he didn't remember seeing or hearing one.

'Do you remember who it was who was burgled?'

'No.'

'Can you describe what the man looked like? Did you see his face?'

'Sorry, no. I'd guess he was about the same height as my dad, but that's it.'

A beat passed, pregnant with disappointment.

I took a deep breath.

'I think a guard may have come to our house, too,' I said. 'I *think*.'

The two men turned to look at me with such intensity that I immediately regretted saying those words aloud – because what I remembered was more of a *possibility* than an actual event.

The doorbell going after dark, sounding strange and intrusive at that hour. Me leaving my homework to go stand at the top of the stairs to see what I could see, drawn by this unusual event but knowing better than to rush down and pull open the door myself. The light coming on in the hall. A stretched shadow in it. A man's voice saying words I couldn't make out. And then my mother saying something like, 'Oh God, who is it? Ross? Colette?' – my father and grandmother's first names, which I never heard her use. The unseen man saying more and my mother making the sounds of relief. Then her saying something about not even locking doors.

'That's all I remember,' I said. 'I don't know when it was, but that could've been a guard, right? She thought he was coming to tell her someone had died, that there'd been an accident. But he was telling her – probably – about a burglary. Right? It sounds like it could've been that?' Neither of the two men answered me and I blushed with embarrassment. 'I know, I know, it's all very vague. I'm not even one hundred per cent sure I didn't dream it. Never mind.'

Ed looked from me to Tommy.

Tommy looked at him.

Ed said, 'That's it. That's it. That's it.'

The words swam in front of Jim's eyes. He closed the book and let it fall on to his lap. His hands were shaking.

So they knew. They knew and they didn't know. They had gathered the puzzle pieces and it would only be a matter of time now before they put them together. It was hard to gauge how much time he had left, but the clock *was* ticking.

He could see that now.

Feel it.

Jim was in the living room, reading Katie's copy of *The Nothing Man*. Noreen had gone to bed hours ago, not long after they'd got home from the event, muttering something about having a headache. She'd been looking for one of those painkillers that she liked because a side effect of them was a good night's sleep. He had considered going out to the shed as before, but it was cold out there, and Katie's copy of the book was in *here*, where it was warm and there was a comfortable chair.

Even if Noreen came downstairs, which he doubted she'd do, he'd have no questions to answer. He was just having a flick through, he'd say. He knew Ed. Turns out he'd met Eve Black at Togher station while she was researching the book.

While she was looking for *him*.

She may not have found him, but she had found the path that led his way.

Jim set the book aside and headed for the drinks cabinet, a foreign land to him. He almost never drank. But he needed something to take the edge off, to settle the electricity sparking inside his brain, to quieten things down so he could think a bit more clearly.

He selected a dusty, half-drunk bottle of whiskey and poured what he thought was a measure of it into a short glass filled to the brim with ice. He took it back to his chair and set it on the table. He watched it sweat for a while, the condensation dripping down the outside of the glass. The ice began to melt.

He took the barest of sips and winced at the taste, then at the burn as it slid down his throat and into his chest.

Jim picked up the book again but didn't open it. Instead, he ran his hand over the dust jacket as he had done before, but which he hadn't been able to do since he'd discarded the jacket on his own copy as a precautionary measure.

Now there was no need to be as careful.

The letters were embossed, smooth and glossy. They raised up to meet him.

The Nothing Man.

Emerging from the shadows, now. After all this time.

Or being dragged from them.

Only if he let it happen.

All because of a casual comment from Tommy O'Sullivan. A teenager at the time. Another one! Him and Eve, in cahoots.

All of Jim's work, his caution, his skills, his planning, his *genius* – it was all being undone by two overgrown children.

How fucking infuriating.

The idea had come to him in July 1990.

Back then, Jim was the new guy at the station in Mallow. He'd been reassigned after a situation had arisen between him and his superintendent back at Millstreet, where he'd been for three years – his first assignment out of Templemore. All he'd done was pick up a mug and throw it at the wall, but the super had been standing in front of that wall and the mug had been filled with hot tea. Jim had just attended a scene where a seven-year-old boy had been ejected through a windscreen and thrown twenty-five feet further down the road, where he was then run over by an articulated lorry driving in the opposite direction. They hadn't had to remove his body so much as scrape it up. Jim said he'd been struggling with what he'd seen and pushed out a few tears to add plausibility, and the performance got him disciplined and a move to Mallow. But the truth was Jim had had his fill of being treated like an idiot *by* idiots, and that day he'd finally blown his top.

Outside the station, he got the respect he deserved. The uniform was a power differential, separating him from the gormless public and criminal lowlifes, the idiots who drove too fast and drank too much and came stumbling out of the pub at closing time to punch *other* idiots just because they'd looked at them the wrong way. Whenever he walked down the street, thumbs hooked into his vest, the weight of the belt and everything that hung from it pushing down on his hips, he felt good about himself. Taller. Stronger. He could see passers-by clocking him but pretending not to, having second thoughts about crossing before the green man or leaving their car in the disabled spot or littering. Little things, yes, but it was about them noticing him.

Seeing him.

Deferring to him.

Whenever he had to attend a scene, interview witnesses or get someone handcuffed and into the back of the car, it was the same feeling only turned up to the max, practically pumping out a bass-line he couldn't hear but could feel in his chest. Those moments made him feel like his whole life had just been a series of events to bring him to this place, to this point, to this job. That he was doing what he was supposed to.

Inside the station, it was a different story. He was the lowest member on the totem pole. A joke, even. No one respected him. No one even liked him, although he didn't give a fuck about that. They *tolerated* him and, he'd begun to suspect, traded jibes about him behind his back. One of the guys had a buddy in Millstreet who'd told the whole station about Jim losing his shite over the boy in the car accident. A couple of times since other members had come back from scenes wiping away pretend tears, asking for a mug and looking for the super.

All because he was better than them and they knew it. They knew it and they just couldn't stand it.

Even on *that* day, the day that started it all, when the call came in about Meadowbrook and Jim and David Twomey were directed to go help with the house-to-house, Jim caught the other man making a face about the pairing. They'd driven to the scene in stony silence, which was probably just as well because David was a terrible driver and Jim didn't want to make things worse by distracting him.

What had happened was this: the night before, in a sprawling estate of affordable semi-Ds called Meadowbrook, three separate houses had been burgled while their occupants slept. The thieves had taken living-room electronics, cash and whatever jewellery they found on the sleeping female's side of the bed. The targets were dotted throughout the estate but whoever had done this had moved quickly, hitting one right after the other and getting in and out before anyone even knew they'd been there. Clearly pre-planned. A white van had been spotted in the area at the time and on a number of occasions in recent weeks. Jim and David Twomey were to help knock on every door in the estate to see if any other residents could recall seeing this white van too.

They could've done this as a pair – there were enough warm bodies already on the scene – but when they met with the member-in-charge, David piped up with a suggestion: they could split up and cover twice the ground in the same amount of time. This was factually correct, but Jim knew why David had said it: because he wanted shot of him. That was fine with Jim, because he wanted to be shot of that streak of shite as well.

They divided a long row of houses in two, with Jim taking the doors on one side of the street and David the ones on the other. The first four knocks were standard fare. There was the usual over-eagerness to help the Gardaí, so people kept him talking on their doorsteps, or invited him in, and made him wait while they racked their brains over the endless monotony of their days looking for something, *anything*, they could offer up to the man in the uniform. They wanted him to be pleased with them, to impress. They wanted him to think *they* were important too. But no one had anything substantial.

And then, at the fifth door, there was Alba.

She'd opened the door in a state of distraction, frazzled, already readying herself to turn back towards the screeching noise that was coming from the space beyond.

Jim saw dark eyes and a huge mess of tightly curled hair.

She saw his uniform and her face changed. She stepped forward, into the light—

And Jim saw Jean standing there.

It wasn't Jean, of course. It couldn't be. Truth be told, the two women didn't even look very much alike. It was more that they *felt* alike. Somewhere deep inside of him, a door opened. Up until that moment on the doorstep of a house in Meadowbrook, he had thought only Jean possessed the key.

Jean had been his babysitter. Between the ages of seven and fourteen, nearly every other Saturday night, she'd come to look after him while his aunt Agnes went out on the town with whatever toy boy she was into that week. Jean was fun. She would organise elaborate games, bring funny films for them to watch and make him toasted cheese sandwiches with honey inside which, she said, was her trademark secret ingredient. She was a bright light in the darkness and after every visit, Jim counted down the days until she was due to come again.

Somewhere along the line, though, they both got older. She had always seemed so much older than him but as the years passed, it started to seem that, by some alchemy, he might be able to catch her. Over years' worth of Saturday nights, Jean lost her braces, changed her hair and started to wear things that made her look different. And then she *was* different, a different shape. And Jim – Jimmy, she always called him – began to notice this, and feel a certain way about it, and think about her when she wasn't there beyond waiting for her to come back. This made him act differently when she did come around, charging their Saturday nights together with a new, treacherous tension – at least on his part.

Jim ached for her. The only balm for it was to think of her, to bathe himself in thoughts of her, to close his eyes and sink into them. In his imagination, they were together all the time. In his fantasies, he could touch that pale pink flesh, push his hand up to the band of her bra and then under it, while Jean closed her eyes and moaned. The next steps were blurry and vague, the exact process unclear to him, but he could see them in a bed together afterwards, her lying with her head buried against his neck. He dreamed of this sometimes, waking up alone with a cold, sticky dampness berating him for it beneath the sheets.

Then one night that last summer, Jean was making pizza in the kitchen when she stretched to pull her sweatshirt off and lifted her T-shirt too, offering Jim a glimpse of, first, pale skin and the smooth curve of her right side and, then, the edge of the blue band of her bra. There was something about the movement – it was oddly slow, deliberate, *performed* – that made him think it had been for him. Convinced him it was. She was sending him a message, he thought. Letting him know that whatever he was feeling, she was feeling too.

But it was a lie. A tease. Because when Jim reached for her the way he had seen men reach for women on TV, she recoiled.

Then she got angry.

Then she *laughed*.

She laughed until she was doubled over and her eyes had filled with tears. She laughed until the smell of burnt bread filled the kitchen and she had to go and open the oven, which billowed smoke. She laughed until every cell in Jim's body was a burning white fireball of hot, sticky shame. She was still laughing when Jim turned and ran, upstairs and into his bedroom, and banged on the walls with his fists until his hands were numb and his knuckles were split and there were smears of red on the wallpaper.

Jean never came back after that night. No one did. Agnes called him 'a little pervert' and said he was old enough now to stay at home on his own. But she believed this only up until midnight, at which point she'd come home, bringing whoever she'd gone out to meet back with her. Jim would be sent to bed and they'd stay in the living room. The first time this happened, he heard strange noises and went down to investigate, thinking that maybe the man wasn't being very nice and Agnes needed his help. To save her now would undo some of the damage from the incident with Jean. But she wasn't in trouble. From what he could see through the open living-room door, Agnes was enjoying what the man was doing. And after a few minutes hidden in the shadows on the stairs, Jim realised he was enjoying watching it.

He hadn't thought of Jean in years. She'd be older than him now, wrinkled and loose, fattened and spoiled by having children like they all were. But here, on the doorstep in Meadowbrook, was Alba. She was probably seventeen or eighteen. When she spoke, it was in a thick Spanish accent. She didn't live at the house, she was staying there as the family's au pair. She hadn't seen any white van but maybe the owners had. Both mother and father would be at home later that evening. The hem of her T-shirt, the neckline of which was cut in a deep V, didn't quite reach the waistband of her jeans, and the skin she'd left exposed was smooth and darkly tanned. He wanted to touch it. He wanted her in the same way he'd wanted Jean.

But he wasn't fourteen years old any more. *She* was younger than him, so much younger.

And he was a guard now, standing in front of her in uniform.

She wouldn't laugh at him. She wouldn't dare to.

That night, after dinner, Jim told Noreen he had to go back to the station for an hour. He took his uniform with him in a bag and changed into it in a lay-by off the Cork-Dublin road. Then he drove to Meadowbrook. He parked his car in a turnaround at the rear of the estate, got out and started walking to Alba's house, keeping his hat off until he was right outside it.

But he hadn't thought it through. Now that her employers were home, there was no need for her to come to the door. The owners were a pleasant, professional couple in their thirties who worked in the city. He asked them about white vans and suspicious characters, but they had seen nothing.

'We're hardly ever here,' the husband said. 'Unfortunately. And you spoke to Alba already, right?'

Jim said he had. 'She's your, ah' – he pretended to refer to his notebook – 'au pair?'

The couple nodded enthusiastically and launched into a spiel about how amazing the young girl was, how they'd never cope without her, how they hoped she'd stay with them for longer than the last one had. They told him how old she was (nineteen), where she was from (Girona, Spain) and what days off she had (half of Saturday if they could manage it, and all of Sunday). They told him that since the only spare bedroom was the tiny box room upstairs, they had converted the garage into a little self-contained studio, and that Alba stayed there. Still, they said, it was a small enough space, and she was probably looking forward to the following week, when the couple and their two young children would go to London to visit his family and Alba would have the whole house to herself. Well, they added, not *all* to herself: her sister was coming from Girona to stay for a few days.

People, Jim mused on the drive home, can be so fucking stupid.

He came back the following week, on three separate occasions, to watch Alba and her sister from the shadows outside the house. On the last one, he entered the house while the women slept, moving through the kitchen, pocketing a couple of delicate things from the laundry basket, standing in the open doorway of the room where Alba slept. He watched her turn over, one bare leg thrown on top of the blankets. She had got up to go to the bathroom and passed right by him as he hid in a recess in the hall and never even knew he was there.

It set him alight, that night. Switched him on, brought him to life. He didn't care about how bad the days were any more when there could be nights like this. Everything that happened elsewhere – pasty, soft Noreen; the crap he got at the station; the things he saw Aunt Agnes doing when he closed his eyes at night – it all just slid off him, melted away.

This was how everyone else must have learned to live in the world, Jim thought. This is how they managed to move around it calmly, with a smile on their face, taking shit day in, day out. They had found an outlet, a remedy, an antidote. It was the only explanation.

And now he had found his.

But Meadowbrook was spent. The morning after his third and final visit to Alba, he'd come into work to discover a neighbour had reported a prowler the previous night. He'd *just* missed a car containing two of his colleagues.

He needed to find somewhere else.

And then somewhere else after that.

What Jim needed was a *supply*.

One night soon after, he told Noreen he was on a surveillance op and drove to a new housing estate fifteen minutes outside the town. He changed into his uniform while parked on the side of the road. He started knocking on doors.

When the occupants opened them, he flashed his badge. He had slipped a new ID card into the clear pocket below it, which had his own picture but a different name. He had photocopied his own ID, modified the details by hand, then photocopied that. It was just a slip of paper with faded ink and wouldn't stand up to scrutiny, but on a doorstep after dark with his fingers partially obscuring it – and when you just saw it for a flash – it did the job fine. 'Sorry to bother you, but there's been a burglary in the area, and we're just canvassing residents to see if they've noticed anything strange in the last few weeks or months, seen any suspicious vehicles, that kind of thing ...'

One thing immediately became apparent with this approach: all the questions were being directed at him. Because there hadn't actually *been* a burglary, this was the first time the residents were hearing of one. They were shocked and concerned and demanding of more details. Jim fluffed the first two homes but, in the third, he found himself face to face with the chairman of the local residents' association. The following day, that man would ring the station asking about the supposed incident. Jim got lucky: he was the one who took the call. But he couldn't risk a similar thing happening again.

It was easier, he realised, to hide in plain sight. Jim started watching out for small, residential incidents – burglary, theft, vandalism. Sometimes they'd necessitated an actual house-to-house, sometimes not. He'd wait it out a week or more, until he was sure the investigation had tied itself up or petered out, and then he'd drive to the area in the evening with his modified ID and his uniform on the back seat of his car. The burglaries he was 'warning' them about had really happened, but his visits had three, unrelated objectives: evaluate the residents, observe the homes, collect information.

For *himself*.

Jim got braver and braver. He began returning to the houses he liked during the night, sometimes watching from outside, sometimes letting himself in. Occasionally he watched the women sleep, standing just inches from their beds. In one house he stood in the shower with the curtain drawn while the woman who lived there took her make-up off in front of the sink.

But over time, the same old feelings crept back into his days: frustration, rage, shame. If his nocturnal activities were the antidote to the pain of being alive, then life began to develop a resistance. Noreen broke an arm. There was another incident at work. This time he was getting moved into Cork City, to Togher Garda Station, where he'd be confined to desk duty.

Jim needed something new. Something stronger.

– 10 –

Password

Burglary. After nearly twenty years, we thought we finally had the password that would unlock the entire Nothing Man case.

What we needed to do now was to try to confirm that Tommy and I were remembering these events correctly, and then to determine if the same thing had happened at the other three Nothing Man homes. If we could establish that we were and they had, our next step would be to verify the nature of those visits. Was that man really a guard? Had there really been burglaries? *How* was this the connection?

Ed quickly established that there had indeed been a burglary near Tommy's family home on Bally's Lane in September 1999. On the afternoon of 5 September, a property had been burgled during the funeral of its elderly owner. Numerous antiques worth thousands of pounds had been stolen, presumably in a van that had been spotted in the area at the time emblazoned with the name of a (fake) moving company. The theft had made the news, with the deceased man's adult son growing tearful as he spoke live on air to a local radio host, pleading with the public to assist in the return of the items his late father had spent a lifetime collecting.

This was the kind of crime the Gardaí called theft-to-order. It hadn't been your run-of-the-mill home burglary – whoever had done this had known what was in the house and how to offload the goods afterwards. The way to solve this type of crime was through the cooperation of antique dealers. Someone would try to sell them one or more of the items; they'd alert the Gardaí; the Gardaí would trace the item back, seller to seller, until they got to the person or persons who had stolen them in the first place. It made no sense that anyone involved in the same investigation would be calling to local houses to warn them about it. Unless they *also* had a house full of antiques and were going to leave them unattended while the whole family went to a funeral, there was zero danger of them suffering a similar fate – which was why the Gardaí hadn't done that. There was no record of any members being sent anywhere to do house-to-house calls aside from the homes immediately neighbouring the target, whose occupants had provided witness statements in the hours after the theft.

There was no record of Christine Kiernan being visited by a guard in the weeks before her attack and after a delicate conversation with her parents, I determined she hadn't mentioned such a thing to them either. But there *had* been talk at the time of installing gates at the entrance because of a recent burglary in the area. I'd already met with Maggie Barry, the neighbour who'd found the rope and knife, and I called her again to ask if she could remember anything about this or a visit from a guard. She said no. But Maggie was the current secretary of the Covent Court Residents' Association and one of her duties was storing the association's files, which included minutes from their AGMs and special meetings. She went through them and found this very issue raised at a special meeting at the beginning of June 2000, six weeks before Christine was attacked. The minutes referred to a 'break-in on the Blackrock Road'. Whoever had recorded them had written this with the word 'Florida' in brackets afterwards.

When Ed went searching, he found a report about a burglary in a detached house on the Blackrock Road reported on 29 April 2000. A family had returned from a fortnight's holiday at Walt Disney World in Orlando to discover their entire home ransacked and vandalised. What neither Ed nor I could find was any mention of this incident in the media. This meant one of three things: there *had* been media coverage and we just couldn't find it; one or more of the residents of Covent Court personally knew the family involved or someone who knew them and had heard about it that way; or one or more residents of Covent Court had had a visit from the Gardaí warning them about it. It didn't rule out anything and, as Ed liked to say, an absence of evidence was not evidence of absence. Our theory that this was somehow the connection between the victims could remain alive.

Ed found two candidates to support my vague memory about the visit to our house. There had been equipment stolen from a farm in Monkstown, and electronics and cash taken from a house on Monastery Road on the outskirts of Passage West itself. Both of these incidents had occurred within six weeks of my family's murders. The records kept by the investigating Gardaí were incomplete but one of the detectives involved was still an active member, and he told Ed he had no recollection of any house calls in relation to these events except for the homes, again, actually neighbouring the targets. It wasn't much, but we had to take what we could get. When I asked Ed if there could've been some home safety initiative where members of the Gardaí, separate to official investigations, called to houses in an effort to prevent them falling victim to property crime, he laughed at me. There was no scenario, at any time or in any place, where the Gardaí would have had the resources to do that.

We didn't need to go searching for burglaries in Westpark or its surrounds, as Ed himself had investigated a spate of them, albeit before the residents arrived. He could find no reports of any subsequent incidents. We couldn't, of course, ask Marie or Martin if they'd had any visits from a guard.

There were five Nothing Man targets in all. In two of them, we had visits prior to the attacks from a lone guard warning of a recent burglary in the area – but one of these was based on my own very vague memory of a man at the door who made my mother call my father and grandmother by their first names. In four of them, we could confirm that burglaries had taken place nearby, prior to the attacks – but burglary was a fairly common crime and if we picked five Cork homes at random at any date in time, we would probably find similar incidents to connect to *them*.

If this really was the connection between the Nothing Man's victims, if this was the key that would unlock the mystery of why *us*, it was still just a blurry shape in the distance.

But we still had Linda O'Neill in Fermoy to check out.

We had only recently made contact with Linda O'Neill after months of unanswered calls, emails and even a handwritten letter sent to her place of work. Shortly before Ed and I met Tommy at Dublin Airport, I had given up on her and resigned myself to completing the chapter about her attack with the materials I had, namely Garda reports and media interviews she'd given at the time. Then Ed tried in an official capacity and finally got her on the phone, but she only stayed on it long enough to tell him – and me – that she had no interest in being involved in this book. It wouldn't be fair to contact her again, now, to ask if she'd ever had a visit from a guard at the house in Fermoy, and honestly even if that didn't present a moral problem for me, I just couldn't stomach another six months of trying to track her down. Instead, Ed went to someone else who had spent a lot of time at the house in the weeks leading up to the attack and who was happy to talk to us: Johnnie Murphy, the foreman.

Johnnie was still in the construction business, although he was now the head of his own firm and was, as he so poetically put it, no longer freezing his balls off on building sites but burning them on space heaters in Portakabins. And as soon as Ed asked, 'Do you remember any Garda calling to the O'Neills' house before the attack?' Johnnie said, 'Yeah, I do – that little prick.'

He didn't know the exact date of the visit, but he thought it wasn't long after he and his team had started on site. That would've made it early March 2001, around the time the O'Neills' planning application had been approved. It had been late in the day, maybe five or six o'clock, and Johnnie was in the utility room on the ground floor, off the kitchen. He was using it as a make-shift office. That evening he was staying late to sort some paperwork and was the only person left on site. Linda and Conor were gone to Cork to collect some bathroom fixtures. When he heard a noise in the kitchen he thought it was them, back earlier than expected. But when he went to investigate, Johnnie found himself face to face with a uniformed guard.

Johnnie had lived in Fermoy all his life and was a regular face at committee meetings, on the sidelines at GAA games and holding fort in the local pubs. He knew the guards who worked out of Fermoy station just from seeing them around and running into them at these same places. But he didn't recognise this guard and didn't like the fact that he'd found the man inside the house. When he flashed his badge, Johnnie made a point of studying it and committing the name on the identification to memory: Garda Ronan Donoghue. He thought the ID looked a bit fishy but he'd never actually seen one up close and didn't know what they were supposed to look like, and the badge sitting next to it in the guard's little flip-up wallet seemed legit. Johnnie had had a bit of trouble with the guards when he was a teen, a time in his life he deeply regretted, and as an adult his default setting with them was deferential, obedient and polite.

'What can I do for you?' Johnnie had asked.

Donoghue said there'd been a burglary in the area. He was looking to speak with the owners about securing their property, especially while building work was going on and 'all sorts of people' would be coming and going. Case in point: he'd just been able to walk right into the house through the open front door. (Johnnie didn't think he'd left the door open but he wasn't sure, so he said nothing.) Donoghue asked about the owners – who they were, whether they were new to the area, if they had kids, whether or not they were living there while the work went on.

Johnnie felt like Donoghue was criticising him, that he was intimating that Johnnie and his team were doing a shoddy job of securing the site, and he didn't like it – especially when the man was clearly new around town and Johnnie was a permanent fixture in it. The more Donoghue talked, the more annoyed Johnnie became. But he had to hold it in. He felt he couldn't say anything antagonistic. By the time Donoghue left, steam was practically coming out of Johnnie's ears. *Who the hell did this prick think he was, eh? Who did he think he was speaking to? The fucking cheek of him.*

Johnnie doesn't think he ever mentioned this visit to Linda or Conor, but he did to Gerard Byrne, a friend of his who taught at the primary school. Byrne said he thought Johnnie was paranoid and totally overreacting. But he also said that as far as he knew – and he tended to be a man who knew such things – there was no Garda Donoghue working out of Fermoy station.

Johnnie did nothing with this information. He didn't call the station to check. He didn't report that someone was impersonating a member of An Garda Síochána. He didn't mention the visit to anyone other than Gerard Byrne – even *after* Linda was attacked when, in my opinion, the visit could only have taken on a greater and worryingly sinister significance. Johnnie just forgot about it. He told us he didn't think he'd ever even thought of it again until Ed called and asked him specifically if such a thing had happened.

I desperately wish I could rewind the clock and set off alarm bells at the point in this story, when someone claiming to be Garda Ronan Donoghue leaves the house in Fermoy while Johnnie Murphy stands in the doorway and watches him go. Forget alarm bells – let's have air-raid sirens. Because that's the moment. That's the point at which two paths diverged in a wood and had we chased him down the other one, my family would still be alive.

But I am armed with the knowledge of what's to come. I know that someone will enter the O'Neills' house to move things, to interfere with things, and to take something – Linda's diary – away. I know that Linda will suffer a heinous attack in her own home that will almost kill her. I know that in a few months' time Ed will link that case to four others, including the murder of my own family members, and that nearly two decades after that, he and I will find another connection that involves a man pretending to be a guard.

But Johnnie didn't know any of that. He had an annoying five-minute conversation one day and complained about it to a friend who mentioned that he didn't think there was a guard by that name in the local station. So what? It was a minor detail in an unimportant event on an unremarkable day, and it soon fell straight out of Johnnie's mind.

You open your door one evening to find a uniformed police officer standing outside. Nothing's wrong, don't worry. This is just a courtesy call. There's been a burglary in the area and they're just letting you know so your home isn't next. Lock your doors and windows. Keep valuables out of view. Think about installing an alarm. You chat for a few minutes. You might mention the door at the back that doesn't lock. Or that fact that you live here alone. Or that the couple who owns this construction site is living here while the work goes on – or, well, one of them is, because her husband is going back to San Francisco for a few weeks next week. Maybe you don't reveal any information, but while you speak he's still gathering it. The integrity of the front-door lock. The layout of the ground floor. Whether or not he likes the look of you. If he'd like to do to you what he's already done to the others.

That's how he was choosing them, we felt sure. Donning a Garda uniform and doing door-to-door calls in the aftermath of a real burglary. But was he really a guard?

Neither Tom nor Johnnie could remember seeing a Garda car, and we thought it would be relatively easy to convince a member of the public that you were wearing a Garda uniform when in actual fact you were wearing an approximation of one. He could've also easily got hold of a real uniform – if he was prepared to murder innocent people, he was probably willing to steal items of clothing too. Moreover this behaviour would have been an incredible risk for a serving member to take, when one phone call to the local station would've been all it took to bring his little rogue scouting missions crashing down.

Ed never said this to me, but I felt he had another objection to the theory that our Ghost Garda was the real deal: he thought there was no way a Garda could do this. Would the kind of man who'd rape Linda O'Neill and then leave her for dead also want to work in the force that protected civilians from men like him? Ed couldn't bring himself to believe the answer was yes.

I have to admit that I found it easier. A real guard would do a much better job of acting like one. He would have access to reports and operational details, so he'd know where there'd been a residential burglary and when his colleagues would be out officially knocking on doors. He'd also be familiar with investigative methods and know the importance of leaving no physical evidence behind him. And he'd already have a real uniform and badge.

We arranged for a sketch artist to meet with Johnnie Murphy so we could get some picture of 'Garda' Donoghue, but Johnnie's memory of the man's face wasn't as detailed as his memory of their conversation. He did, however, remember a lot about the man's uniform. He mentioned epaulettes with numbers sewn on and, although he didn't remember what they were, he could recall that one of them was askew, hanging – literally – by a thread.

This made Ed think that even if the man wasn't the real deal, the uniform was. Numbers coming loose was a common problem that Ed himself had suffered when he was in uniform, keeping a supply of paperclips on him just in case. (They were the best way to reattach them in a hurry.) Rank-and-file Gardaí have to report to superiors if any issued items go missing or get misplaced, but looking for such a thing nearly two decades later would be a fool's errand. However, spit-balling about this scenario made Ed think of another kind of missing property report: the evidentiary kind.

It wasn't common, but sometimes things went missing between crime scenes and the evidence room. Money and drugs, mostly. Corruption plagued the force just as it did every other area of society. If it was noticed, it took a brave and principled member to report it, but it did happen. Ed went to his superintendent, Kevin Taylor – who had already helped us so much – and, through him, managed to get a look at such reports for Cork county for the twelve months before the Nothing Man's first attack. Taylor wanted the same thing Ed and I did: to finally solve this case.

In October 1999, a handgun, one of thirteen weapons seized in a raid in Ringaskiddy, disappeared somewhere between the farmhouse in which it was found and the evidence room to which it should've been delivered. There was no way of knowing if that gun was the same one the Nothing Man had used, but the model didn't clash with the description of the gun as provided by Linda O'Neill. Had the Nothing Man got a gun by stealing it from a crime scene? If he had, then we had our answer: he *was* a real guard. But investigating every member of An Garda Síochána who theoretically had access to that gun nearly two decades ago was a step too far for Ed, if not morally or logistically then certainly legally and procedurally, when we had no evidence that the missing gun and the gun used at the O'Neills' house were one and the same.

And just like that, we found ourselves at another dead end.

What else could we do? Put a call out asking people if twenty years ago they'd had a five-minute visit from a uniformed guard? Even if anyone remembered that they had, we'd need a team of people not only to get the word out there, but also to effectively collect and deal with the responses.

I couldn't quite believe it – I refused to, at first – but after the dust had settled on this heady rush of new information, Ed and I were stuck once again. We had run our Ghost Garda lead down and it had led us absolutely nowhere.

Burglary. After nearly twenty years, we thought we finally had the password that would unlock the entire Nothing Man case.

But we didn't.

– 11 –

The Nothing Man

Dr Nell Weir is associate professor of forensic psychology at Trinity College Dublin. She is in her mid-forties and was born in Port Talbot, Wales. If you visit her profile page on the university website, you will not find the kind of professional headshot her colleagues have all opted for. Instead, Dr Weir has chosen what looks like a holiday snap, taken outside the Lizzie Borden House in Fall River, Massachusetts, where the bodies of Borden's father and stepmother were found covered in axe wounds in 1892. Today it is both a macabre tourist attraction and a thriving bed and breakfast. It's only a tiny glint of light in the photograph, but Dr Weir is wearing one of her favourite accessories on her coat's lapel: a small pin in the shape of a pair of pursed, full lips that says, *Let's talk about serial killers*. That's what Dr Weir does on a freshman module called 'Ordinary Monsters: Inside the Mind of the Serial Murderer'. The course is so popular that she teaches it twice a year to keep up with demand and, even then, enrolment has to be decided by a lottery of student numbers to keep things fair. 'It is surely the only class on campus,' Dr Weir told me via email, 'where we have to station someone outside to stop students from sneaking *in*.'

On a Tuesday morning in January 2017, I sat in on the introductory lecture. It was held in a theatre that seated at least a hundred people, but by the time I arrived – early, I thought, a good ten minutes before Dr Weir was due to – it was already standing room only. I hovered by the doors until a gaggle of teenage girls took pity on me and squeezed up so I could fit on the end of their bench. The room was overheated and I felt slightly sick with nerves, although Dr Weir had assured me the next forty-five minutes would be free from gory details and that she wouldn't be talking about the Nothing Man.

The girls beside me were trading the names of their favourite true-crime podcasts ('That's the one about the kids who went missing. It's so good, oh my God, I was *obsessed!*') when Dr Weir arrived and descended the central stairs to the front of the room. When she turned on the projection screen, we were treated to an extreme close-up of Anthony Hopkins in his most famous role, as the food and wine and human flesh connoisseur, Hannibal Lecter.

Dr Weir took her place behind the lectern and smiled at us. She didn't have to wait for everyone to quieten down; that had happened automatically when she'd entered the room. The air buzzed with giddy anticipation.

Before she began the lecture proper, Dr Weir announced, she wanted to gauge our existing knowledge. She asked anyone who knew the name of a serial killer to raise their hand and keep it up until she called on them, or until someone else she'd called on said the same name first.

Almost everyone in the room put up a hand and Dr Weir started pointing at random.

Ireland's own Will Hurley, aka the Canal Killer, was back in the news, so it was unsurprising that his was the first name said aloud. Then came all the usual American and British suspects. Ted Bundy.

Jeffrey Dahmer. John Wayne Gacy. Ed Gein. Fred West. Peter Sutcliffe. Harold Shipman.

'The Nothing Man,' one student said, 'but we don't know who is he yet,' and I silently thanked her for that *yet*.

After those names, barely half the raised hands were still up. Then came the ones whose nicknames were better known than their given ones. Gary Ridgway aka the Green River Killer. Richard Ramirez aka the Night Stalker. Dennis Rader aka BTK. Ted Kaczynski aka the Unabomber.

Now, only three hands remained. When Dr Weir called on them, she got Arthur Leigh Allen, suspected of being the Zodiac Killer; Andrew Cunanan, the man who shot and killed Gianni Versace; and Aileen Wuornos, executed in 2002 for the murders of six men and famously played by Charlize Theron in the movie *Monster*.

'Well,' Dr Weir said, 'I'm very impressed. Give yourselves a round of applause.' The students were happy to oblige. 'Now let's do the same thing again, but *this* time, I'm looking for names of their victims.'

Silence – and not a single hand.

'Even just a first name,' Dr Weir said.

The students shifted in their seats. Some of them turned to their neighbour to exchange nervous smiles. There were a few throat-clears and coughs.

'Anyone?'

Dr Weir waited them out and, eventually, the student who'd named Andrew Cunanan tried to offer her Versace, but Dr Weir said that didn't count because he'd already mentioned it and Versace was famous for other things. A girl in the front row put up her hand and said the name Caroline Ranch, uncertainly, phrasing it as more of a question. *Caroline*

Ranch …? Dr Weir told her good try, but she was thinking of Carol DaRonch who had had a miraculous escape from Bundy's car and later testified against him at trial. Another student thought the Canal Killer's victims might have included a 'Paula Something' (they didn't), while another, who had recently watched David Fincher's *Zodiac*, said the name 'Paul Avery'. That was the crime reporter at the *San Francisco Chronicle* played by Robert Downey Jnr in the movie and definitely *not* a victim of the Zodiac.

'And that,' Dr Weir said, 'is the problem.'

Dr Weir knows exactly what she's doing with her Lizzie Borden house picture and her funky lapel pins. (Others in her collection include *Hey! Ted Bundy isn't hot!* and *Talk true crime to me*.) She puts things like *Psycho*, *The Stranger Beside Me* and *The Silence of the Lambs* on the module reading list for a reason. They reel the students in. Once Dr Weir has them in her class, she can proceed to tell them the truth: that everything they think they know about serial killers is wrong.

'It's fine to be fascinated by serial killers,' she tells me in her office after the lecture. 'I am myself, obviously. They *are* fascinating because even though they look just like the rest of us, they do things the rest of us would never, ever do. But they are *not* especially intelligent. They *don't* outsmart authorities. You know David Berkowitz? Son of Sam? They caught him because he got himself a parking ticket at the scene of one of his crimes. They are boring, ordinary, failures of men – not always men, of course, but predominately – who can't even manage to live, love and process their feelings in a world where the rest of us have all managed to master it by the time we're in our teens. These are no dark magicians. They have no special skills. People seem to forget that we know their names because *they got caught*. In fact, the only remarkable thing about them is what they took from the world: their victims. It's *their* names we should know.'

I met with Dr Weir primarily to try to get an answer to one of my most burning questions: *why did the Nothing Man stop?* How had he been able to? Or was it more likely he hadn't stopped at all but instead had moved or changed his methods or died? After her lecture, I was beginning to suspect that the answer wouldn't be the one I was expecting – and I was right. When I finally asked my question after more than an hour in her company, Dr Weir shrugged her shoulders, held up her hands and said, 'The boring truth is that he probably just stopped.'

She told me about a symposium the FBI held back in August 2005, which brought together more than a hundred experts in the field of serial killings. Catching serial killers presents a special kind of challenge for law enforcement but, again, probably not for the reasons you might think. Serial killings are exceptionally rare, accounting for less than one per cent of all homicides in any given year, but because of the public's endless fascination with them, they draw the most publicity. A hugely disproportionate amount of it, which thrusts investigations into the spotlight from the get-go, which in turn amps up the pressure on police to make progress, fast.

But because serial killings are so rare, there's relatively little scientific data available about them. The general public get their serial killer info from Hollywood movies, Netflix and the crime section of their local bookshop, and that's okay, because the general public are only looking for entertainment. The problem is that, consciously or unconsciously, rank-and-file police officers get *their* serial killer info from the same place – and that's *not* okay because they're looking for the actual perpetrators. This FBI Serial Killing Symposium was an attempt to correct some of the most pervasive myths and misconceptions surrounding serial killers and equip law enforcement with the actual facts.

Serial Murder: Multi-Disciplinary Perspectives for Investigators, the 2008 report on the symposium, lists the most common misconceptions about serial killers:

– Serial killers are all dysfunctional loners.

– Serial killers are all white males.

– All serial killers travel and operate interstate.

– All serial killers are insane or are evil geniuses.

– Serial killers cannot stop killing.

In fact, serial killers are often married with families, have jobs and are involved in their community. The racial diversification of serial killers tends to match that of the population in which they operate. The vast majority commit their crimes in a defined geographic area or 'comfort zone'. These offenders may suffer from debilitating mental conditions or personality disorders, but they are not insane, and as a group they display the same range of intelligence as the general population. Serial killers often stop killing long before capture due to changes in their lives that reduce triggering conditions such as stress – a new, better marriage, for instance – or because they find a substitute in another activity. Dennis Rader, for example, also known as BTK (Bind, Torture, Kill), murdered ten people between 1974 and 1991 but wasn't captured until 2005. He was a married father of two, had served in the military, had a job in local government and was a leader at his church.

Another possibility, Dr Weir said, is that serial killers stop because they simply 'age out'. Unlike other sexually motivated crimes such as paedophilia, it is exceptionally rare for a sexual homicide to be committed by someone over the age of fifty. Perhaps when these killers reach their half-century, they find testosterone levels have depleted to such an extent that their drive to kill just fades away, if not dissipates entirely.

'When we talk about serial killers stopping,' Dr Weir told me, 'the key thing to remember is that we are almost never talking about compulsive acts. Some of what Hollywood tells us about these offenders is actually correct. They do plan and prepare. They wait until they have the opportunity and then they make a choice to commit the act. They're not walking about gripped by some overwhelming compulsion to kill, like some kind of crazed, blood-thirsty animal. They're not out of control. They don't *have* to do it, they *want* to. There's a big difference between drive and compulsion. So as they get older, and tired and slower, it's entirely plausible that they just stop wanting to kill people. In the same way I once used to want to party all night but now that I'm five minutes from fifty, I'm desperate to be in bed by ten. It's not sexy, it's not Hollywood and it's not very dramatic – but it's almost certainly the truth.'

I asked Dr Weir what she thought the Nothing Man might be like, based on what she knew of his crimes.

'God,' she said, 'don't even get me started on so-called' – she made air quotes with her fingers – '*profiling*. But I will say this: he'll be boring. Boring and ordinary and unremarkable. He may have friends, but not many who really like him. His marriage won't be great. He won't be really good at anything and he'll probably have some mind-numbing, unfulfilling job. As in, he won't be curing cancer. Essentially, except for the fact that he's raped and murdered people, he won't be much of anything at all. The Nothing Man is an exceptionally apt name for a serial killer, Eve. When you find him, you'll probably be shocked at just how much of *nothing* he really is.'

When we think back on our lives, we tend to shape our memories into neat, linear narratives with beginnings, middles and ends. As Joan Didion wrote, we tell ourselves stories in order to live. That's what I'm supposed to be doing here: telling my story so that I can live, so that I can have more of a life in the future than I have had in the past. Starting at the beginning, tying everything up neatly at the end.

But when you are trying to find a killer and a publisher is waiting for you to deliver the manuscript of your book and you *haven't* found him (yet), you have no choice but to put 'THE END' in an arbitrary place of your choosing. I'm going to put it here. But this isn't the end. Our search goes on. I'm typing these words at my desk while four feet away, a very tired Ed rubs his eyes and squints at the screen of his laptop. It's almost midnight but I know neither of us will be quitting anytime soon.

For legal reasons, I cannot include everything we discovered about the Nothing Man in the course of our research into this book but know this: there are still several leads that Ed and I are chasing. These threads are small and delicate, filaments really. We're not sure where they will take us but we're both hopeful that it will be closer to the truth. One lead in particular is looking very promising.

Books must be finished long before they get stacked on a shelf and, perhaps, by the time this one is finally in print, the Nothing Man's name will already be known. Perhaps you, dear reader, even know what he looks like. Maybe you've already seen his face on the news. Did you get to watch as he was led out of this world and into some dingy, dark cell with *his* wrists and ankles bound? Was I there? Did I get to watch too? I hope so. It's the hope that sustains me. It's what has kept me going all these long months and the painful, lonely years that led up to them. The ending – the real ending – feels tantalisingly close, closer than it ever did before.

But just in case we haven't found him yet, I must ask of you a favour: help us make this ending the beginning. We have presented as much as we can of what we know about the Nothing Man. This includes almost everything from the original investigation and the fruits of our research over the past couple of years. This, as my editor promised, is an era of armchair sleuths and amateur detectives. I know because I have occasionally lurked in the forums and Facebook groups where they gather. So now, I hand the baton over to you. Please, help us find him.

Someone must know who the Nothing Man is. Perhaps you recognised the sketch back then, or now, or you've long held suspicions about where the person you live with went on the nights of the crimes. Maybe you just have a feeling. Please, think of us, the victims' families. Think of your own. Please pick up the phone and call the Gardaí. They have a confidential tip-line which can be reached on 1800-666-111. There is never a wrong time to do the right thing.

People ask me how I am now. By *now* they mean, post 'The Girl Who', post coming out as a survivor of the Nothing Man, post abandoning all attempts to have a normal life and instead dedicating my time and resources to finding the man who took my family from me. It's difficult to answer because I feel sure that how things are now is not how they will be for much longer. I'm hopeful that when this book comes out, if not before, we will capture this faceless killer, and he will be charged with his crimes and locked away. That might give me a chance at something resembling closure.

Until then, I can only continue to do what I've done all this time, which is to do my best to stay afloat. Keep moving forward. I don't stop to take stock. I fear doing that. My feelings constantly move and shift and tumble, like the contents of the drum of a washing machine in motion. It's hard to pin them down and separate one pain from the other but I know that one day, that drum *will* finally still. So, ask me again later. Ask me when we get him. I'm convinced we won't have long to wait.

Finally, we may not have *his* name yet, but we do know these: Alice O'Sullivan. Christine Kiernan. Linda O'Neill. Marie Meara. Martin Connolly.

My father, Ross, and my mother, Deirdre.

My little sister, Anna.

Remember them, please.

Jim was so engulfed in rage that he was only dimly aware of his actions. He heard the *thunk* of something hitting the wall of the living room and the smashing of glass that followed it, but it sounded like it was coming from far away. He didn't realise he'd gone outside until he felt the sharp shock of night-time cold. He didn't know why he was going into the shed until he was lifting the old Goblin hoover out of the tool cabinet, ripping off its cover and pulling out the bag inside.

It had a little bulge to it and felt heavy. He felt for the slit he'd made in its back. Pushed his hand in and touched soft cloth and then, through it, the reassuring hardness of something steel.

Jim sank to the floor, knelt next to the hoover.

He took out the items one by one and laid them gently on the stone floor of the shed in a neat row.

Mask.

Gloves.

Gun.

The knife he'd discarded long ago, off the back of a passenger ferry that Noreen, Katie and him had taken to France on their first – and last – foreign holiday.

But no matter. He'd do Eve Black with his bare hands and enjoy every single second of it.

That fucking *bitch*. He should've killed her when he had the chance.

By the time the sun came up again, he would have.

He wouldn't need the rope; she wasn't going to live that long. His old head torch had been thrown out more than a decade ago, but he had a newer one in the tool cabinet somewhere. Jim started rooting—

It's there.

He stopped.

His name ... It's there.

Eve had said his name was in the book.

But he'd read to the end and hadn't come across any mention of Jim Doyle or, come to think of it, Eve visiting Togher Garda Station.

He went back out into the night and crossed the garden to the patio door. The book was splayed open, spine-up, on the floor behind the TV. The dust jacket had ripped.

There was glass and spilt whiskey all over the place but cleaning it up could wait. One problem at a time.

Jim picked up *The Nothing Man* and flipped to the end to check if he'd missed something.

But all that came after the last chapter were the acknowledgements.

Acknowledgements

It would not have been possible for me to write this book without Ed Healy, Jonathan Eglin, Bernadette O'Brien and the entire team at Iveagh Press. For being so giving of their time and assistance, thank you to Maggie Barry, Gerard Byrne, Brendan Byrne, Joan Connor, Aisling Feeney, Peter Fine, Elaine Grady, Graham Harris, Patricia Kearns, Jean Long, Johnnie Murphy, Denis Philips, Kevin Prendergast, Geraldine Roche, Kevin Taylor, David Walsh and Dr Nell Weir. Thanks also to Melisa Broadbent, Rae Broughton, Andy Carter, Kevin G. Conroy, Kent Corlain, Anne Marie Gleeson, Cathy Hanson, Iain Harris, Holger Hasse, Catherine Ryan Howard, Sheelagh Kelly, Christ McDonald, Henrietta McKervey, Henry Molnar, Renee Nash, Marie O'Halloran, Johanna Pérez Vásquez, Sara Pickering, Frances Quinn, Sasha Reeds, Laura J. Roach, J. H. Siess, Sandie Smith, Nikki Telling, Oliver Troy, Heather Webb, Judith Whelan, Valerie Whitford and Crystal Williams. I am especially thankful for the generosity of An Garda Síochána. To Tommy O'Sullivan, Nancy Kerr, Breffany and Elizabeth Kieran, and Linda O'Neill: I can't thank you enough.

His name wasn't there.

Jim flipped to the back, where there was an index. He ran a finger down the columns of tiny text, checking for every possibility. He looked under D, for his last name. J, for his first. G, where he found *Gardaí* and *An Gardaí Síochána, members of*.

His name wasn't there.

He tried to recall exactly what Eve had said. *I'll tell her that her husband helped with the book. To keep an eye out for his name. It's there.*

Why would she say that if it wasn't true?

Jim flipped back through the book, intending to go to the beginning of the bit where Eve commenced her research, and move forward while scanning each page quickly just to double-check he hadn't missed his name. But he went too far, all the way back to the start, opening it at its title page.

The Nothing Man.

His other name.

The one he hadn't chosen.

The one no one knew was his.

No one except for Eve Black. She'd found out somehow. She hadn't put it in the book and she hadn't, apparently, reported him to the Gardaí, but she wanted him to know that she knew it.

Why? Was she trying to communicate something to him? Was she letting him know that actually she *did* remember everything from that night, that she did—

'Have you finished it?'

Noreen was standing by the door, holding a copy of *The Nothing Man* in her hand.

Another one.

Jim stared her, confused.

'I bought it,' she said. 'Tonight. I got Katie's copy signed and then I bought another one on the way out.' She lifted the book, looked at the cover. 'I haven't read it all, but I've read as much as I can. I had to skip the … The descriptions.'

'What are you doing up, Nor?' Jim took a step forward in an attempt to hide the broken glass from her view. 'I thought you weren't feeling well.'

'I'm not.'

'Then why—'

'*Katie* is going to read this, Jim. Katie will—' Whatever was supposed to come after that got swallowed by a sob.

Tears started to roll down Noreen's cheeks.

'I'll talk to her,' Jim said. 'Tell her it's unsuitable. She'll listen to—'

Noreen screamed.

The sound was high-pitched, raw and primal. And excruciatingly loud.

For a moment Jim could only blink at her, stunned that such a noise had come out of her mouth. He'd never heard her make anything like it before.

Then he wondered if she was having some kind of mental breakdown.

'Noreen—' he started.

But now she was screaming and coming towards him, *at* him, and then the book in her hand was in the air, coming down—

She was attacking him with the book.

Hitting him with it. Repeatedly. Hard. On the chest and against the sides of his head and his forearms once he'd lifted them up to try to fend off the blows. While continually screaming and sobbing.

No, not screaming.

Not *just* screaming.

After enough repetitions, Jim could make out the words.

'How? *Why*? How could you *do* this to us? To *Katie*? To *me*?'

Jim got hold of the book and threw it across the room.

Then he did the same to Noreen.

Silence. Finally. He closed his eyes.

He opened them again when she started whimpering.

Noreen was slumped on the floor against the opposite wall, gingerly touching a hand to the back of her head. When she pulled it away, there was a little bright red on her fingertips.

'Noreen,' Jim said evenly, 'I don't know what's got into you, but you need to get a hold of yourself. It's four in the morning. The neighbours will hear.'

'I won't let you do this.' Her breathing was laboured but otherwise she sounded eerily calm. 'I won't let you ruin Katie's life. I won't let her find out what her father is.'

'What the hell are you on about?'

He had no idea.

Because Noreen couldn't know. It wasn't possible.

'I was pregnant with Katie.' She winced as she slowly pulled herself up on to her knees. 'I woke up in the middle of the night, in pain ... I thought something was wrong. I rang the station to tell you, but they said you were off-duty. And when you came home you were ... You were different somehow. Excited about something, I thought. Or especially pleased with yourself. And you weren't wearing your uniform. But you told me you *had* been at work.' Noreen smiled weakly. 'I thought you were just having an affair.'

Jim didn't know where she was going with this, but he didn't like it.

'Have you been drinking, Nor? Is that what this is?'

'There was another morning, when you came home from work wearing your own clothes, and I wondered if it had happened again. Whatever *it* was. As soon as you got into the shower I rang the station. Whoever answered didn't know my voice. I said I was trying to get in touch with a Garda I'd spoken to the night before, and that I thought his name might be Jim something. Jim Doyle? "Can't be him," she said. "He was off."'

'Stop this,' Jim said. 'You're only making a fool of yourself.'

'I was wondering what the hell I was going to do when I saw the news.' Noreen wasn't looking at him any more. Her gaze was directed at the floor by his feet. 'That family, in Passage West. Four dead, they thought at first. And that made me think about the other time, about how I hadn't had a chance to ask you where you'd been, to work up the courage to confront you, because you'd got a call about the murder in the house on the Maryborough Road – what was it? Westpark? That young couple. The man trapped under his car, his wife dead upstairs. It was all hands on deck and you had to go.' She paused. 'And then all the stuff about the Nothing Man came out, and that sketch was everywhere, and you were suddenly obsessed with your weight, doing all this exercise, changing how you looked … But it was the eyes, Jim.' Noreen lifted her head and looked into them now. 'I knew those eyes. I'd know them anywhere.' She struggled into a standing position, swaying slightly before leaning back against the wall for support. 'I didn't want to believe it, but I knew in my heart that it was true. I was the wife of a Garda, I knew how it would go if I tried to report you. All your buddies down the station, they'd take your word over mine. I wouldn't even blame them. Who'd believe the man the Gardaí were looking for was hiding among them? And I knew what you'd do to me afterwards. So …' Noreen sighed resignedly. 'I'd nowhere else to go and Katie was nearly here, her arrival was days away. I had only one option: to stay and say nothing. And to protect her. To protect my daughter.'

'*Our* daughter,' Jim corrected.

While Noreen droned on, he'd been considering his options. All she had right now was a blunt-force injury to the back of her head that had happened when she'd impacted the wall. She might have a bit of bruising on her upper arms from where he'd grabbed her but then again she might not. He could pull her by the hair to the top of the stairs and push her down. But the screaming. What if the neighbours had heard it? How would he explain that away?

And what if she survived the fall?

Noreen started shaking her head, as if she could read his thoughts.

'There's a letter,' she said. 'With a solicitor. If anything happens to me, he'll make sure Katie gets it. Then she'll know the truth. I don't want that to happen. And I don't think *you* want it to either.'

She straightened up, moved away from the wall, tested her balance.

'I prayed for you to die, Jim. Every morning and every night. May God forgive me, but I did. But here we are, all these years later, and no such luck. And now' – she pointed at the books, both copies of which were lying discarded on the floor – 'it's all in there, in that bloody *book*, and that book is out there in the world, all over the place, and it's only a matter of time before there's a knock on our door and I can't …' She took a deep breath. 'I can't protect Katie any more, Jim. Only you can. So I'm asking you to. I'm asking you to protect her.'

Noreen took one wobbly step forward, then another one after that. Towards the hall.

Jim could only stare after her.

'It's time for you to end this,' she said, pausing at the door. 'Do what needs to be done. Tomorrow night. No later. If anyone comes asking, I'll swear you were here, with me, all night. But' – she turned to jab a finger in his direction – 'that's *it*, Jim. That *will* be the end. We won't speak of it and you will *never* do this again. Or I'll be telling Katie about you myself. Do you understand?'

After a beat, Jim nodded.

'Good.' Noreen disappeared into the hall. 'I'm going back to bed.' Jim could hear her slippered feet shuffling on the floor out there, then her calling to him as she started up the stairs. 'Clean up that glass before someone gets hurt.'

Friday mornings were the busiest at Centrepoint. Normally Jim liked them because they were his last shift of the week and the hours passed quickly, but today it was taking everything he had just to look like a functioning human being. He'd forgotten to set an alarm and so had to skip his shower and shave, and he'd only realised after he'd got to the Centre that he was wearing yesterday's sweat-stained shirt. A dull ache was gathering at his temples.

Because Noreen knew.

Had known, all this time.

No matter how many times Jim replayed the events of last night, he couldn't quite believe that they had happened.

Beep-beep.

The noise brought Jim back to now, to the display of newspapers and magazines by the start of Grocery. His radio. He pulled it from his belt and pressed the TALK button.

'Go.'

'Jim, come see me. I'm upstairs.'

Steve.

'Can it wait? I was just about to—'

'I can see you on the cameras, Jimbo. You're not busy. Get up here. *Now.*'

Jim lifted his chin and glared for a long moment into the fish-eye lens on the ceiling a few feet in front of him. Then he set off for the STAFF ONLY doors at the back of the frozen food section, behind which some metal stairs led him to the door of Steve's office.

Steve was sitting at his desk eating a breakfast roll. The crumb-filled paper bag it had come in was ripped open and resting on his laptop's keys. The man's face was smeared with brown sauce and a tiny piece of what might be fried egg-white was clinging to his lower lip. The room smelled of grease and stale coffee.

Bile rose in Jim's throat and for a moment he thought he might gag.

The dull ache at his temples was ramping up to a thumping pulse.

'Jim,' Steve said through a mouth full of masticated meat. 'Have a seat.'

On the wall to Jim's right was a bank of TV monitors showing various black-and-white views of the supermarket. He searched for the camera feed that Steve had been watching him on. The view was so zoomed-in that Jim could read the newspaper headlines.

He sat on one of two empty seats in front of the desk. Steve set down his half-eaten roll and leaned back, looked at Jim. He smiled. His lips were shiny with grease.

Whatever he was about to say, he was looking forward to saying it.

'We have to let you go, Jim.'

Steve paused, apparently waiting for a reaction.

Jim refused to give him one.

'We had a complaint,' he continued. 'From a customer. Yesterday afternoon. She said that, twice now, you've been staring at her as she moved around the store. *Leering* at her is how she put it. I've checked the cameras, Jim. Seems to me like she's telling the truth. You've already had a warning for insubordination, and another for that thing with the guy you thought had stolen the beer who tried *repeatedly* to show you his receipt. We have a three-strike rule. As you know. You leave me no choice but—'

One fluid motion.

A charge.

Jim got up and grabbed what was left of the breakfast roll and leaned over the desk and gripped the back of Steve's neck with one hand and pushed the roll into his mouth with the other.

Smashed it against his teeth.

Forced it in, deeper and deeper, until the man started to cough and splutter and choke.

Jim stopped and stood back to watch as Steve rose from his chair and bent forward, over the desk. He clawed at his throat. His eyes were wide and bulging. His mouth was open but only a wet, wheezing sound was coming out of it. His face was rapidly turning red. The man couldn't breathe.

Jim did nothing for ten, fifteen seconds.

Then he calmly went to the other side of the desk, stood behind Steve's back and thumped him hard five times.

Reached around to the man's front, pressed a fist just above his navel and knocked it in and upwards with his other hand. Steve immediately sprayed bits of bread, sausage and egg out of his mouth and across the desktop. He fell forward, over the desk, coughing and spluttering and gasping for breath.

'You should be more careful,' Jim said.

Steve turned to look at him, his eyes wide with fear. He took a step back, away from him. Then he took another.

He backed up all the way to the opposite wall, his eyes never leaving Jim's.

Jim smiled, satisfied.

Then he turned on his heel and left.

By the time Jim got back to the house, his headache was so bad it felt like his brain had turned into a hammer and was trying to knock its way out of his skull. He nosed the car slowly into the driveway, relieved he'd managed to get it home without incident despite the pulsing pain behind his eyes.

Derek was in the driveway next door, unlocking his car. Karen had just stepped out of the house carrying the geriatric shit machine awkwardly in her arms. The dog was whining loudly, as if in pain.

Karen was also carrying a small, clear plastic bag. Jim couldn't say for sure at this distance, but it seemed to him as if there were a couple of dog biscuits inside.

She turned and saw Jim, sitting in the car looking at them.

He raised a hand in salute.

She glared at him murderously.

Jim smiled back. Karen could make all the faces she wanted. They'd never be able to prove it was him.

He waited for them to drive off before he went into the house.

He hadn't even withdrawn the key from the lock in the door when Noreen appeared in the hall, her face pinched in concern.

But was it concern? After last night, he couldn't be sure of anything any more.

Especially not anything to do with Noreen.

'What are you doing home?' she said. 'What's wrong?'

'I have a headache.'

Noreen peered at him as if evaluating the likely truth of this.

'You're exhausted,' she said then. 'Go on up to bed. I'll bring you some paracetamol. What you need is a good rest.'

On any other day, Jim might have argued with her. Even when she was right, that's what he liked to do. But he felt so horrible, the pain in his head so intense, he didn't say anything. He just trudged his way up the stairs and into their room.

He kicked off his shoes, drew the curtains and crawled into bed, pulling the blankets up over his head to shut out the light. But in the dark, the pain seemed to grow even stronger.

It was so bad now he couldn't think about anything else.

Noreen came into the room with a glass of water and two white pills. Jim didn't even pause to check what they were. He knocked them back and then lay down again, burrowing beneath the blankets.

He was so tired.

But he had so much to do.

He needed to plan for tonight.

To prepare.

As soon as the distant edges of the pain in his head began to dull, Jim slipped into a dreamless sleep.

Hours passed.

When he woke, it was getting dark outside. His headache was gone. He felt rested, refreshed, clear.

Ready.

The smell of cooking food was wafting up from downstairs.

When Jim got to the kitchen, he saw Noreen stirring something on the stove.

'Sit down,' she said. 'Eat.'

He did as he was told.

She served him a steaming plate of roast chicken and then sat in the seat opposite, at the other end of the kitchen table. There was nothing in front of her except for a small glass of water.

A full minute passed where the only sound was the noise of Jim eating.

Then Noreen said, 'I don't want to see you tonight, okay?'

Jim stopped, a forkful of chicken paused halfway to his mouth, and looked at her questioningly.

'When you're leaving,' she clarified. 'I don't want to see you when you're … When you're ready. When you're dressed.' She paused. 'I don't want to see *him*. Do you understand me? I don't want to … To meet him.'

Jim said nothing. He resumed eating.

He found a pair of black sweatpants, a black sweatshirt and a black hooded jacket in the wardrobe. Having double-checked they were free from logos or other identifying marks, he changed into them. He slipped his feet back into his black work boots and tied the laces. He set his mobile phone to silent and put it into the drawer of his bedside table. Then he went downstairs and slipped out the front door, around the side of the house and into the shed. It was nearly midnight.

The mask, gun and gloves were still sitting on the floor where he'd left them the night before. He stashed them in various pockets along with the other items that formed his kit. He crossed the garden and pressed his back against the rear wall of the house, just beside the patio doors. He stole a quick look inside the living room, being careful to remain out of sight.

Noreen was sitting on the couch. Her body was facing him but her head was turned away, towards the television.

He scanned the surrounding houses, checking their windows, making sure each one was either dark or had its curtains drawn. Satisfied, he took out the mask, put it on his head and pulled it down. He pulled on the gloves. He reached inside his jacket and withdrew the gun.

Then he slid open the patio door and slipped inside.

Noreen immediately turned towards the noise and let out an aborted scream when she saw him.

But she didn't move. She didn't run.

She stayed sitting on the couch, her body rigid, wide-eyed with fear.

'Please, Jim,' she said, her chin trembling. 'Please don't ...'

He turned to slide the door closed behind him and paused for a moment to admire his reflection in the glass: a tall, broad-shouldered figure dressed all in black. Covered in it, except for the slit in the mask that revealed his eyes.

It had always disguised his identity but now, in doing so, it also disguised his age. Unless you were close enough to see the wrinkles around his eyes and the white hairs in his eyebrows, no one would have any idea what age the man behind the mask was. They would only know that it was a man, stronger and taller and bigger than them, and that if they had seen such a sight before, it was in their nightmares.

The reflection of the living room behind him, a scene of warm domesticity, only seemed to heighten the effect. People were terrified by the idea of masked men appearing at the end of their beds in the dark, but surely seeing one moving silently around your fully lit living room was far more horrifying a prospect.

He turned back around to face Noreen.

He moved towards her.

'*Please*, Jim.' Her voice was a nervous whisper. 'I asked you not to do this. I said I didn't want to see. *Please.*'

He stood over her and waited until Noreen lifted her head and looked up into his face.

Into his eyes.

The only bit of Jim she could actually see.

He raised the gun and touched the cold barrel of it to the side of Noreen's face. Stroked her with it. Gently. A caress.

'*Please*, Jim.'

He traced her jawline with the butt of the gun, then pushed it into the fleshy part of her neck.

She was crying now.

'Think of Katie, Jim.'

He pushed harder.

'Please, Jim. Don't. I'm sorry.'

He leaned down until his mouth was level with her ear and whispered, 'Who's Jim?'

Not in his own voice, but in *his*.

The Nothing Man's.

Noreen's whole body began to shake.

It came back then, crashing over him in a ferocious wave. Soaking into his skin. Filling him.

Fuelling him.

The Nothing Man had returned.

And he was ready to end this once and for all.

He straightened up and stepped back. He slipped the gun inside his jacket. He pulled the mask up over his head, folded it up and put it away in a pocket. He pulled off his gloves and stowed them away too.

Noreen looked up at him, scared and uncertain.

'I'm doing this,' Jim said, 'because I was going to do it anyway. You're not my master. I don't take orders from you. Now or ever. Do *you* understand *me*?'

Noreen nodded.

'Good.' Jim moved to go. 'Don't wait up.'

He stuck to back roads and secondary routes, avoiding traffic cameras.

The house in Passage West wasn't in the village proper, but down a narrow lane that turned sharply off the main road before you got that far.

Jim drove past the turn.

Two hundred yards further down the road was a derelict pub called The Harbour Master. Fifty yards beyond it was a small, unlit lay-by. Jim pulled in there, turned the car around and headed back in the direction he'd come from. When he got to the lane that led to the house, he used it to turn around and come back once again to the lay-by. He had to repeat this move three times before he reached the Harbour Master just as there was a gap in passing traffic. No one saw him turn in there and once he'd parked behind the derelict building, no one passing could see his car from the road.

He killed the engine and settled in to wait.

At 2:00 a.m., he headed towards the Black house on foot, crossing the main road and slipping down the lane. His gun was secured inside his jacket. In the pockets on its outside were his gloves, the mask, the head torch and the shiny new toy he was excited to use.

There was no traffic at all on the lane, no streetlights, no noise. He'd forgotten how, in the countryside, it got *actually* dark. He nearly tripped in a pothole and, after a couple of minutes, began to feel his bearings slipping away. Was he in the right place? Had he already passed the house? He didn't think it was quite this far down the lane …

But then he saw the familiar gates and the shadowy shape of the house beyond.

The Black family home looked exactly the same. It stood in the middle of its plot as if it had been absently dropped there, as − to this day − no garden or landscaping had ever shaped the field around it. There was one car parked outside the house, lit by the light over the front door. A small hatchback, grey in colour. Jim presumed it belonged to Eve. All the curtains to the front of the house were drawn but through the glass of the front door he could see a dim glow: the light in the hall was on.

Jim walked past the house, continuing on down the lane, scanning for a parked car hidden in the hedgerow with a Dublin registration plate and two bored figures sat inside, or any movement at all elsewhere in the dark. He saw neither.

Satisfied, he started to double back.

He had never really believed that Eve would be under any kind of police protection. She thought she was looking for an old man who hadn't felt the urge to kill in nearly two decades, and the Gardaí would assume that an offender who'd got away with what he'd done for this long would want to keep it that way. Jim had been counting on it.

He reached the gates.

Now that his eyes were better adjusted to the dark, he could see that they *had* changed. Eighteen years ago they'd been cast-iron railings, hanging lopsided, paint peeling off. To open them, all you'd needed to do was reach through and lift the latch. Now they were solid wood, at least two feet taller and firmly locked. And electronic: the buttons on a small keypad glowed green in the dark.

He couldn't climb over them. Not these days. He was going to have to force his way through the perimeter hedge.

Now was as good a time as any to suit up.

Gloves first. Two sets. White latex ones, the kind they might use at a hospital. He had chosen these over the standard blue type the Gardaí used, for obvious reasons. He pulled them on and up his arm as far as they would go, which was a couple of inches past the cuffs of his jacket. Then, over them, the black leather set. The double layer restricted his movement somewhat, but it prevented hair-shedding and protected him from fingernails.

He took the same approach to the head. First: a rubber skull cap. He wasn't entirely sure what it was supposed to be used for; he thought maybe women's hairdressing. He pulled it down over his forehead and tucked his own hair up underneath it. The black knit mask went on afterwards. He rolled it down, over his face and neck, tucking the hem of it into the collar of his jacket. He adjusted it until it felt comfortable and only revealed his eyes.

He touched a hand to his chest to check for the reassuring bulk of the gun and then went looking for the thinnest section of the hedge.

He pushed his way through it.

It was easier than he'd thought it was going to be: he only had to make a big enough hole to climb through. He landed hard on the ground on the other side, sending a shooting pain through his hip and guaranteeing him a bruise there tomorrow, but he was in. He was on Eve's property.

From here on in, patience was his greatest asset.

He crouched down with his back against the hedge and held his breath while scanning the area. No sounds. No movement. When he was confident he was the only one out there in the night, he began advancing towards the house.

Up close, he saw that he'd been right: there seemed to be only one light on inside and it was the fixture on the ceiling in the hall.

Combined with the silence, that told him Eve was at home but already in bed.

He walked all the way around the house once, checking each window for signs of life and the walls for an alarm-bell box. He found neither. No motion-activated security light surprised him, and there were no barking or scratching dogs.

Just as he'd hoped.

Jim went to the back door. He fixed the elasticated band of the torch around his head, crouched down until he was at eye-level with the lock and reached up to turn the light on. When a bright spotlight fell on the lock, it was as if eighteen years fell away.

Four people had been asleep in their beds inside this house – or so he had thought.

One of them, it turned out, was awake.

And she would prove to be no victim.

The house in Bally's Lane had had a conservatory door that wouldn't lock. The girl in Covent Court habitually forgot that *closing* her front door wasn't the same as *locking* it. Fermoy was a building site with people coming and going all the time. But this house and the one in Westpark had required a homemade bump-key to get Jim past their back-door locks.

Tonight he had a new toy.

Jim reached a hand into his pocket and carefully withdrew the pick-gun. It looked like a silver electric toothbrush with a long, thin needle instead of a brush head. He'd taped a picking needle to its handle with masking tape, which he pulled off now.

He'd bought it a few years back just because he thought it'd be a handy thing to have around. Tonight, it would be the most important part of his kit.

Moving quickly and quietly, Jim slid the picking needle into the lock on the back door, then pushed the pick-gun's needle in after it. There was a knack to this — he had to move them around until he got the tension just right — and the gun made a mechanical clicking noise, but it was so much better than his old bump key. Within seconds, the door was unlocked.

Jim switched off the head torch and held his breath, listening.

Nothing.

He stowed the pick-gun and needle, depressed the handle of the back door and slowly pushed it open. It happened silently, with no creak or whine from the hinges.

He stepped inside, into the darkness of the kitchen.

The air was still. The light in the hall was just detectable through the gap between the kitchen door and its frame. As his eyes adjusted to the dim, he could see that very little had changed. There appeared to be fewer items of furniture in here now, fewer things, but the layout was the same.

Jim crossed the kitchen, opened the door and stepped into the hall. The front door faced him now, at the other end of it. He could see that since he'd been here last, a second dead bolt had been added to it along with a safety chain.

Two doors led off the hall, one on either side. Both were standing slightly ajar. The living room was to the left, the study to the right.

Jim took three steps forward and turned to look up the stairs.

He had been standing in this very spot on that night eighteen years ago when it happened.

The moment that had changed everything.

When he'd looked up these stairs back then, he'd seen a ghostly little figure standing at the top, looking down at the broken body lying splayed across the bottom steps.

'Dad ...?' she'd said.

Quietly. Uncertainly. As if she were confused about what was happening in the house.

About what had *just* happened, moments before.

Jim had been confused, too. He had come downstairs, leaving — he thought — the man a floor above, secured and waiting, and the other little girl hiding in a bathroom whose door he'd easily be able to kick open when it came time. But then he'd heard a noise and returned to the hallway just in time to see it happen.

A little figure on the landing, running with arms outstretched.

An adult body tumbling down the stairs.

Coming to rest at the end of it.

Silence.

It was the man. The blue rope Jim had bound him with was still tying his wrists and ankles, but he had somehow slipped the one that had tied him to the radiator. The arrangement of his limbs seemed utterly incompatible with life but just to be sure, Jim bent down to put an ear close to the man's lips, to listen for the sounds of his breath or even to feel the weak tickle of it.

There was nothing. He was dead.

Jim looked up, to the girl at the top of the stairs. Her eyes were on the man's body.

'Dad ..?'

Then her gaze lifted and she looked right at him.

At Jim.

Who realised then that he wasn't wearing his mask.

It was sitting on the table in the kitchen. He'd taken it off when he came downstairs. The light in the hall was enough to illuminate her face for him and since he was standing practically underneath it, it was surely more than enough to illuminate his face for her.

Eve Black *had* seen him, the real him, clear as day.

But she'd never told anyone that because *he'd* seen what she'd done.

She had written in her stupid book that she had a list of questions for the Nothing Man. Maybe tonight he'd let her ask them, but only if he could ask her his question first.

He only had one.

Tell me why, Eve. Why did you kill your father?

He checked the living room first, using only the light that spilled in from the hall when he pushed open the door. The curtains were drawn. The TV remotes were lined up neatly on the coffee table, next to a half-drunk cup of stone-cold tea. He pulled off one leather glove and touched a hand to the back of the television, but couldn't feel any heat through the latex. No one had been in this room for hours.

Eve had written that she was sleeping in the study. He paused outside the door to replace his glove, to collect himself, to prepare.

But something was missing.

Eighteen years ago, this moment – just before he revealed himself – would've felt like the peak. Adrenalin would've been surging through his veins, filling him with strength and power. The anticipation would have been palpable. The promise of the night would have felt endless, the hours ripe with infinite possibilities. He would have been excited.

But Jim didn't feel that way tonight. He was strangely detached, as if he were a spectator at his own crime scene. Maybe things would change when he saw her, when it started for real.

He pulled out the gun. He pushed open the study door.

And knew immediately that there was no one in there.

The light from the hall illuminated the empty bed but it was more than that. He could feel it. The air was too still, too dead. He stepped inside anyway, to double-check. An old, hairy blanket was thrown on the bed. He repeated his glove removal and heat check. Cold. No one had been sleeping in here tonight.

Jim went back out into the hall and paused to listen for the tinkle of urination or the rush of water from a tap. There was nothing. No humming appliances. No settling of the house. No creak of a mattress spring.

He decided then that Eve Black had lied.

Again.

She hadn't taken to sleeping in the study. She was upstairs, in one of the bedrooms. He could see why she might not want to admit it. Both options were bleak: sleep in the room where her mother died or in the one where her younger sister did.

Jim started up the stairs, ascending with excruciating slowness, careful to test each step with an increasing amount of weight before trusting it to hold him without creaking.

Halfway up, something changed. The air. It suddenly held a presence, like a muted television in an otherwise empty room.

She was here. In one of the bedrooms.

He could *feel* it.

When Jim reached the landing, he saw both bedroom doors were slightly ajar, offering only darkness in the spaces beyond.

The third door, the bathroom, was standing wide open. He made a cursory check of it. Empty. The cistern was silent and the sink was dry. He went back out on to the landing and moved to the next closest door.

Her door.

The bedroom Eve had once shared with her sister.

He didn't even have to go inside. Standing on the threshold, he could already hear her. Breathing, steady and regular.

She was in there and she was fast asleep.

Jim pushed open the door. He watched as the light from the landing raced across the carpeted floor and rushed up on to the bed.

She was a shapeless mound beneath the sheets, one bare foot sticking out and over the side.

For a little while, he just watched her.

As he did he felt it like a wave in the distance: the feeling.

Gathering.

Building.

Coming this way.

He stepped into the room. Moved deeper into the dark. He went to the side of Eve's bed and stood above her sleeping form. She was on her side, head resting on a bare arm.

Still asleep, breaths deep and regular.

It was time, after all this time.

Finally.

He closed his eyes and listened to Eve breathe and braced himself for the impact of the wave as it reached its peak and broke and roared and crashed against him, *through* him.

Washing away Jim Doyle.

Leaving only the Nothing Man.

He pointed his gun with one hand and reached up and switched on the head torch with the other.

And saw that Eve Black was wide awake, looking up at him.

He shoved the butt of the gun into the side of her neck and whispered, '*Let's play a game.*'

Eve squinted in the beam of the torch but otherwise barely reacted.

He pushed the gun in further, harder, as far as it would go into the soft flesh just under Eve's jaw.

She released a painful moan, but didn't move or squirm.

She's resigned, he realised.

She knew this day would come and now it's here and she knows she can't do anything about it.

'Jim,' she said.

He put his mouth to her ear and whispered through the fabric of the mask. '*I'm not going to tie you up. I'm just going to kill you.*'

When he directed the beam of the torch back to her face, he saw that her eyes were wide and her breathing had become shallow and rapid.

Good.

'Do what you want,' she said. She sounded breathy, panicky. 'But please talk to me first. Tell me why. Why did you do it? After all this time, I deserve an answer. And what difference does it make if this is the end anyway?'

Jim considered this.

He was in total control. He should take advantage of it. Press the gun against Eve's flesh and pull the trigger. He'd be out of the house in less than a minute. Back at his car in two. Home in ten. He'd have disposed of his clothes and covered his tracks before anyone even discovered that the Nothing Man's most famous survivor was dead.

But he had a question he wanted answered too. And Eve had a point: here, at the end, what difference did it make?

He sat down on the edge of the bed, keeping the gun pressed into Eve's neck and the beam of light from the head torch focused on her face. With his other hand he cupped her chin and roughly pulled her face towards him.

He leaned close until his mouth was mere inches from hers.

She said something that could have been a desperate, '*No,*' and shut her eyes tightly against the blinding glare of the light.

He whispered, '*You first.*'

Then in his normal voice – there was no need for performance now, here, in these last few minutes – he said, 'You answer my question and then I'll answer yours.' He sat back, moving the light away from Eve's face, but staying close enough to keep the gun in place. 'Why did you do it?'

Eve opened her eyes, blinked at him.

'Do what?' she whispered.

'You know what. If you're going to lie I'll just end this now.'

But she still seemed confused.

'I saw you,' he said. 'I saw what you did.'

A beat passed, then Eve's face changed.

She started shaking her head and saying, 'No. No. No, I *can't*. Please.'

He moved the muzzle of the gun to her temple and his free hand to her neck. Spread his fingers around it. Squeezed as hard as he could.

Eve cried out.

He gripped the skin until she was gasping and had started to struggle and thrash.

'*Tell me*,' he spat.

He released her and waited while she gulped down air.

'Last chance, Eve.'

She was crying now, hard, the tears on her cheeks glistening in the beam of the torchlight.

She whispered something but he didn't catch it.

He told her to repeat it.

She said, 'I thought it was *you*.'

Her voice had become raspy.

'I was trying to save my family,' she said. 'I pushed my father down the stairs because I thought *he was you*.'

But of course.

He felt foolish for not realising it sooner. When she'd suddenly come running out of that bathroom all those years ago with two hands stretched out in front of her, and charged up against the man standing at the top of the stairs, she'd thought it was *Jim* she was pushing down it.

But then she'd seen the body in the light of the hall, and Jim standing there looking up at her, and realised her mistake.

Her terrible mistake.

But now he saw that *he'd* made one, too.

He should've charged upstairs and killed her, right there and then. No hesitation. She'd seen his face and he had been planning on doing it anyway before he left the house. But he'd just seen her kill her own father. A twelve-year-old girl had murdered her daddy in front of him and he had no idea why. Was it because the girl was bad? Or because the daddy had been? What had been going on in this house?

Jim didn't know. He was suddenly missing most of the information. His control ran away.

And then *he* did, turning and running through the kitchen, out the back door and into the night.

But he wouldn't make the same mistake twice.

The gun was at Eve's neck. Jim put his left hand to his mouth and pulled off the leather glove with his teeth. Slowly. Keeping his eyes on Eve's the whole time. Then he did the same thing to the latex glove underneath.

'What about my questions?' she asked.

He ignored her.

'Just tell me why,' she said. 'Why us? Why didn't you just lock us up like the O'Sullivan children?' Her voice cracked. 'Why did you destroy my family? For what purpose? And why did you leave me alive? Why Anna? Why a *little girl*, you sick fuck?'

Jim made a *ssshhh* noise. He pushed back the blankets with his bare hand and lowered his jaw so the torch shone directly on the smooth, pale skin of Eve's neck and, below it, the curved promise of her breasts.

He touched his bare hand to her skin. Pressed it against it.

Eve started protesting, squirming.

Her skin was warm and soft. She was wearing a top with a low, round neck and no sleeves. He traced the edges of the material from one shoulder to the other with a single finger.

Once left to right. Once right to left.

Then he slipped the finger underneath and on to the soft pillow of her breast, pulling the material away from the skin, putting his whole hand inside, cupping her bare breast, feeling the nipple turn hard against the palm, moving to squeeze it—

Eve screamed.

A sound as loud and as piercing as anything Jim had ever heard.

But not, then, the only sound.

Beyond it, underneath it, there was an oncoming rush of noise.

What the—

Footsteps.

Shouting.

People.

Then suddenly bodies were rushing into the room and someone was shouting.

'Drop it! Drop your weapon! Drop it *right now*!'

Jim didn't have time to react.

There was a flash and an impact that rocked his entire body, sending him backwards off the bed and on to the floor. He lost the gun. He landed on his side and rolled until he was face-down on the carpet. He touched a hand to his left side where the epicentre of whatever had just happened seemed to be. When he lifted it to his face, he saw that it was covered in blood, glistening and red.

'Are you okay? Are you okay?'

A new voice. Male.

Jim tried to say, 'No,' but no words came out.

He tried to roll over on to his back so he could see what was happening. He only made it halfway, but that was far enough.

Ed Fucking Healy.

He was on the bed, gathering a crying Eve into his arms.

There were dark figures all around the room, coming towards him, bending down.

Gardaí.

With guns and baseball caps.

The Armed Response Unit.

The pain began to subside but Jim understood now what was happening, that that wasn't good news.

It's time for you to end this, Noreen had told him.

The darkness came creeping slowly on to the edges of his vision, then suddenly rushed in from all sides until there was nothing left but a tiny pinprick of light in the middle.

And then there was nothing at all.

ONE YEAR LATER

Katie lies awake, waiting for her alarm to go off. The tent is hot and stuffy and smells of someone else's body odour. She can feel the springs of the camp bed's thin mattress poking into her back. Her sleeping bag, only pulled up to her knees, holds a warm sweat that glues the synthetic lining to her calves.

She lasts another minute before she gets up, disables the alarm and pulls on her uniform of brightly coloured cotton shorts and a matching T-shirt. She grabs a towel and walks outside.

The campsite feels deserted at this hour. The only sound is birdsong and the soft rhythm of distant waves. The forecast has promised another thirty-degree day and the air is already warm.

Katie takes a long, cold shower in the toilet block and has a breakfast of coffee and two cigarettes at the site's poolside café. Technically staff are not supposed to sit in guest areas in uniform and certainly not while they're smoking, but no one else is here yet except the waiter and the guy with a net lifting leaves from the pool. They speak to each other in French and act as if Katie isn't there. That's the best she can hope for these days: to be ignored.

She's been here, a seaside resort on the south-west coast of France, for months. She heard about the job while eavesdropping on a couple of British Inter-Railers at a restaurant in the nearest town, where she'd just spent her last ten euro on a hot meal and was facing a second night of sleeping on the beach. She'd hitched a ride here with a Frenchman who was leering at her before her seatbelt was even on, but Katie is no longer afraid of men. It feels pointless to be. She's already seen the worst of them and called him her father.

She doesn't often think about time and dates but now that the season is winding down, the new arrivals thinning out, it's hard to ignore the fact that in a few days, it'll be September. The first anniversary of the end of everything.

Katie is in exile. The rest of the world feels separate here, far away. She has no phone. The only TVs on site are the ones in the bar, which always seem to be tuned to football matches. The work is menial so she doesn't have to think about it, the accommodation monastic, her days monotonous and simple.

It suits her.

It's penance.

'Excuse me?' A customer – the short, smiling, chubby woman who's been staying with her family in one of their Riviera Deluxe models for the past week – is standing in front of Katie, blocking her sun. 'Sorry to bother you, love, but we're about to hit the road to Roscoff and I'm just wondering if there's any chance you can let me into reception for a second just to switch out these books ...?' She's holding two bloated, battered paperbacks that have been evidently tarnished by sea water and sunscreen. Her other hand is pointing over her shoulder at a car stuffed with children. The husband is in the driver's seat. When he sees them looking, he pointedly raises his watch to the window.

'Sure,' Katie says, stubbing out her breakfast in the ashtray. 'No problem.'

Whenever she speaks to customers she does her best to shave the Irish edges off her accent. She learned her lesson back at the start. *Is that an Irish accent I hear? What part? Oh, I have a cousin there! What's your last name?*

Reception is a modified mobile home steps from the café. Katie unlocks the door and lets the customer in ahead of her, giving the thick, airless heat inside a chance to become a shade more bearable before she herself steps in.

The books are on a stand just inside the door. It's an exchange: leave a book, take a book. The woman returns her paperbacks and tilts her head to study the spines of the others.

'Hmm,' she says. 'I don't know … Have you read any of these? Anything you'd recommend?'

Katie steps closer so she can see the books too. She spies a historical saga another customer raved about last week.

'That one is really good,' she says. 'And it's set in Perpignan, which isn't far from here.'

The customer takes that and a memoir about restoring a chateau in Provence.

After she leaves, Katie takes a second to tidy up the books. Her hand is already on it before she realises what it is. She's never seen it in this smaller size, with a soft cover. It must be new. The colours on the spine are different. The font is, too. It looks absolutely nothing like the book she read, actually. The only thing that's the same is the title and the author.

The Nothing Man: A Survivor's Search for the Truth.
Eve Black.

And at the bottom of the spine, in tiny lettering: *UPDATED WITH A NEW POSTSCRIPT.*

The aftertaste of cigarette smoke is suddenly sour on Katie's tongue and the bitter coffee swirls sickeningly around her otherwise empty stomach.

She should put it back. It won't do her any good. She doesn't need to know any more details. Her nightmares already have more than enough fuel for years to come.

Katie is still telling herself this when she slides the book from the shelf.

She sees her father's face on the cover – half of it. The other half is covered in a black mask except for the eye. The two images have been blended into the other. She traces a finger down the seam in the middle.

But really, she has no interest in *him*.

It's Eve she wants to know about.

She wants to know how she is, if she's okay, if she's managing to somehow move on and live a life. Katie desperately hopes so. She's not religious but she has been saying silent prayers to the universe asking for this very thing.

Her father was a rapist and a murderer but she had eighteen years of a happy childhood before she found that out. He ended Eve's at twelve. He took both her parents from her. Robbed her of her little sister. Left their bodies in the house so Eve could see exactly what he'd done to them.

Katie holds all his victims in her heart. This includes her mother, at least the version of her that was young and naïve and didn't know what she was in love with. The woman she mourns, because she may as well be dead now. The woman that's still alive knew what he was but she stayed and helped him anyway. Katie feels nothing for her. She may as well be a stranger.

But it's Eve she thinks of the most.

Katie locks the door to reception from the inside and goes into the closet-sized office at the back. She locks that door too, just in case. She sits down and flicks through the book until she reaches the new part.

She takes a deep breath of hot, musty air.

She starts to read.

– POSTSCRIPT –

The Woman Who

When I was twelve years old a man broke into my home and murdered my mother, father and younger sister, Anna, seven years old then and for ever. When I was thirty years old I wrote a book about it. Eight days after it was published, on 6 September 2019, that same man broke into that same house and tried to murder me. He was shot and killed by Gardaí. His name was Jim Doyle.

Now, I must come clean and tell you the truth. I left out one very important detail in the first edition of *The Nothing Man*: his name. I knew it was Jim Doyle. I knew what he looked like and where he lived and what kind of a person he was. Ed and I had found him before I'd even finished the first chapter of the book. But our evidence was circumstantial. At best, writing about our discovery would be pointless and, at worst, doing so would get me charged with libel and slander in a case that Jim Doyle would definitely win. For a time, I thought having to leave this detail out made writing the book itself pointless and I came close to calling the whole thing off. But Ed convinced me that the book might be the very thing to draw him out. It might be the *only* thing that could. So I wrote it and it was published and thousands of you went out and bought it, and I thank you deeply for that. I hope you'll forgive me for not telling you the whole story – until now.

When I visited Maggie Barry, Christine Kiernan's neighbour in Covent Court, she told me about the knife and the rope being mislaid at Togher Garda Station. What I didn't include in the first edition of this book was that Maggie remembered the name of the guard who told her that: Jim Doyle. It meant nothing to me at the time. I presumed the loss of the knife and the rope had been a team effort and it had merely fallen to this Garda Doyle to deliver the bad news. It was just another detail to add to the master file Ed and I had been building during our re-examining of the case.

But Ed knew Jim Doyle, a little. He'd worked with him at Togher. He also knew that before that, Doyle had been in Mallow – which was just thirty kilometres from Fermoy. Moreover, Togher was just off Cork's primary orbital road which linked various southside locations, as well as the N28 to Carrigaline. Blackrock and Passage West were easily accessed from it. In fact, if you plotted Fermoy, Mallow and Cork City on a map, you'd make a neat triangle. What interested Ed the most, however, was *why* Doyle had been moved to Mallow from his previous posting in Millstreet: because in a fit of rage, he'd thrown a cup of hot liquid at his boss's head.

Ed found a photo of Jim Doyle in his navy blues, taken in the summer of 2004. When I saw it, I had a visceral reaction. That's the only way I can describe it. I felt hot and light-headed and panicky all at once and, as I held the print-out in my hand, it began to flutter wildly. I was shaking. I felt as if I might be on the verge of a panic attack. Because it was *him*. I was looking at a picture of the Nothing Man. I knew it on an instinctual level.

And yet on an intellectual one, there was no way for me to know that for sure. I never saw the Nothing Man in our house that night – or at least, I couldn't remember seeing him. But there were discrepancies in what I did remember that suggested the version of events as I recalled them were not entirely trustworthy. Now I couldn't help but wonder if there was a whole reel missing from my memory of that night. Perhaps the most important one. Had I actually seen the Nothing Man and then blocked it out? What were the circumstances? Did we speak? Did he try to hurt me? Was that something to do with why he left me alive?

The only way I would ever get answers was if the Nothing Man himself told me them. But we couldn't approach Doyle. A physiological reaction to a photo does not a successful prosecution make.

We showed Doyle's photo along with four other Garda headshots to Johnnie Murphy, the foreman in Fermoy, and at first he picked out Doyle's. But then, on second thought, he decided another photo was more like 'Ronan Donoghue' and ultimately he settled on that as his choice. We were unable to track down Claire Bardin, the woman whose sighting of a man on Bally's Lane had given rise to the police sketch, but when we compared the sketch and Doyle's photo, there were clear similarities. This was by far the most promising lead we'd ever had that included a name but, when we took my reaction out of the equation – and we had to – we weren't left with anything near enough to justify fingering Doyle as the man who had murdered my family. We needed more. Much more. Undeniable, empirical evidence. If Jim Doyle was indeed the Nothing Man, how could we prove it?

As Ed had warned me the very first day we met, the Nothing Man was a meticulous offender. He had never left any physical evidence behind that would connect him to his crimes and the way he chose his victims was so subtle that it wasn't discovered until nearly two decades later. Even if we found him, a conviction would be impossible without a confession. And why, with no physical evidence to back up the charges, would he ever confess? The publication of the book might stir him up a bit, might make him do something stupid like contact the media or make a drunken confession to a friend, but there were no guarantees there either and the only action we could take was to wait and see.

'The only other way,' Ed said to me late one night, 'would be if we caught him in the act, but we're about twenty years too late for that.'

That's when the idea first occurred to me. I could use *The Nothing Man* – and myself, its author – as bait.

In the summer of 2017, Ed had an apartment overlooking the waters of Cork's inner harbour at Jacob's Island and, that July, we packed up our rented office space and moved Operation Write *The Nothing Man* into his spare room. Our research and investigations, for the most part, were over. The case files had been returned to Anglesea Street. It was now time to actually start writing the book.

Although Ed could help, this part was really my responsibility. I wrote the story of the Nothing Man and what his visit that night long ago had done to my life, but I also wrote *to* the Nothing Man. I imagined him reading every sentence I typed. When it came to his crimes, I put in just enough detail to rekindle his memories. I made sure to tell him what I really thought of him. I wanted to make him mad and, specifically, mad at me. After a lifetime spent hiding away, of being paranoid about my personal safety, of not even telling close friends my real last name, I told every reader of this book where I would sleep at night when I was in Cork: back in the house where, for me, this had all started.

Every reader including *him*.

The Nothing Man was to be a true-crime book that, if all went well, would lead the Nothing Man to commit one more crime. But I had absolutely no idea if my plan would work.

The book came out on 29 August 2019. Exactly a week later, on 5 September, my publisher organised an event at a bookshop in Cork city centre. Just before it was due to begin, Ed appeared by my side and whispered something into my ear: *Jim Doyle is here.* In a move that surprised us both, I turned to him and said, 'Introduce me.'

As Ed led me to him, I had no plans to do anything other than pretend this was a normal exchange, that I was merely meeting an old colleague of Ed's, another Garda. But when the crowds parted and I saw him standing there, I recognised him – not just as the Nothing Man, but as someone I'd met in the course of my research. The Nothing Man was youthful and strong and lean, as was the picture of Jim Doyle in his Garda uniform that Ed had found. But this Jim Doyle was grey and balding, with a turkey-neck of loose skin and a bulge around his middle, and he looked sweaty and ill-at-ease under the harsh lights of the shop. He also looked like the man who'd been on the reception desk at Togher Garda Station when I'd visited there looking to speak with someone about the missing knife and rope.

I told him we'd met before but that I'd looked different then. I admit it: I was toying with him. I also admit this: I enjoyed it. I didn't feel afraid. I was in a public place filled with people and Ed was by my side and Doyle didn't know what I knew. For once, the power was mine. When Ed said that Doyle had been 'dragged' to the event by his wife, I told him his name was in its pages because I wanted to ensure that he would read it too. Technically, that wasn't a lie. If Ed and I were right about him, his name – his other name – *did* appear in my book, probably more than a hundred times.

Since publication day I had been staying at the house in Passage West. Over Ed's objections, I was staying there alone. He wanted to put protection outside or even keep a guard in the house, and failing that have other people staying with me, but I vetoed it. If Doyle was the Nothing Man, he was also a former guard. He would know the signs of a police presence, no matter how hidden, and I didn't want to inadvertently put anyone else in danger. We compromised on a panic button. If I pushed it, it wouldn't make any noise but it would ring an alarm in Carrigaline Garda Station, where the members were on alert for it. Officers would arrive within minutes.

The night after the bookshop event, Friday 6 September, the Nothing Man returned to the scene of his last crime at around three in the morning. I don't sleep well and was awake when he broke his way in via the rear door. He was probably thirty feet from me. I pushed the panic button, threw an old blanket over my bed and ran upstairs into my room, the one I had shared with Anna. For several minutes I listened to the sounds of him moving around a floor below, then the suspicious silence that I correctly assumed was him ascending the stairs. I saw him appear in the bedroom doorway, masked with gun drawn, and realised I was seeing the very same thing that the women I had written about – Alice O'Sullivan, Christine Kiernan, Linda O'Neill and Marie O'Meara – had also seen.

That my mother had seen.

And Anna.

I felt, in a weird way, closer to them. *With* them. Part of their exclusive, awful club.

But I wasn't scared. What I was, honestly, was relieved. I was relieved that the thing I had been scared of my entire life was finally happening. It meant I wouldn't have to be frightened of it any more.

The night he died, Jim Doyle was sixty-three years old. He'd been married to his wife for more than thirty years and their only child, a daughter, was about to start her second year of university. He lived in a nondescript semi-D in a southside suburb of Cork City known for its high property prices and good schools. He had been a guard but not a very good one. There had been further incidents after the mug-throwing, although not as serious, and for most of his career in the force he'd been 'put on paper', essentially blocked from doing anything except the most menial of tasks. On the day he banked his requisite thirty years, he retired.

There were signs that he was unravelling, losing the control he'd maintained for so many years. I have no idea if it was the book that prompted this, but no fewer than three copies of it were found at his home. (One of them even had handwritten notes inside the front cover.) Hours before he arrived at my house to kill me, he was fired from his job as a security guard at a supermarket following complaints that he'd made female customers uncomfortable. After he was given the news, he'd assaulted his boss in a bizarre attack, forcing food down the man's throat. That same morning his next-door neighbours, a couple called Derek and Karen Finch, called the Gardaí to report that someone was trying to poison their dog. They presented the officers with dog biscuits they'd found with pellets of rat poison pushed inside. A bag of that same rat poison would be found in Doyle's garden shed, along with an old hoover whose bag contained DNA traces that matched Linda O'Neill, Marie Meara and my mother. When Gardaí interviewed Doyle's wife, she had visible injuries to the side of her face. She would only speak to Gardaí long enough to tell them that she wasn't going to speak to them, that she knew nothing about the Nothing Man.

Doyle was born in Castlebar, Co. Mayo, in July 1956, seven months after his parents married. Sean Delaney was forty-two to Emer Doyle's twenty-one at the time. After the wedding, Emer moved into the house on Delaney's farmland. There is no written record of what their marriage was like and no one left living who can tell us about it, but we do know this much: Delaney was known around town as a fella driven mad by the drink – a violent drunk – and on 26 December 1961, he shot his wife in the head before turning the gun on himself. Five-year-old Jim was unharmed but spent two days alone in the house before a neighbour raised the alarm. When Gardaí entered they found the boy sleeping soundly in bed, curled up against his mother's dead and bloodied body.

After that, Doyle was sent to live with his mother's sister, Agnes, in Rathmines in Dublin. She gave him his mother's maiden name and enrolled him in the local school, where he was a good if unexceptional student. Agnes was a single woman who enjoyed socialising and on Saturday nights, young Jim was often left in the care of teenage babysitters. One of them, Jean Long, contacted me after his death. She described him as an intense little boy who grew into a somewhat unnerving adolescent, prone to staring and saying inappropriate, sexualised things. He had once tried to grab her breasts.

As soon as Doyle turned eighteen in 1974, he tried to enrol in the army but failed the fitness test. Agnes died suddenly the following year, in April 1975, of a brain aneurism. After that, public records lose Doyle for more than a decade, until a marriage certificate marks his wedding to eighteen-year-old Mary White*, of Enniskerry, Co. Wicklow, in January 1986. Months later, Doyle joined the ranks of the Gardaí.

Why did he do what he did? I didn't get a chance to ask him. Armed Gardaí burst into the room, saw that Doyle was armed and shot him dead before either of us could speak. We might, however, have an answer for why he stopped, for why the attack on my family was his last. Dr Weir said that one of the reasons serial killers stop killing is that they 'age out' and Doyle would've been forty-five in 2001. But she also said that sometimes their stopping is down to a change in their circumstances. 2001 is also the year his daughter was born.

The short version of Jim Doyle's life is that he was a wholly unremarkable man. He failed at everything he tried to do. He didn't get into the army, he failed to advance in the guards and he even got himself fired from the supermarket where he worked security. As far as I'm concerned, the injuries to his wife's face on the day of his death also indicate that he had failed as a husband, and his daughter having to live the rest of her life knowing who he really was qualifies as a fatherhood failure too. Everyone who knew him disliked him and physically he was well past his prime. In the absence of contrary information, it seems as if his motivation for committing his crimes is standard Serial Killing 101: misogyny. He didn't like women because they didn't like him. Even that is unremarkable, unfortunately. As Dr Weir had pointed out, the Nothing Man is an exceptionally apt name

---

* Not her real name.

for a serial killer. 'When you find him,' she'd said to me, 'you'll probably be shocked at just how much of *nothing* he really is.' She was right.

A few months ago, Ed gave me a book called *Savage Appetites: Four True Stories of Women, Crime, and Obsession* by Rachel Monroe. On its cover was a picture of a dead little girl in a yellow dress whose face was smeared with blood and whose dark hair was matted with it. It was only on second glance I realised that the girl was in fact a doll. I looked to Ed for an explanation, half-wondering if the man had lost his mind. He pointed to a page he'd marked with a Post-It note. When I turned to it, I found a phrase underlined in dark, smudgy pencil. *You bought me a ticket to a planet where I lived by myself.* It was part of a section of the book called 'The Victim'. The shock of recognition was electric.

For years I collected descriptions of grief, looking for the one that would put into words what I was feeling because I didn't have the words for it myself. But none of them had ever fit. Now I know why. What I went through in the wake of my family's visit from the Nothing Man wasn't grief. It wasn't *just* that. To lose family members to illness, accident or time, while just as painful, is a different *kind* of pain to losing a loved one to a violent crime. This one is more complex. Nowhere near as many people can relate to it and so it separates you from everyone else. I've been separated since I was twelve years old. I don't know what it feels like *not* to be.

I also carry a tremendous amount of guilt. I wish I had acted differently in the house that night. I wish I had told someone about the knife and the rope. I was the only one to get out alive and I didn't deserve it. If there was to be one survivor, there should've been three other names on the list above mine. Why didn't I do something? Why didn't I run downstairs and raise the alarm? Why didn't I protect my sister? How can I call myself a victim or a survivor when nothing happened to me, when I wasn't even hurt?

And what did I do with this blessing, with my escape, with all this extra time? Until very recently, nothing. I sleepwalked through life. I existed more than lived. I gave into the pain. That, in turn, gave rise to even more guilt. Because I know for sure that if *Anna* had lived, she'd be making the most of every moment. She'd have a family and a career and be a wonderful person who gave back as much if not more than she took. She would be *worthy* of surviving the Nothing Man. I feel like I will never be. People tell me to forgive myself but, trust me, that's easier said than done.

In the meantime, all I can do is try to make the most of my time on earth. That started with writing this book. My mother, father and Anna are immortalised in it. Everyone who reads it will know they were here. Writing this book also helped catch the man who took them away. And weirdly, inadvertently, it led me to the wonderful man who earlier this year became my husband. In a few weeks' time, our daughter will arrive.

A friend told me recently that when my daughter reaches the age I was on the night the Nothing Man entered our home, I will see how innocent and small and young that is, how much of a child remains even right on the cusp of their becoming a teen, and I will finally understand how young *I* was. She says if I haven't already, I will forgive myself then. I don't know about that. We'll see.

Nearly nineteen years ago, Jim Doyle bought me a ticket to a planet where I had to live by myself. I didn't want to go but I had no choice in the matter. I was too young and too numb to recall the journey, leaving me utterly lost, disorientated and unable to find my way back. I'm still here. Until recently, I had resigned myself to the fact that I would be for ever.

But something unexpected has happened. A visitor has arrived and he knows the way back. He says he'll take me with him. We leave soon. I'm finally getting to go home.

EVE BLACK

Dublin 2020

About the Author

Eve Black lives in Dublin with her partner Ed and baby daughter Anna. *The Nothing Man* is her first book.

Acknowledgements

Thank you to the people who continue to make it possible for me to do my dream job: my agent Jane Gregory and everyone at David Higham, Corvus/Atlantic Books, Blackstone Publishing and Gill Hess Ltd. To Sara O'Keeffe: thank you, thank you, thank you, thank you (one for each book!). Best of luck in your new adventures. Thank you to Casey King, Garda procedure consultant extraordinaire, and my followers on Twitter who volunteered to have me use their names in Eve's acknowledgements. To my fellow crime writer Mason Cross (and Pearl Jam) for the title, which turned out to be a perfect name not just for the book but for Jim, too. To the booksellers, reviewers and readers who so kindly support my work – I deeply appreciate it. To Hazel Gaynor and Carmel Harrington for keeping me sane, entertained and in excuses to drink French 75s. To Mum, Dad, John and Claire for everything but, really, you shouldn't be moving stock around in bookshops unless you work there, okay? We've talked about this …

You can really buy a *Let's talk about serial killers* lips pin (I got mine from Krystan Saint Cat) but *Hey! Ted Bundy isn't hot!* was printed on a bottle opener in real life (also by

Krystan) and *Talk true crime to me* was on a greetings card I bought from Greenwich Letterpress in New York City.

I got the idea for *The Nothing Man* from reading the late Michelle McNamara's *I'll Be Gone in the Dark* less than a week after Joseph James DeAngelo was arrested in California. I would urge you to read it too if you haven't already, and to listen to the Audible Original *Evil Has A Name* as well. I also highly recommend Rachel Monroe's book, *Savage Appetites*.

Finally, a disclaimer: this is a work of fiction. That means I made everything up, including the facts.